To Melt a Frozen Heart

An Enemies to Lovers Winter Romance

The Anderssons
Book 1

Helena Halme

HELENA HALME

The Anderssons Book 1

TO MELT A FROZEN HEART

An Enemies to Lovers Romance

Chapter One

All the cafés in Helsinki airport were crammed with people. Kat spotted a seat in a fancy champagne bar, hoping they served coffee. She'd been awake most of the night, not able to sleep, due to the torturous images in her mind. Her flight from London left at silly o'clock and the worry she would oversleep and miss her alarm had made it even more difficult to relax. She now needed an injection of caffeine to keep her eyes open and to stay alert.

Setting her rucksack on the floor, Kat perched on a leather seat. Immediately, a waiter approached from the other side of the counter. He looked her over, clad in jeans, a long (second-hand) Uniqlo down coat, and a pair of Doc Martens. It was obvious he thought she was in the wrong place.

'A glass of champagne?' he said with a sneer.

Without thinking, and to show him up, Kat replied, 'Yes, please. That would be wonderful.'

She didn't usually drink alcohol before a flight. She might have one of those small bottles of wine with her meal onboard, but she liked to keep a clear head before boarding. She was always late for everything and was terrified she'd lose track of time and miss her flight. Especially now when she was travelling on her own.

While Kat watched the waiter pop open a fresh bottle and with a flourish, pour a glass, her eyes settled on a guy at the other side of the crescent-shaped bar. He had a deep tan and teeth that looked too white. His blond hair was slicked back, and he wore a dark-blue jumper with a logo.

'Eurotrash.' She heard Jacques' voice in her head.

She shook her head to dislodge her ex's words.

Kat smoothed her short hair with her hand, stopping at the nape of her neck. She'd had long hair for as long as she could remember.

The guy wasn't her type, the Jacques in her head was right. All the same, she had to admit the stranger was very good looking.

Yet, Kat was definitely not in the mood for flirting. For the first time in her life, she'd decided to stay single for longer than a few weeks. She had absolutely no interest in men. Not after what had happened.

Lifting his glass, the guy winked at Kat.

Who winks at a stranger?

She smiled briefly to be polite, then took her phone out of her pocket and began scrolling through her emails, pretending to be engrossed in whatever was on the screen.

In truth, she had been avoiding looking at her phone. She didn't want to read any more messages from Jacques, or from *her*. This trip was supposed to be special. She'd arranged the perfect setting so Jacques could give her the perfect ring she'd suspected he'd already bought her. Thinking about it, anger boiled inside her.

She took a large gulp of the sparkling liquid. My, it was rather nice. The bubbles stayed on her tongue for just a moment, and after swallowing it, her head grew light and her limbs relaxed slightly. This was the break she'd been dreaming about for months. Why not enjoy herself a little?

Kat leaned back in her chair and took another sip, trying to avoid looking at the guy opposite.

Scanning the busy departures lounge, she spied a departure screen displaying the flights. She found hers and gasped when she saw a notice next to her flight: Boarding. Please go to Gate.

Typical!

Kat drained her glass and indicated to the waiter for the bill. All she'd really wanted was a cup of coffee. While she waited to pay, she cursed under her breath for showing off to the barman. Why was she always so worried about what other people thought? The alcohol was already making her forget herself.

'It's been taken care of by the gentleman over there,' the barman said, indicating with a nod across the bar.

'What?'

Kat looked over at the winking guy again, who was

grinning now. She gave him a nod, not able to bring herself to smile at the weirdo.

She heaved her rucksack onto her shoulder and escaped into the throng of people all hurrying in different directions.

After negotiating the busy concourses of the airport and finding her gate, she saw two women in Finnair uniforms sitting like statues and the area bustling with people beginning to queue up.

A piercing shriek alerted Kat to a woman struggling with a toddler. The boy was silently crying, while the mother seemed to be frantically looking for something on the floor and the seats around her. Kat spotted a battered looking brown teddy right underneath the woman's legs. She hurried to retrieve it.

'You looking for this?'

The little boy's tears dried immediately, and the woman gave Kat a weary smile.

'Thank you,' she said in broken English.

Kat gave the boy a smile but got an angry stare back, as if it was she who had stolen his beloved toy.

'Can't win them all,' someone said behind her.

Kat knew who it was even before she turned around. The Eurotrash from the bar.

The call to board saved her from an awkward conversation with the guy. As she glanced at her ticket, she saw she was in the second group. Because of the specialness of the trip, she'd decided to treat Jacques and herself to front cabin seats in Economy. She prayed, as she queued up for the boarding card check, that the woman with a blue Finnair uniform and short blonde hair didn't ask where the second passenger was.

She'd completely forgotten that she'd already checked both of them in online. At the departures desk in London that morning when she had dropped off her luggage, they'd made an almighty fuss when Kat had told them she would be travelling alone. She'd wanted to shout at them and tell them the whole sorry tale of his betrayal but instead, she'd just apologised and said it had been 'a last-minute change'.

Now walking the endless airport corridors to the gate and fuelled by the buzz of the champagne, her thoughts went back to the reason for this holiday to Lapland.

This was supposed to be a trip of a lifetime. She had wanted to take Jacques to the magical land where her family was from, to a romantic place where he could finally pop the question. She had even imagined the scenario: snow falling outside; a fire blazing; a soft rug where they had just made love. Then from his pocket, Jacques would pull out a velvet box. He would struggle onto his knees and open the box, tell Kat how much he loved her and ask her to marry him.

Jacques was an old-fashioned man; Kat knew he would want to plan the proposal himself. All she had been doing was giving him a gentle push.

And look where that had got her.

How could she have read him so wrong?

Was it because he was older?

Kat wondered if having no dad was the reason she'd hooked up with him. Although Jacques wasn't *that* old. At forty-three, he was nearly twice her age, but they'd had so much in common that age wasn't a factor.

They laughed at the same weird jokes, and they were both foodies. Jacques was a romantic. Whenever he was attentive, Kat felt like a princess under his gaze. The men – boys – Kat had dated before Jacques only wanted to party. They hadn't held open doors for her or sent her flowers. When she'd hinted at wanting more than just a night out in the pub followed by drunken sex, they'd immediately ended things with her.

Not that Kat had always been the one who'd been dumped. She'd done a fair bit of breaking off relationships herself. She'd started dating at college – too young, in her mum's opinion.

Lying awake last night and not being able to sleep, she had thought back to her relationship with Jacques. Although she was still angry – *so angry and hurt* – at what he'd done, she'd never been as happy and felt as comfortable with anyone as she had with him. Tears of self-pity had soaked her pillow then, only to be dried by the blind rage she continued to feel.

To her surprise, sitting in what was supposed to be Jacques' seat was someone else. Kat stopped in the aisle when she saw who it was.

How is that possible?

She'd paid for the seat, so how could they have given it to someone else already? On the flight from London to Helsinki, she'd sat alone in her row on an otherwise full flight. At first, she'd felt a lump in her throat at the sight of the empty seat, but was soon grateful that she didn't have to talk to anyone else. She had needed space to reconcile to her new future without Jacques.

A young girl with dreadlocks gave her a gentle push, making Kat move forward. She uttered an apology.

The tanned man smiled widely at her and greeted Kat as she got to her row.

'You the window?' the guy asked unnecessarily, and got up.

Kat nodded. As she awkwardly made her way past him along the tight space, she accidentally brushed the guy's arm with her chest.

'Sorry,' she said before finally settling in her seat.

'Pleasure is all mine,' the guy said, and gave her another stupid grin.

'Did you enjoy your champagne?' he added, after she put her rucksack under the seat in front and fastened her seatbelt.

Kat recognised his accent.

He's Finnish?

To be polite, she replied, 'I did. That was very kind of you, thank you.'

Kat couldn't help but meet his gaze. She noticed he had blue eyes, and that he was a bit younger than she'd first thought. In his mid-twenties like her, or perhaps only a couple of years older?

'You looked like you needed it,' the guy said, smiling.

'You think so? I'm not really a champagne person,' she lied.

His face fell at Kat's brush off. To her relief, he turned to face the front.

'I'm not being funny,' she said, 'but can I ask you how come you're in that seat? I thought I'd bought for a friend who couldn't make it. Still...'

The guy snapped his head back to her.

'Oh my God, you think I'm a stalker, don't you?' He looked embarrassed. 'I was on standby and they allocated me this seat. I didn't know it was your friend's seat, obviously. Isn't it free?'

Kat shrugged. 'It is. I was just curious.'

'Right,' the guy said, raising his eyebrows at Kat.

Kat ignored him and took her laptop out of her rucksack, angling it away from the guy as much as she could sitting next to someone on a plane. She tried to concentrate on the article on the melting snowcaps in the Andes but couldn't. Instead, she gazed out of the small window and watched the suitcases below being loaded onto the hold.

When she turned back, she came face-to-face with the guy, who was also watching the bags. Their eyes locked and for a moment, time stood still. The guy's lips were parted a little, revealing his straight, white teeth, which didn't seem as bright as they had from across the bar. He lifted his hand up to brush his blond hair out of his eyes. Kat followed the movement. Somehow, the gesture made him appear more vulnerable.

She blinked and concentrated on the article once more, shaking her head to try to break the spell.

What on earth are you doing, Kat? Didn't you just decide to stay off men for the foreseeable future?

Chapter Two

Soon after takeoff, the air stewards started delivering meals.

'Two specials with champagne, one vegan, one with meat,' the woman said, adding, 'Are you celebrating a special occasion?'

She looked from Kat to the Finnish guy while holding the plastic containers out and smiling widely.

Without a pause, Kat's neighbour said, 'Yes, we are.'

He took the meals from the steward and handed one to Kat.

He lifted a brow. 'I presume you're the vegan?'

Colour rose to Kat's face. She'd completely forgotten about the little surprise she'd arranged. The pre-purchase of two meals with small bottles of champagne was another little treat she'd arranged to make this trip special. Another clue for Jacques that this would be the perfect holiday to pose that question.

Damn you, Jacques!

The guy lifted the miniature bottle from his tray and, with a mischievous grin, said, 'I thought you didn't like this stuff?'

There was laughter in his voice, and his blue eyes twinkled as he gazed at Kat. For a moment she was transfixed, but when she looked down at his tray, she spied a signet ring on his pinkie. It was silver with a dark violet stone on it.

Who wears something like that?

'You're welcome,' she replied pointedly, and took her tray.

This stopped the guy in his tracks.

'I'm sorry,' he muttered.

For a moment he was still, barely breathing. Then he spoke again, 'I'll tell them this isn't for me. Or I can pay you for it? How much was it?'

Kat looked at him and saw he was sincere. There was an urgency to his words, which only embarrassed her even more.

'No, I should be sorry. It was meant for my friend, who couldn't come on this trip, so please go ahead. It's the least I can do for buying me the champagne at the airport.'

Again, there was a brief silence between them. The guy hung his head over the food, like a dog waiting to be told he can eat.

She touched his arm, suddenly sorry for him. Kat felt a hard muscle underneath and something in her tummy flipped.

She removed her hand quickly and indicated to the

food in front of him. 'Please have it. It'll only go to waste otherwise.'

'Thank you,' he said simply.

They smiled at each other, and Kat's heart leapt for a moment. But it faded when she saw the ring again and noticed he was wearing bright-pink socks inside his leather winter boots.

Could he be more of an upper-class show-off?

'My name is Mikael.' He reached the hand with the ring towards Kat.

'Katherine, but everyone calls me Kat,' she replied. Again, she forgot herself for a moment, sinking into the bright-blue pools of his eyes.

Control yourself, Kat.

'Um, we'd better eat before it gets cold,' she said, turning away. She peeled off the coverings from the food containers.

Eating brought welcome respite from Kat's embarrassment over the whole situation. She refused when Mikael offered to open her bottle of champagne. At first, she decided she wouldn't drink it, to keep up the pretence of not liking the stuff, but then that seemed stupid. It was as if she was so bothered by her lie to the guy sitting next to her that she was refusing to enjoy herself. She was on holiday, after all. She'd decided to come on this trip to get away from the rat Jacques, so she might as well have some fun.

A little tipsy, she also opened the bottle of wine that was included in the meal.

After the stewards cleared away the empty trays, she tried not to look at her neighbour or involuntary touch him again. But it was proving difficult because he was hogging the armrest. His legs were too long for the gap between his and the seat in front, so his knees were also wide, brushing Kat's thighs.

Manspreading. But then it hit her that it must be very uncomfortable to be so tall that you couldn't fit into your seat.

She closed her eyes, trying to sleep, but images of Jacques with *her* flooded her mind, and her fury at the unfairness of the situation hit her again. The betrayal was so complete that it had taken her two weeks just to comprehend what had happened. She wanted to cry right there, but that would elicit more unwanted attention from her neighbour, so she picked up her laptop and read the same sentence she'd already read three times.

Her thoughts wandered back to Jacques. She wondered what he was doing right now. Was he thinking of her? Was he regretting what had happened? Was he wishing he could be with her now? Kat concluded that he probably wasn't, because otherwise he would have made the effort to come to the airport.

She hadn't opened any of his messages since she'd left his flat. She had done the classic thing of packing all her belongings into whatever bag she'd found, flinging items in while Jacques had begged her to stay.

She'd stayed in her best friend Toni's house, who was away filming in Somerset.

Before leaving, she had turned around and seen the surprise on Jacques' face. It had caused her to laugh through the tears that fell down her cheeks. She had banged the door shut with such force that she heard his fine glassware shatter inside the living room cabinets. It had felt as if she was in a badly made TV drama as she ran down the stairs and out of his life for good.

A small cough from the guy next to her – Mikael – brought her back to the present.

'You didn't like it?'

He stared down at her food, which Kat had barely touched.

'I'm not hungry,' Kat said. She immediately regretted her words, because now she was inviting a conversation with the guy. Mikael nodded and looked past her out of the window.

Kat noticed his strong jaw line and couldn't help but be drawn in by his rugged good looks. She shook her head to clear her thoughts. She couldn't be thinking like this. Jacques had only just betrayed her, and she was not ready to move on. Besides, this guy was hardly her type.

'I'm always starving,' Mikael said, smiling.

'Hmm,' Kat said, not knowing how to reply. He wasn't fat; quite on the contrary, he had slim hips and a wide chest. He was at least a head taller than her, and had strong arms. *He must work out,* she thought absent-mindedly.

Stop it!

Kat could feel his eyes on her. She tried to ignore him and focus on her article again, but her mind kept wandering.

She remembered the first time she had met Jacques. He'd been charming and witty, and they'd hit it off immediately.

They'd been together for two years, and Kat had thought they were happy. But then she'd found him in *her* bed.

Chapter Three

Kat managed to avoid Mikael after they'd landed and disembarked from the plane. Because she was in the window seat, he had got up first. She'd pretended to fuss with her rucksack so that she could stay seated until he'd disappeared out of the aircraft.

When she spotted him in the small arrivals hall, she made sure to stand a little farther away, on the opposite side of the baggage carousel. Half hiding behind a large pillar, she looked out through the open automatic doors to where people were coming in from outside, wearing padded coats and trousers, and stamping their boots to get rid of the excess snow. The light was fading and all she could see was a row of dark pine trees, heavy with snow, beyond the frost-covered car park.

Memories of a childhood holiday here filled her thoughts. Her Finnish grandparents had accompanied Kat and her mother, and they'd all skied both downhill and cross-country during the fun-filled week. Kat had never seen so much snow in her life.

One evening, she'd seen the Northern Lights. Her mum had woken Kat up late at night and bundled her into a duvet to watch the colourful display from the porch of their rented cottage. Kat had always wanted to come back and share with Jacques the spellbinding spectacle of one of nature's most fantastical displays.

'Which resort are you going to?'

Her neighbour off the plane broke Kat's train of thought before it went off the rails and ran into Jacques' betrayal.

Mikael stood with his hands in the pockets of his open padded jacket with his booted feet apart. His wide smile was infectious.

Kat's breath caught in her throat, and she felt butterflies in her tummy. Mikael was annoying as hell, with all his designer gear and perfect teeth, so why was she feeling like this?

'Oh, Y-ylläs,' she stammered.

'Same here! Actually, I work there.'

His eyes settled on hers. To keep her composure, Kat had to look away.

At that moment the luggage carousel came to life, and bags started to appear on the belt.

'I'd better...' Kat said, and moved closer.

She didn't turn to check whether Mikael was following her, but she thought she could feel his presence close behind her. When she saw her bag, she moved forward, but before she could grab it, Mikael was right behind her, taking hold of the handle of her suitcase.

'Let me,' he said, and flung the heavy baggage effortlessly off the belt and onto the floor.

'Thanks,' Kat said, quickly fleeing the guy and his eyes. She headed for a woman with long, pitch-black hair who was next to the name of the company she'd booked the holiday with.

'Katherine Wootton?' the woman asked.

Kat nodded and the woman looked down at her clipboard. She ticked a line and said, 'Two of you?' She glanced behind Kat, her expression a question mark.

'Just me. The other person had to cancel,' Kat replied.

'Oh,' the woman exclaimed.

Kat blew air out of her mouth. Was this what it was going to be like the entire holiday? Would she not be allowed to forget about Jacques at all? Would it be an issue everywhere she went and everything she did?

'Yes, my boyfriend isn't with me because he is a cheating rat,' Kat replied in frustration.

'Oh,' the woman said again. Kat wasn't certain she'd understood her.

Just as she was about to ask where she should catch her transport, the woman's eyes moved to someone behind her. Too late Kat realised Mikael had witnessed their exchange. He said something unintelligible in Finnish to the woman and she nodded.

'Welcome to Lapland,' she said, turning back to Kat with a smile this time. 'We will find you a good Finnish man here!'

Two men next to the woman, also holding lists and displaying various holiday company logos on their shirts, smiled knowingly at her. Kat wished for the floor of the arrivals hall to swallow her.

'So where should I go?' Kat asked, trying to ignore everyone except for the woman in front of her.

The woman's eyes widened. 'To find a man?'

Kat sighed. 'No, to get to *Ylläs.*'

'The bus is waiting right there. It has all the resort names on it.' She pointed at the small parking lot, visible through the open sliding doors.

'Thank you so much,' Kat said in her most British-sounding accent. She ignored Mikael, who was standing right behind her.

I never want to see that man again, she thought, as she settled on the bus.

The beauty of the snow-filled scene calmed her, and she inhaled the crisp, clean air. This was going to be good for her. She needed to be able to stand on her own two feet.

What Jacques had done to her was terrible. To carry on behind her back for such a long time was the worst betrayal she had ever experienced. But compared to what the other woman had done, his deception was nothing. Not only had Kat lost her boyfriend, who she thought was going to be the person she'd spend the rest of her life with, but she had also lost someone who should have loved and cherished her. She was totally on her own now.

Chapter Four

As the bus drove along narrow, deserted white-covered roads towards the ski resort, dusk settled on the snowy landscape outside. First, a pink glow filled the sky as the sun sank below the horizon. Kat looked at her watch and saw it was only just 3pm.

The dark light made the high banks of snow glimmer, like tiny diamonds had been scattered on top of them. The trees on either side of the road were weighed down with snow, giving the landscape an enchanted look. Kat craned her neck to see if she could spot any green or yellow Northern Lights in the sky, but when she saw a thin layer of clouds, she knew there would be no Aurora Borealis tonight. The Northern Lights mainly occurred in clear skies.

Kat was beginning to feel better. Perhaps this holiday would be good for her after all.

The bus was only about a quarter full. There were

two families, a group of young twenty-somethings, and two couples. Kat avoided looking at them, their heads close to one other.

That should have been Jacques and me.

She couldn't escape the images playing in her mind. Was Jacques with *her* right now? Were they talking about Kat, laughing at her naivety, at her youth?

How could you have expected a man like Jacques to want to spend his life with you? You are a child compared to him!

These words haunted Kat as she surveyed the landscape, which, with the intensifying darkness of the skies, had become even more spellbinding. They passed a small hamlet with a group of houses topped with fresh snow, soft blankets of white covering their roofs. Their little, lit-up windows suggested warm, cosy interiors. Kat imagined open fires and comfy sofas covered with blankets.

She closed her eyes for a moment and, once more, resolved to forget about Jacques and enjoy this holiday.

That's when her phone pinged with a message.

How are you, hon?

It was her friend Toni, who was also her current landlady.

Kat had begged her to take Jacques' place on this trip, but Toni had just started working on a new reality show, *Farmers on the Hunt for Love*. Leaving the set and the production without its newly promoted assistant producer would have been a career-breaking decision.

Kat and Toni had met two and a bit years ago when they'd both been runners on another cookery show set in a seaside town. They were both green and eager to work their socks off. They'd felt lucky to have the chance to work in the glamorous (or what they'd thought then was glamorous) TV world. The hours they'd put in were ridiculous.

Even now, when they both had proper titles and designated responsibilities in different production companies, the days were long. The competition was fierce, because there was always someone else ready to take their place if they didn't work their asses off.

In more ways than one.

As the bus stopped to let a couple sitting in front of her out, Kat typed a reply.

I'm OK. Regretting coming a bit, to be honest. But it's beautiful here.

She snapped a photo of the sunset which was now a line of pinks and purples against the darkening sky and white snow.

Wow! You need to have a good time, girl! Find yourself a handsome rebound guy to help you forget about you-know-who. You're better off without him.

Kat smiled at the message.

If only it was that easy.

She gazed out of the window again just as the bus came to a roundabout. She could see the signs for Ylläs.

I'm nearly there. Call later?

A reply came quickly.

Got it, girl. We've just finished for the day so I'm chilling at the hotel.

Kat misjudged the amount of travelling left. As the bus made its way along the dark, snowy landscape, her thoughts went back to that first year of her TV career.

Her second job had been on The Culinary Kingdom. Jacques had been the presenter on the hugely popular cooking show where, each week, contestants faced various challenges to ultimately win the title, King Chef.

Originally from France, Jacques was a bit of a celebrity in the UK. Before The Culinary Kingdom, he'd been a chat show host on morning TV, and had even written several books about food. One of them *Maman's Kitchen* was a bestseller. In it he recounted the dishes his French mother cooked.

Kat gave a snort.

She remembered how he'd told her that he had invented the stories in the book. His own mother, a selfish Parisian ex-model, hadn't prepared anything more complicated than *Croque Monsieur* in their tiny one-bedroom flat in the less-well-to-do suburbs of Paris. It was his dad who was the foodie.

Jacques had left Paris for the 'culinary wasteland' – as he called the UK – on a whim after meeting an English girl. He'd followed her to London, but the relationship had ended soon after.

'We found we had nothing in common,' he'd told Kat.

Before London, after leaving school and from the age of sixteen, Jacques had worked in various kitchens in Paris. He was following in the footsteps of his father, who was a chef in a small brasserie in *Le Marais* district.

'The *arrondissement* wasn't as fashionable then as it

is now,' Jacques had said, his mouth turning down and giving a Gallic shrug.

Kat had been quiet, eagerly waiting to hear more about Jacques' past, which he had always been very tight-lipped about.

'I have a new life in your beautiful country,' was all he'd say whenever Kat asked what his life in Paris had been like.

She'd been to the city twice while studying at art college and she'd loved the city. She'd desperately wanted him to take her there, and couldn't think of anything better than have a Parisian show her the secret places to visit and eat, but Jacques never did.

Kat could never understand why he didn't want to go back. Now, she wondered if he'd ever even lived there. She couldn't trust anything he'd told her.

Chapter Five

Mikael was excited to be back in Lapland. The call to return a week early had been a relief. He was getting tired of his mother Ulla's not-so-well disguised hints about his future and how he was wasting his time as a skiing instructor.

Or 'ski bum' as she'd put it.

Words that were not hers, Mikael knew, but his fathers. Erik Andersson rarely spoke to his son about anything important, preferring to use his wife to communicate his displeasure of his children.

Instead, his father preferred to talk to Mikael about ice-hockey, and the latest wins of his team, the Helsinki HIFK. He never once mentioned Mikael's latest job, or the fact that he'd wanted his son to join the family firm. Mikael had learnt all this from his mum. Ulla was originally from Lapland, but for the past thirty years, she had lived in Helsinki after meeting and having married his father.

It was being half-Lappish that had pulled Mikael to the north – he was sure of it. He also knew that his father blamed Ulla for Mikael's love of skiing. Not that Erik had anything against the sport itself. Slalom was – in the rest of Europe, at least – a rich man's pursuit, but working with one's hobby as he, through her mum, put it, wasn't right.

It was selfish.

'It's time to grow up, Mikael,' his mother had said. 'Look at your brother. He's got his own apartment and a girlfriend. He is being such a support to your father and the business.'

Mikael had raised his eyebrows at the mention of his brother's girlfriend. Victor was a serial philanderer, picking up women with his flashy car and designer clothes, and dropping them as soon as there was a whiff of a serious relationship on the horizon.

Mikael hated that his mother would compare him to Victor. Although she was just repeating what his father had told her to say.

Still, it hurt, especially when Mikael was nothing like his brother. Two and a half years older than him, Victor was the golden boy. Everything he did ignited praise from his parents.

It had always been that way.

Mikael loved skiing, and was good at it, but he was not sporty. He'd never been any good at ice-hockey or baseball at school. He'd always been the last to be picked, whereas his brother excelled in everything that moved.

(Nowadays this included the sport of dating as many women as he possibly could).

Surely his parents must have noticed how different Mikael and Victor were?

When Mikael had first learnt to ski at an early age, he immediately understood this was his sport. He'd loved the crunch of the snow under his skis, the wind in his hair, and the rush of adrenaline that came from going downhill at breakneck speed. It was something he'd never experienced before, and it was addictive. But his parents had never tried to understand him. They'd always thought it was a phase that he'd eventually grow out of. That skiing would be something he'd do on holidays. Not something he'd want to make a career out of.

His parents' large apartment in the older part of Helsinki, Ullanlinna, which his brother had long since escaped, had become stifling to Mikael, after having been forced to spend days there before this trip. He felt sorry for his colleague up in Ylläs, a local guy who'd injured his knee while descending the mountain. But his misfortune meant that Mikael's forced holiday at home had been cut short. So, he was glad for himself.

Mikael hadn't been able to breathe in Helsinki. The city and the large apartment (his chalet in Ylläs would have fitted into his parents' bedroom) had made him panicky.

After waking up in his old bedroom, he'd tiptoe into the kitchen and listen out, to hear if his father had left for the office. Once certain the coast was clear, he'd pour himself a coffee from a thermos his mother always left out for him.

Except for one morning, when Erik Andersson had returned without warning. His entering the kitchen had made Mikael jump.

He had nearly poured the hot liquid onto his lap when his father had barked, 'Day off, is it?'

Erik stood in the doorway, with his heavy, woollen ulster buttoned up and his briefcase gripped tightly in his gloved hand.

Mikael glanced at his own T-shirt and tracksuit bottoms.

'I'm on holiday. Going back to work next week.'

His father harrumphed and after giving his son a steely gaze, turned on his heels and left the apartment.

His mum came into the kitchen right after to find Mikael still staring at the doorway where his father had stood.

'You look like you've just seen a ghost,' Ulla said, pressing her hand to his back.

Mikael sat down at the kitchen table and muttered,' Oh, just Dad giving me his usual death stare.'

Ulla peered at her son's face and sat opposite him.

'He only wants what best for you, you know that.'

Mikael lifted his eyes to his mum's. 'More like what he has *decided* is best for me. For him and the company. He doesn't give a crap about what I want!'

His mother's face fell and Mikael felt bad. He didn't mean to upset her, but he was so fed up with his father's attitude.

He took Ulla's hands into his and said, 'I'm sorry, Mum, but it's so frustrating when he refuses to even talk to me about it. You know I love skiing, and being able to teach people is my dream.'

'I know,' she said, brushing his cheek briefly, and continued, 'You father is an old-fashioned man, but I believe he is acting in your best interests. What you are doing isn't really a career. You can't make a living out of it. Besides, what will happen when you get older and you can no longer ski? You're young now, but you must think about your future.'

'But I love it up there. The snow, the pure air, the wilderness ...' Mikael smiled at her. 'It's your half in me that makes me love Lapland, I'm sure of it.'

His mother pulled her hands out of Mikael's grasp.

'Don't say that! Your father is already blaming me for your obsession with the Sami culture.' She rose from the table abruptly.

On her way out of the kitchen, she said, 'There's some homemade granola in the cupboard and fresh milk in the fridge. Help yourself.'

Mikael had sat at the table for a long time after his mum had left. Amid the repressive stillness of the apartment, he heard her close the door to his parents' bedroom.

It was always stifling being at home and in the city. He'd missed the pure air and quiet of the mountains and he missed the snow. He missed the vast skies that seemed to touch the snow-topped cliffs.

That's why he'd been in such good mood at the

airport and had bought the glass of champagne for that miserable-looking girl with the cropped hair in the bar. It wasn't something he made a habit of doing. He wasn't like most of his classmates in the School of Economics in Helsinki who'd try to impress any pretty female they came across.

All he'd wanted was to spread his good cheer, but she didn't seem to appreciate it. Instead of having a quick conversation with him, she gave him a look as if he'd spat in her champagne. That's why he'd laughed when she had struggled to find her transport to take her to the resort. It wasn't the nice thing to do, but the girl had been so serious. She needed to lighten up.

He hoped experiencing the wild beauty of Lapland would make her relax a bit.

Chapter Six

The chalet hotel was a wooden, two-storey building, which looked magical in the twilight surrounded by blankets of white snow. A few other people alighted from the bus who were staying at the same hotel with Kat. All of them were couples. Then she spotted the annoying guy, Mikael.

Kat swore under her breath. She couldn't understand how she'd missed seeing him on the bus. Not that she had been looking for him. He must have got on while she was putting her luggage into the hold.

Not only did she feel out of place as she walked into the hotel lobby with the couples who were oohing and aahing, but she felt awkward in his presence.

When she looked around the hotel, Kat could see what the fuss was all about. The space was filled with low-slung seats covered with reindeer skins. There were chandeliers made from what she guessed were reindeer antlers. The lighting was low, showing off a large open fire in the centre of the room.

There were a couple of friendly looking receptionists behind a long desk set against the back wall, standing in front of a picture of the snowy landscape they had all just travelled through. The other holidaymakers formed a queue in front of each receptionist.

Mikael didn't join the queue but stood to one side of the reception desk, nodding to the woman closest to him. He leaned on the desk and spoke in a low voice to her. They seemed to know each other. They exchanged a few words in Finnish, while the woman checked in a couple in front of Kat. Kat purposely chose the other queue, but regretted it, as the couple in front were taking forever. They asked hundreds of questions about their holiday and booked several excursions.

Kat shifted from one foot to the other, releasing a long sigh and trying to catch the receptionist's eye.

'You can come over here. Salla can check you in.'

Mikael was suddenly next to her, gesturing towards the woman he had been chatting to. His eyes, however, were on Kat. There was a smile twitching on his lips.

She gave the desk in front of her another glance, but the older couple were still deep in conversation with the receptionist.

Kat could hardly refuse.

With a sigh, she went to grab her suitcase, but found that Mikael had already moved it. She walked slowly towards the smiling woman.

How more in your face can this guy get?

'Hi, welcome to Ylläs!' the receptionist said.

'Thank you,' Kat replied, and tried to return the woman's warm smile. She glanced at Mikael, who also smiled at her.

Kat addressed the receptionist.

'I had a large chalet booked for two but it's just me.'

'Oh yes, her friend couldn't make it,' Mikael added, his eyes shining with mischief.

'You know each other?' the receptionist asked, clearly surprised.

'Not really,' Kat replied. 'We sat next to each other on the flight from Helsinki and shared a glass of champagne.'

Mikael grinned at her, and Kat couldn't help but smile back.

When Kat saw the huge bed in the middle of her chalet, a pang of longing tugged at her heart. The sight of the inviting mattress, overlooking the snow-covered woods, reminded her of the romantic getaway she had planned with Jacques. It was meant to be a shared experience, a celebration of their love and a step towards a future together.

But as she dropped her bags and lowered herself onto the soft mattress, a sense of desolation engulfed her. The weight of loneliness settled heavily in her chest, squeezing her heart with a pain so piercing that she wanted to double over. She longed for the solace of tears, but they refused to come. It seemed that she had exhausted her tear reserves, having squeezed them dry in the tumultuous two weeks leading up to this trip.

Unpacking her belongings, Kat's mind drifted unchecked, filled with images that she couldn't escape. Visions of Jacques entangled in bed sheets with *her* haunted her, coupled with a cocktail of anger, betrayal, and heartache.

As she had done for the past two weeks, Kat frantically tried to piece together the timeline in her mind, torturing herself with the thought that Jacques had never really been hers, and hers alone.

With Toni away, Kat had no one to talk to about the betrayal. At work, she had carried on as normal, supporting Jacques as the show lead as she had always done. She'd felt numb, but was secretly glad that no one in the company had known about their relationship. Jacques had wanted it that way.

Had it been because of the affair with *her*?

They had shared intimate moments, laughing, whispering secrets that had once been reserved for Kat and Jacques. The knowledge that it had probably gone on for almost as long as her relationship with Jacques was unbearable. A sharp pain pierced her gut.

Unable to bear the weight of her heavy thoughts any longer, Kat pushed herself off the bed and walked to the window. The soft flakes of snow were falling gently from the sky, blanketing the ground and covering treetops in a pristine white. The serenity of the scene contrasted sharply with the turmoil in her heart.

She spotted stars glimmering in the now clear night

sky, their distant light offering a glimmer of solace. Closing her eyes, Kat took a deep breath, attempting to find a sliver of peace amidst the chaos within. She reminded herself that this trip was not about Jacques or his new lover.

It was about Kat's healing, her growth, and finding a sense of self that didn't rely on the presence or approval of others.

With a new determination, she dragged herself away from the window and undressed herself. She'd seen a sauna in the corner of the bathroom, and decided to allow herself the luxury of a relaxing steam. The warmth lulled her exhausted body into submission, wrapping her in a cocoon of serenity. The low lighting inside the sauna created an atmosphere of hushed introspection.

In the sweltering embrace of the sauna, Kat let her mind drift back to her life so far, the journey that had led her to this point.

Her grandparents were from Finland, but Kat, born in London to their only daughter, had only seen them once, when she was very little. Her mum had taken her to Finland before her *pappa* died and her gran, *mummi*, had ended up in an old people's home. Kat didn't even remember her grandparents. She only had a vague memory of a funeral, but she wasn't certain if it was because of her mother's stories and the photographs she'd occasionally dug up and showed her. Kat had only been six at the time.

After her grandparents had passed, Kat's mum seemed to lose all contact with her home country, concentrating instead on her translating business. Simona was a single mum of three, and always working, so Kat and her younger sister and brother had spent their childhoods being looked after by her mum's friends and her English grandparents.

Her dad was another missing person in Kat's life. He'd disappeared when Kat's mum had been expecting her younger brother.

Memories of her childhood with her single mother, Simona, flickered through her mind like an old movie reel. The struggles Kat had faced head on with her siblings; the laughter they had all shared; and the unbreakable bond that had cemented their family's foundation.

But a bitter realisation cut through those cherished memories. The betrayal of Jacques struck at the core of her being, threatening to unravel the very fabric of her identity. Her father's abandonment had already left a void within her, and now, the infidelity of the man she loved felt like a second abandonment, a reopening of old wounds.

Kat's fists tightened as she felt anger and pain surge through her. She had vowed to herself that she would rise above this. She wouldn't let the actions of others define her. This trip was her opportunity to rebuild, to find strength within herself, and to forge a new path forward.

Kat stepped out of the sauna, took a shower, and wrapped herself in a warm robe. She resolved to make the most of the days ahead. She would immerse herself in her surroundings by learning to ski, and experiencing the beauty of Lapland and its breathtaking landscapes. She would find solace in the serenity of nature and the exploration of new adventures.

She stared at her reflection in the mirror, seeing only a flicker of determination in her eyes. Fresh tears fell and she swiped them away. She refused to let Jacques' actions interfere in her happiness any longer.

As she slipped into the warm embrace of the huge bed, she looked out the large window once more. The snow was still falling, a reminder of the cleansing purity that could come if she let go.

With a deep breath, Kat closed her eyes, ready to embrace the possibilities that lay ahead and to forge a new chapter in her life, one defined by her own choices.

Chapter Seven

'Of course, you'll be able to ski. You're just being a scary cat as usual. You're half Finnish, for goodness' sake. Act like it.'

Kat's mother's words reverberated in her mind as she trudged up the small slope, burdened by heavy skis and poles. She couldn't help but feel a mixture of frustration and defiance at her mother's comment.

If she'd been given the opportunity to experience Finland and its winter wonderland more than once, then perhaps she would have been more confident about the lessons ahead. A surge of resentment bubbled within her as she recalled the brunch with her mother and Jacques at the expensive coffee place in Hampstead.

'*Ma petite chérie*, I will take care of you. I have been skiing since I was a small boy!'

Simona's remarks had made Jacques laugh.

Jacques had put his arm around Kat and kissed the

top of her head. She had felt special then, looking forward to their magical trip together.

Of course, that was before.

But now, in the wide-open landscapes of Lapland, Kat would have to look after herself. Which she was fully capable of doing.

She heaved her skis onto her shoulder, the edges digging into her skin, even through the insulation of her jacket and salopettes. She clenched her teeth, reminding herself that these fleeting discomforts were nothing compared to the emotional pain she carried.

As she caught her breath and took in the slope ahead, Kat's heart skipped a beat. The piste loomed before her, wide and steep, filled with confident skiers gliding effortlessly across its surface. Doubt crept in, whispering that she would never be as skilled as these seasoned skiers, that she will only embarrass herself or worse, get injured. But there was a flicker of determination within her, too, a resolve to prove herself, not only to Jacques but to *her*.

Chapter Eight

London, before

The piercing shriek of car horns shattered Kat's reverie as she gazed out the window of the double-decker bus rumbling through London. The traffic had come to a standstill and many drivers were protesting.

As if that ever made any difference.

With Kat's stop only a few yards away, she moved towards the door and gave a pleading glance to the bus driver. His eyes met Kat's through the rear-view mirror and suddenly the doors flew open. Kat gave him a wave and a quick smile while securing her canvas tote of vegetables, nuts and spices on her shoulders. She hopped off and opened her umbrella. Just as it had every day that week, it was raining hard. As Kat walked towards the massive warehouse that housed the set of The Culinary Kingdom, she wondered if the sun would ever show its face again.

Passing a row of shops, she spotted a thin, little dog, tied outside Tesco, shivering and whimpering. The sad creature kept glancing at the doors of the store, waiting for its owner to remerge. Kat glanced at her watch. She was running late, but the pleading eyes of what she thought was a miniature whippet stopped her in her tracks.

'You poor little thing,' she said, as she moved closer to the dog. She knelt down and extended her hand for it to sniff while covering the dog's head with the umbrella. The creature gave Kat a grateful lick, then lifted a wet paw and placed it on her knee.

'Oh, I'm so sorry!' An older woman came out of the shop and gazing at the wet mark on Kat's jeans, put a hand over her mouth.

'That's OK,' Kat said. Smiling, she added, 'He's lovely.'

'I don't usually leave him outside, but I just had no choice. The manager wouldn't let me take him inside.'

When the woman kept on speaking, Kat had to stop her.

'It's OK, really! I must go, I'm late for work.'

Once inside the studio, Kat switched to work mode. Blocking out the cacophony around her, she chopped the cabbage, julienned the carrots, and toasted the quinoa. Her hands moved swiftly and precisely, as they had so many times before.

'Rolling in thirty seconds!' The panicked voice of the producer crackled through her headset. Kat nodded, not looking up from the cutting board.

The familiar sounds of the show's dramatic theme music began to play as the host strode onto the set with his usual bravado. Kat kept her eyes down and continued slicing, though she couldn't help listening to the host's booming introduction.

'Welcome to The Culinary Kingdom! Our contestants will face their biggest challenge yet – creating a gourmet, three-course vegan meal with only locally sourced organic ingredients and one hour on the clock!'

One hour. Kat breathed in the earthy scent of the vegetables, took in the cool sleekness of her knife, and began to chop faster. Thirty minutes to get the ingredients prepped. Fifteen minutes to help the contestants. Fifteen minutes to clean the set.

The timer was running. The kingdom awaited.

Kat risked a glance up as Jacques fronted the set, smiling and waving to the live audience. His piercing blue eyes scanned the kitchen, landing on Kat for a brief moment. She looked away quickly, focusing on the mushrooms she was slicing.

Though they had been together for over two years, Jacques still made her nervous. His presence dominated the room, a larger-than-life personality who demanded perfection from his staff and the contestants.

'*Mademoiselle!*' Jacques barked, making Kat jump.

She looked up to see him glaring at one of the contestants, a young woman with shaking hands who was attempting to make pastry.

'Your dough is too dry! Did you not follow the recipe?'

The contestant stammered an apology, cheeks turning bright red under the hot studio lights. Jacques sighed – the picture of Gallic impatience – and shoved her aside.

'I will do it myself, as always,' he muttered, snatching the rolling pin from her hands. Kat winced in sympathy and returned to her *mise en place*. Jacques's temper was legendary, and she didn't envy the contestants one bit.

As Jacques began rolling out the dough, Kat finished prepping the ingredients just in time. The host was announcing the start of the cook-off, the dramatic music was rising to a crescendo, and the contestants were rushing to claim their stations.

Kat handed them baskets of ingredients, wishing them luck, and then began cleaning up the prep area. Through it all, she kept an eye on Jacques – and on the timer ticking down to the end of another chaotic day in The Culinary Kingdom.

Kat wiped the sweat off her brow. Taking a moment's rest, she leaned against the stainless-steel counter of the prep kitchen on the far side of the set. The on-set kitchen was a flurry of activity, with contestants shouting and pans clanging, and the aroma of shallots, wine and freshly baked bread wafting through the air.

In the midst of the chaos, Jacques glided with preternatural grace, correcting contestants and charming the studio audience with equal aplomb. But Kat noticed something odd; he kept glancing over at the door to the pantry, a small smile playing on his lips.

After the take, when Kat was helping set up the next cook-off and Jacques went missing, she remembered his strange behaviour during the show. Her heart beating too fast, she crept towards the pantry to investigate.

Peeking through the door, her worst fears were confirmed: Jacques had cornered one of the new interns there, a pretty blonde girl who was barely twenty. He was whispering in her ear and running a finger down her arm in an unmistakably intimate gesture.

Kat reeled back, bile rising in her throat. She had suspected Jacques was unfaithful, had ignored the signs, but to see the evidence so plainly before her eyes shook her to the core. How could he do this – and right in front of her, on the set of their show? It was a betrayal too far.

In that moment, Kat realised the truth she had long denied: Jacques did not care for her at all. She was merely a convenience, another ingredient in his recipe for success and fame. Their relationship, like so much else in his glamorous world, was artifice.

Kat curled her hands into fists, rage and sorrow warring within her. She had given him her love, her loyalty, her life, and this was how he repaid her.

For a moment, all Kat saw was white light in front of her eyes. It was as if Jacques' latest betrayal had tipped her over the edge and blinded her. Heat rose in her throat, reaching her face; it felt flushed as if the blood running around her veins was literally boiling over.

Kat went back to The Culinary Kingdom prep kitchen. She took a couple of deep breaths and her vision gradually returned to normal. She began chopping vegetables again, this time with quick, angry strokes.

Through the window she saw Jacques. He was now filming at the judge's table, laughing and preening for the cameras. His eyes met hers for a brief moment, and she saw a flicker of guilt pass across his face. But then he turned away, playing the charming host for the viewers at home.

Kat's hands clenched around the knife handle until her knuckles turned white. How dare he? How dare he pretend that nothing was wrong?

One of the sous chefs approached her nervously.

'Kat? Are you alright?'

She rounded on him, eyes blazing.

'Does it look like I'm alright?'

The *sous* chef backed away, hands raised in surrender. Kat exhaled sharply through her nose, trying to calm her frayed temper. She couldn't afford to lash out – not here, not now. She needed to keep it together until the cameras stopped rolling.

Through the window, Jacques looked at her again. Their eyes met and she saw a flicker of unease in his gaze.

Good. He should be worried.

Kat returned her attention to the mirepoix in front of

her, dicing the carrots and celery with quick, precise strokes. To any outside observer, she would have appeared completely calm. But inside, she was seething. The rage bubbled just under her skin.

Knowing she had to keep her emotions at bay, she put all her emotions into her work.

Chapter Nine

'There you are! We were beginning to worry.'

Mikael stood in front of the other would-be skiers as Kat finally reached the ski lifts.

Oh no!

The others were sniggering at her lateness, but one of the women, whose husband was as round as he was tall, touched Kat's arm and said, 'Don't worry, dear, he's exaggerating.'

Kat gave the woman a weary smile but didn't lift her eyes to Mikael's. She should have guessed he would be their ski instructor.

She was close to regretting this trip. What had she been thinking, going skiing alone, trying to catch the Northern Lights, staying in a huge chalet obviously meant for romantic getaways for two, all the way in Finnish Lapland?

But standing at the bottom of the pistes, she suddenly appreciated the splendour before her. The Ylläs Fell, a regal giant, reached towards the heavens, its majestic peaks bathed in the golden rays of the sun. A stunning contrast unfolded between the snow-capped summits and the azure sky.

The ski slopes, meticulously cared for, danced like ribbons of pure-white silk, inviting adventurers to embark upon an exhilarating journey. Several skiers were already traversing the mountainside with a grace that mirrored the elegance of a waltz, leaving temporary imprints on the virgin snow.

All around Kat, laughter mingled with the soft crunch of boots on snow, as skiers descended upon the slopes, their movements as fluid as poetry in motion. In this winter haven, time seemed to stand still, granting respite from the bustle of the world.

Up ahead, Mikael paused a moment, as if waiting for her to speak or to acknowledge the joke. But she pretended to busy herself with her ski boots. The woman in the rental shop had told her not to do them up until she was about to take the lift, so, with difficulty, she was now trying to get the bindings fastened.

'Here, let me.'

Suddenly Mikael was in front of her. He knelt down and with practiced hands, locked the first two binds, but when he came to the third, which was just over her ankle, he struggled.

'That's a bit too tight, I think,' he said, and smiled up at Kat. His eyes were clear-blue against the orange-coloured jacket and the white snow piste behind him.

'Yeah,' she replied, trying not to blush. They were so close that she could smell his cologne.

That's when Kat remembered that she hadn't taken a shower that morning. For years now, she'd restricted herself to one shower per day lasting just four minutes, to save the earth's resources. The sauna in her chalet last night had been too tempting, so she'd decided not to waste any more water or energy on herself today.

She had then trudged up the hill, her skis and boots making a clumsy racket against each other. Even though the temperature was below freezing, she now felt like she was melting inside all the layers of clothing. Now, Kat couldn't help but worry what she smelt like.

Jacques had once asked her if she had showered that morning during the early stages of their relationship. When she responded she hadn't because of her concern for global warming, he'd given her one of his familiar shrugs. In alarm, she had asked him if she was sweaty. To which he had just replied, 'I love your scent.'

But she hadn't been able to shake off her doubts, and after that embarrassing episode, she always made sure to shower before seeing him.

And now, here she was again thinking about Jacques, even when it no longer mattered what he thought about her, because, in reality, he was an upper-class guy and she was never in his league.

Mikael adjusted something on her boots and expertly got the last bind closed on both.

'Lean forward a bit and bend your knees,' he said. 'The boots will be more comfortable to wear.'

'OK, thanks,' Kat muttered, blushing. Even though it didn't matter what the guy thought of her, she felt embarrassed enough to worry about it.

Mikael turned to the rest of the group. 'That goes for all of you. If you need any help, just let me know. Now, let's go over to the lift.'

To Kat he said, 'I think you're with me. All the others are paired up.'

'Just relax,' Mikael said, when they were seated either side of what appeared to be a flimsy T-bar, moving up the snowy mountainside.

'I'm trying,' she said, giving him a sideways glance.

Mikael had shown her how to hold her skis against the ground. As the lift began to jerk forward, Kat had nearly slipped off the seat. That had prompted Mikael to put his arm around her waist. Of course, that made her tense up even more, but at the same time, his strong grip *had* made her feel safer.

Mikael tightened his hold on her.

'It's OK. You should have seen me when I first tried to get on an anchor lift. I think I fell about ten times.'

'That's a lie right there. I bet you were born with skis on your feet.'

At that moment, Kat's left ski started to veer against her right; tendrils of panic began to creep into her chest.

Mikael squeezed her waist and said, 'It's OK, just keep them pointing up. No big movements.'

Kat made a small adjustment to her feet, and soon they were on a level course again.

'How old were you?' she asked him.

'Oh, when I had my incident with the lift? I can't remember.'

'Another lie.'

When Kat glanced at Mikael again, she saw he looked embarrassed.

'OK, I was three.'

'Right.'

'I don't really remember it, but I've been told I caused a terrible scene. The story goes that I decided to ski downhill about halfway up the mountain while the anchor lift was still moving. My dad had been sitting next to me on the T-bar. He fell over because he was taken so aback by my move, which caused all the people behind him lose their balance. Apparently, it was like a set of dominos falling. My dad was so angry with me. I don't think he's ever forgiven me.'

Mikael fell quiet for moment and Kat took a quick look at him. He appeared deep in thought. Perhaps he was ashamed of having shared too much with her, a perfect stranger?

The lift stopped abruptly.

Mikael turned to look down the hill, causing Kat to nearly fall off the slippery bar.

'Hey!'

The word escaped from Kat's mouth before she had time to stop herself.

'Sorry, I was just trying to see what's happened,' said

Mikael. 'I think someone missed the bar down at the bottom. But they're OK.'

Mikael smiled at her and pulled her closer to him.

'Right,' Kat said, trying to sound casual. But her heart was racing.

She didn't know if it was flimsy seat, the unfamiliar sensation of the skis on her feet, the skiers moving fast downhill on the piste on Mikael's side, or his proximity.

How would she manage to ski if she was this hopeless just going up the hill in a lift?

The bar moved again and this time, Kat managed to keep herself in balance and stay quiet.

'Skiing is much easier than getting used to these anchor lifts,' Mikael said, as if he had read her mind.

'Huh...'

Mikael's smile was wide and lighting up his face. Despite herself, she returned the smile.

He was really good looking.

No, no, no. What am I thinking! No thoughts of Jacques, or other men.

'By the way, I'm digging your retro look,' Mikael said with a wink.

Before she could answer, they'd arrived at the top of the mountain. Mikael took her hand and told her to do exactly as he did.

'Most important thing,' he said, 'let go of the lift, but don't let go of my hand.'

Chapter Ten

Sitting next to Kat, Mikael had wanted to ask her more about herself. But he was annoyingly tongue-tied. Then she'd somehow made him tell the story of when he had embarrassed his father, which was the last thing he wanted to talk about.

Once they had reached the top, Mikael led her to the beginner's slope and began the lesson. It was clear that she had never skied before, but she caught on quickly. Soon, she was making her way down along with the other beginners.

When Mikael skied ahead of his group, he couldn't help but enjoy the familiar rush of adrenaline that came with it. The cold air brushed against his face, sending shivers through his body. He smiled to himself, content in the knowledge that he was where he was meant to be.

The thoughts of his father, and the pressure that was being put on him to 'do the right thing and join the family business' fell away like the snow beneath his skis.

His thoughts returned to Kat. She was quiet and reserved, but there was an air of mystery about her that intrigued Mikael. He couldn't quite put his finger on the attraction, but he felt drawn to her in a way he hadn't in a long time. Her large brown eyes, which were made more piercing by the short, chestnut-brown hairstyle, were noticeably sad, but he'd also seen a glint playfulness in them.

As they made their way back up in the anchor lift, for a second run on the nursery slope, Mikael couldn't help but sneak glances at her. Her eyes were fixed on the mountain ranges around them, and he wondered what she was thinking about. He cleared his throat, breaking the comfortable silence between them.

'So, what did you think of skiing?' he asked.

She turned to look at him, her eyes meeting his. Mikael was taken aback by the intensity he saw there.

'It was exhilarating,' she said, her voice low and husky. 'I never knew skiing could be so freeing.'

Mikael's heart raced at the sound of her voice and the obvious passion that skiing had awoken in her. There was something about the way she spoke that sent a jolt of electricity through him. He found himself leaning in, wanting to be closer to her.

As he took the group down the nursery slope again, Mikael struggled to keep his focus on the task. His mind kept drifting to the woman behind him. He wondered what her story was, and what had brought her here alone.

. . .

By lunchtime, Kat was hot and exhausted. With Mikael's help she and the other beginners in her group had managed to make their way down the nursery slope more than ten times. Flanked by children of various ages speeding past her, Kat had learnt to do a very basic, but terrifying, turn on her skis, while holding them in an inverted V shape – or plough as Mikael called it.

'Tomorrow we will begin parallel skiing,' he said enthusiastically to the group.

At the bottom of the run Kat leaned on her poles. She couldn't remember being this tired ever. She was amazed she hadn't broken some part of her body. Her legs felt like jelly and beads of sweat ran down her back.

'You have great balance and internal control,' Mikael had told her at the beginning of the last run, giving her that same flashy smile as he had in the Helsinki airport bar.

Kat had lowered her eyes and pushed off gently, skiing down the hill. However much she tried not to, the compliment made her smile, as she glided down the piste.

Looking at the group now, Kat realised she was the youngest of the women by some margin.

That's why this guy is hitting on me.

The others were in their forties at least, if not older. All had their partners with them, so that left her as Mikael's only choice.

What is it with men? Why can't they communicate with women without making it sexual?

Not that older women had ever been a problem for Jacques. It seemed he preferred them.

Kat shook her head, trying to make thoughts of him vanish. She was here to learn how to ski, to observe the Northern Lights, and to have some fun. Moping over her ex wasn't part of the plan.

Neither was discovering another man. Kat was done with the opposite sex.

Forever.

'We're having lunch over there, care to join us?' The woman who had spoken to her earlier in the day pointed to a spot by the lifts. While clutching Kat's arm, the vibrant woman with silver hair gave her a gentle smile. 'I'm Pat, by the way, and this is Reg. I reckon we all deserve some refreshment after all that, don't you agree?'

'Let's have a drink!' her husband, a short man with grey eyebrows and moustache, exclaimed. Reg gestured wildly with his pole. 'Come on love, I'm parched.'

'I'll be there in a minute,' Kat said, needing a little breather after the last run.

She turned around to gaze with pride at the slope she had just skied down. The darkness was beginning to settle upon the fell again, and Kat inspected the skies for any signs of Northern Lights. It was too early, but the skies were clear, so there was hope.

With a sense of satisfaction and anticipation building, Kat followed the others to the large building by the lifts.

Chapter Eleven

Kat joined the other skiers at one of the larger restaurants by the lifts. She made her way clumsily through the restaurant with her bulky boots, which she had unbuckled like the girl in the shop had instructed her. Still, her progress was slow and seemingly even more difficult than navigating a slippery, snow-covered mountain.

Pat waved at her from a large table by the floor-to-ceiling windows.

Kat walked over and added her jacket to a pile of clothes on a settee. She slumped down, allowing the exhaustion from the morning's skiing lesson to settle in her bones. Her muscles ached and her eyelids were heavy from the exhilaration of conquering the nursery slope. She glanced around the bustling restaurant, taking in the sight of skiers and snowboarders enjoying their well-deserved break, as the weariness, both physical and emotional from the experience, began to ebb away.

'Can't be that bad, can it?' Reg stood next to her, carrying a tray of drinks. The skin around his eyes was creased, and his lips were upturned into a smile. He put a bottle of beer in front of Kat and added, 'Didn't know what you wanted, so I thought I'd get you the local brew. It's supposed to be excellent.'

Kat's eyes lit up at the sight of the cold beer. It was exactly what she needed after the emotional rollercoaster of the past couple of days. Gratefully, she took the bottle and glass offered by the older man and thanked him with a smile.

'To a great day's skiing!' Reg exclaimed, lifting his glass.

Kat clinked her glass against his, and they both took a sip. The beer tasted refreshing and helped to wash away some of the lingering bitterness from her recent heartbreak. As she glanced at one of the menus strewn on the table, she noticed there was a great selection of vegan food available, further putting her at ease. With the drink and the promise of a satisfying meal, she felt herself relax.

Glancing around the table and her group, Kat saw that all the other skiers looked equally exhausted but were still invigorated after their morning's activities. Laughter and chatter filled the air, as if they had been friends for years rather than mere hours. She couldn't help but inquire, turning to Pat, who was seated beside her.

'Did you all know each other before?' Kat's voice carried genuine intrigue.

The question caused laughter from the entire table, though it was a friendly reaction.

Pat smiled and leaned in closer. 'Heavens no, dearie, but trying to make it off that wretched mountain has made us best pals for life!'

Reg chimed in too, raising his voice to be heard over the din of the boisterous group.

Pat added, 'We're all in the same boat here, figuratively, and literally. We've bonded over shared triumphs and hilarious wipe-outs.'

Kat smiled at the others and the camaraderie with this group of strangers-turned-friends filled her heart. The boisterous energy at the table drew the attention of other diners, as their gazes lingered on the animated skiers clad in colourful winter gear.

Throughout the meal, the group regaled each other with stories of their ski adventures, mishaps, and near-misses. The tension of the morning's lesson dissipated, replaced by an atmosphere of warmth and mirth. Kat found herself genuinely enjoying the company, their shared laughter easing some of the burdens she carried within.

As the meal wound down and plates were cleared, Mikael walked into the restaurant. His eyes scanned the room until they locked onto Kat's. He smiled and made his way to their table, his presence commanding attention. There was an air of confidence about him, accentuated by his perfectly styled hair and his designer clothes.

Mikael slid into an empty seat next to Kat.

'Mind if I join you?' he asked, his voice smooth and

accented with a hint of playfulness. His eyes held a twinkle, a subtle invitation for Kat to let her guard down.

Charm radiated from his every pore.

She studied Mikael for a moment, taking in the Rolex on his wrist and the air of privilege that surrounded him. A part of her resented his opulence and his seemingly carefree existence.

But another part of her was intrigued by his confidence.

Then she remembered that it had also been Jacques's pluck and belief in himself that had first attracted her to him.

She drifted back in thought to the day she'd first encountered Jacques, a bittersweet memory that lingered like an ache in her heart. It had been at a bustling food market in London with a vibrant tapestry of flavours and scents. The vivacity of that day was in stark contrast to the current wintry surroundings of Lapland, where she was now alone, tangled in an unexpected web of emotions.

Kat recalled the electric connection she'd shared with Jacques, the way their conversations had flowed effortlessly, the excitement that had coursed through her veins...

A sudden burst of laughter roused Kat from her thoughts. Mikael had made a joke involving a sports car he had run off the road. As she watched him engage in lively banter with the other skiers in the group, she couldn't help but feel a growing disdain for him.

Mikael's obvious privileged upbringing and the expensive cars he drove represented everything Kat despised. He embodied a world of excess and a life of not caring about the consequences for the planet. Her heart, bruised and battered, saw him as the epitome of everything wrong with the world – a stark contrast to her values of green living and sustainability.

As Mikael caught her gaze, a mischievous smile playing on his lips, Kat's eyes narrowed with resentment. How could he be so carefree, so blissfully unaware of the damage his lifestyle was inflicting on the environment? Here they were in the lap of unspoilt nature, and he was joking about his escapades with his sports car! Her frustration simmered beneath the surface, ready to explode.

Kat unleashed her animosity, unable to contain it any longer.

'Do you know what driving your gas-guzzling car and living a life of excess is doing to the world, Mikael?'

Her voice was punctuated with bitterness and she added a touch of scorn to his name.

Mikael's playful demeanour vanished, replaced by shock and defensiveness.

'Hey, I was only making a joke.'

'Yeah, on the back of poorer people who can't afford your extravagant lifestyle. They're the ones who suffer the most from floods and storms caused by the warming of the planet. Have you seen the news lately?'

He stood up. 'You don't know anything about me.' His voice was laden with frustration.

The tension between them crackled with hostility; their words clashed like opposing forces.

Kat refused to back down, anger fuelling her words.

'I know what I see. I bet you've never taken a train to here from Helsinki. Do you realise how much more environmentally friendly it is? Instead, you live a life of indulgence while the rest of us strive to make a difference.'

Mikael's face contorted with anger.

'You think you have it all figured out, don't you?' His voice matched the intensity of their clash. 'I seem to remember that you are here on holiday and that you flew here, too!'

'That's different...'

'Really?' Mikael snorted.

'Yes. I'm vegan and I don't have a car. I take public transport where I can, but I didn't have enough time to take the train up here. Instead, I planted a tree and paid into the airline's green fund. Did you do that?'

Their heated exchange spiralled into a full-blown argument, words flung back and forth like daggers. Their voices rose above the ambient noise of the restaurant, drawing the attention of fellow skiers and instructors.

'I don't know what I've done to you,' Mikael said, 'but obviously you have some serious issues to work through. Just leave me out of it!'

With that said he turned on his heels and walked out of the restaurant.

Kat's cheeks flushed with mortification at her

outburst. She glanced around the table at the faces gawping at her.

'Are you alright, dear?' Pat said, reaching across Reg to touch her arm.

She couldn't comprehend what had come over her.

'I-I apologise if I ruined your meal.'

Pat waved off her very polite – and very English – rejections, indicating that she hadn't done anything of the sort.

'I'm so sorry, I really don't know what came over me.'

Pat gazed at her and after a brief silence which extended around the table, she said, 'I think it may be Mikael who you need to apologise to.'

Chapter Twelve

Back at the chalet, Kat threw herself onto the vast bed, her frustration and disappointment overwhelming her. She wanted to scream, to release the pent-up anger coursing through her veins. Why had she allowed herself to be drawn into a conflict with Mikael? Why did she even care?

As she lay there, her mind swirling with conflicting emotions, Kat realised that her anger towards Mikael had little to do with him personally. He had become a symbol, a representation of everything she resented and feared in the world. Her outburst had been born out of her own pain and insecurities, and she had projected onto him her frustration and disappointment.

But deep down, beneath the layers of anger, Kat also acknowledged a flicker of something she refused to name. It was a spark of a connection, an attraction that brought butterflies to her tummy and made her heart beat faster when she was close to Mikael. She pushed the thought away, unwilling to explore the possibility that she might be developing feelings for someone so different from her.

Besides, she had decided she was not going to have anything to do with the opposite sex for the foreseeable future.

Convincing herself that she felt nothing for Mikael, Kat resolved to distance herself from the man. She decided to request a change of ski groups, certain she could find another instructor who wouldn't stir up such anger in her. She reached for the phone, and dialled the reception of the chalet hotel.

'Hello?' a polite voice answered.

'Hi, this is Kat Wootton. I would like to request a change of ski groups. Is that possible?'

She injected a hint of hope into her words. She wished to make her desire to escape the turmoil clear.

There was a moment of silence before the receptionist responded.

'I'm sorry but due to an instructor being off sick, there are no available spots in other groups at the moment. Unless you wanted to stop the lessons altogether, you'll have to stick with your current group.'

Kat's heart sank and disappointment washed over her. She had hoped for an easy way out, a chance to avoid any further interactions with Mikael. But fate seemed to have other plans, and was determined to test her resolve.

'I understand,' she managed, her words tinged with resignation. 'Please let me know if any changes become possible in the future.'

As she hung up, Kat realised that she had no choice

but to confront her feelings and the complicated dynamics unfolding between her and Mikael. She couldn't run away forever, especially not in the midst of this winter wonderland that had become the backdrop to her personal journey.

Taking a deep breath, she rose from the bed, determination replacing her previous self-pity. She refused to let the pain in her gut devour her, caused by the betrayal of those she should have trusted the most, or her anger at a stranger to hinder her experience in Lapland. This was a holiday, a chance to learn to ski, to witness the magic of the Northern Lights, and find some semblance of peace.

With her newfound resolve, Kat decided to rise above the irritation Mikael had provoked in her. She would try to tolerate him, just as she would overcome the despair Jacques' infidelity and *her* deception had inflicted on her. It was time she stopped pushing her anger and pain onto a stranger.

She decided to allow herself another hot sauna. It went against all her principles, but the day had been a disturbing and tiring one. She'd have to pay to plant another tree when she got home. She would also re-join the ski group later for the evening meal and face the consequences of her previous outburst.

Relaxing in the warm steam, sitting by the window with views overlooking a snowy landscape, Kat watched the snow falling. As it brightened the darkened pines outside her window, she came to the realisation that she didn't want to see or talk to Jacques ever again. The brief disappointment she'd felt at the airport at him having not joined her on this holiday was turning into satisfaction.

She could learn to ski and have more fun without him – without any man.

Chapter Thirteen

The second day on the slopes was much easier. She kept out of Mikael's way, heading for the lifts first, so that she could partner with someone else. Apart from a few furtive glances in her direction as he gathered the group at the bottom of the mountain, Mikael left her alone.

After a few pointers at the top of the piste, he told the skiers to follow his lead down the slope.

With a deep breath, Kat pushed off, letting her skis glide along the snow. At first, she felt wobbly and unsteady, her body tensing with each small movement, as if it was her first day on the slopes. She was last of the row of skiers but she preferred it that way. It was the farthest she could be away from Mikael.

With each passing moment, she gained a semblance of control; her muscles relaxed and found their rhythm.

Kat's focus narrowed until her attention was solely on the piste ahead. She immersed herself in the joy of skiing, enjoying the wind as it whipped against her face and the exhilaration of each turn. The worries and anxieties that plagued her mind began to fade into the background, as she lost herself and found solace in the act of surrendering to the mountain.

As she descended the slope, she realised that she wasn't alone in her pursuit of freedom. The skiers around her zipped past, their movements fluid and graceful. Even with an array of backgrounds and experiences, they all shared a commonality: everyone wanted to challenge themselves, to push beyond their comfort zones.

Kat reminded herself that this journey was about more than simply proving herself to others. She wanted to embrace her own strength, uncover new passions and rewrite the narrative of her life. She would refuse to let the decisions and desires of others dictate the path she would take.

As she reached the bottom of the slope, a surge of exhilaration coursed through her veins. She had done it. She had conquered her fear and found joy in the simple action of skiing. It was a small victory, but it was a push forward on her path of self-discovery.

Kat stopped to catch her breath, her cheeks flushed from both exertion and elation. She glanced around to see her fellow skiers were applauding each other, their smiles warm and encouraging. It was a warming moment of companionship that reminded her she wasn't alone on this expedition.

'Well done, everyone!' Mikael said, beaming.

Kat smiled back and gave him a slight nod of acknowledgement.

Pat grinned. 'That was fun, wasn't it?' Both she and her burly husband had been surprisingly quick coming down the slope.

Kat smiled at the couple, who, with the other skiers, were making their way towards the ski lift once more.

Mikael said, 'We'll do this run one more time and then we'll move on to a slightly more challenging piste.'

His gaze was locked on Kat.

With a grin she held his eyes, and for a moment forgot how she resented everything the privileged guy represented. The elation she felt had wiped away her bitterness. Then she remembered their argument from the previous day. Should she apologise? It didn't seem the right time with their ski group standing around, taking a well-earned break between runs. Perhaps she would talk to him privately later.

With a newfound purpose, she switched her focus back to the mountain.

That same evening, her group of novice skiers gathered in a vibrant *après-ski* bar to celebrate their triumphs on the mountain. Her new friends, Pat and Reg, asked her to join them, their eyes shining with a new zest for life.

'You have to live life to the fullest, Kat,' Pat said, her hand tightly clasping Reg's.

Kat smiled gratefully at the older couple, appreciating their *joie de vivre*.

The French expression brought up thoughts of Jacques, but Kat pushed them firmly back. Tonight, she'd take a leaf out of Pat and Reg's book and let her hair down.

Earlier in the day, amidst the flurry of laughter and camaraderie, she had learnt of their respective losses. Pat's husband, her partner of more than two decades, had passed away suddenly from a heart attack at the young age of fifty-four. And Reg had endured the pain of watching his wife battle cancer before she'd eventually succumbed to its relentless grip in a hospice.

Yet, despite their lingering pain and grief, Pat and Reg had made a conscious decision to look forward rather than back. They had chosen to honour the memories of their previous partners by embracing the future and cherishing the time they had left on this earth.

Their pain had resonated deeply with Kat, stirring a mix of emotions within her soul. She understood the reason for their choices; life was fragile and unpredictable, and it was essential to seize every moment of joy and connection that came her way.

It was for that reason that Kat agreed to join the celebration. The vibrant bar pulsated with music and laughter; the air came alive with joyful togetherness.

As her skiing group settled into a cosy corner, Kat found herself seated next to Pat and Reg. Kat told them about her TV career, and even let them know that she'd recently suffered a heart break. She didn't – couldn't bring herself – to offer them any details, but Pat was sympathetic all the same, pressing her hand on Kat's arm and squeezing it gently.

'I could tell you had a sadness in you. But life goes on. You're so young, beautiful and obviously very intelligent. You will find someone decent and kind to love, I'm certain of it.'

Pat and Reg's zest for life was contagious, and it was gradually eroding the walls that Kat had built around her heart.

As the night unfolded, Kat caught sight of Mikael chatting with his ski instructor friends across the bar. She had managed to avoid him for most of day and the evening, but now their eyes met briefly, and a flicker of something passed between them. Curiosity and trepidation stirred within her, but she quickly averted her gaze, determined to focus on the present moment and the new connections she had formed.

Pat must have witnessed the look Kat exchanged with Mikael, because she caught Kat's eyes and said, 'He's gorgeous. If I was a few years – or decades – younger I wouldn't say no to him!'

Kat smiled, but replied sharply, 'He's arrogant, though.'

'He's just confident and young, that's all.' Pat nudged Kat and, getting close to her ear, whispered, 'I know you two haven't exactly hit it off, but wouldn't he be perfect for a little holiday romance?'

Kat laughed at Pat's comment, but the type of emotion Mikael aroused in her was not the romantic kind. He was annoying, yes, infuriating, and trouble, yes. Despicable times three, yes.

What she didn't tell Pat was that if she wanted a holiday romance – and she definitely did not want one – Mikael would be the last person she'd turn to.

The hours slipped away; the drinks flowed and the laughter intensified. The barriers that had once separated the group of beginners were now replaced by friendship and shared accomplishment. Kat was surrounded by people who had faced their own struggles and losses, yet had chosen to embrace the beauty of life.

During the revelry, Kat's heavy heart felt lighter than it had in a long time. She danced, she sang, letting go of her inhibitions. The weight of her past reduced.

As the night drew to a close, Kat looked around at her new friends with gratitude. They were more than just fellow skiers; they were a support system, a reminder of the resilience of the human spirit.

Pat leaned in, her voice filled with warmth and affection.

'Life is a tapestry of moments, my dear. Weaving together the highs and lows, the triumphs, and tribulations. Embrace it all, for it is what shapes us into who we are.'

Kat nodded, her eyes heavy with unshed tears. She realised that coming to Lapland had allowed her to not only learn a new skill, skiing, but also to understand herself better, and to try to enjoy life without a man. She alone was enough, but if she wanted to share her life with someone, she would need for them to be genuine and share her beliefs.

All her life her mother had told her what she should do: use her youth and beauty before it vanished to trap a rich man. Not fall in love and be stupid enough to get pregnant with the wrong kind of man (a poor one), like she had. And always, always be watchful for signs that the man was about to leave her.

Her mother's poor choices had turned Kat into a people pleaser. Kat had rebelled against it by believing in good causes her mum openly despised. Despite all that, she had found a rich man in Jacques, but as it turned out, she wasn't very good at making him stay.

Or, rather, not stray. After all, it was Kat who had left Jacques. Her ego was somewhat bolstered by that.

From now on, she was determined to enjoy herself and take each day as it came, rather than worry about what others thought of her.

Chapter Fourteen

As the *après-ski* bar slowly emptied, the group of new friends made their way back to their chalets, their laughter echoing in the crisp night air. Kat walked briskly with Pat and Reg along the snowy pavement in the bitter cold of the Lappish winter. Despite the chill, the warmth of the evening in the bar still enveloped her, and as she glanced up at the bright stars in the sky, for the first time since arriving in Lapland she felt something close to happiness.

Outside the hotel lobby, Kat hugged Pat and Reg goodnight.

Just as Kat was about to head towards her own chalet she heard a voice.

'Hey, wait!'

She turned around and saw Mikael running towards them.

Of course, he had to come along and spoil the evening.

'Ah, Mikael, the best ski instructor this side of the North Pole!' Reg smiled and hugged the younger man, patting him on the back with hands encased in thick mittens.

Mikael looked embarrassed. But she must have seen wrong, because up to then all she'd witnessed the guy display was cockiness. Mikael looked down at his feet and kicked off a bit of snow with his boots.

He clapped his hands together and said, 'A bloody cold night, isn't it? I think the temperature has really plummeted tonight. It might be a bit cold on the slopes tomorrow, so wrap up warm, will you?'

His blue eyes locked on Kat, and she nodded.

A silence followed.

Pat said, 'Er, well, I think we'd better hit the sack – we'll need our sleep if we're going to manage another day of trying to kill ourselves on those pistes! We're not as young as you two.'

Reg gave a wave and Pat smiled at Kat, her eyes glinting with mischief. Remembering their conversation from earlier, she felt her cheeks flush. Luckily, they were outside and it was dark, with only the lights from the hotel reception and the stars above enabling them to see each other. Confident Mikael wouldn't notice her embarrassment, Kat nodded at him, unable to bring herself to look at him properly.

'See you tomorrow,' she said.

As she trudged through the snow towards her chalet, she couldn't help but feel relieved that Mikael hadn't tried to make conversation after Pat and Reg had left them alone. She'd had wanted to apologise but at same time, she didn't want to continue the argument from the day before.

She was fumbling with the key to her chalet, when she felt someone behind her. Turning around, she saw Mikael standing there with a smirk on his face.

'What do you want, Mikael?' she snapped.

'I just wanted to see you to your door.' he replied smoothly, his blue eyes glinting under the moonlight.

Kat was trying to find the words to say sorry for what he said to him, but before she had time to open her mouth, Mikael added, 'I didn't want you to get into an argument with a wolf or a bear. You might come worse off with them than you did with me.'

His eyes were peering at her in the dark and his lips were pulled into a wide grin.

Kat was fuming. Was he making fun of her?

'I have nothing to say to you.'

The words were out of her mouth before she could stop them. She owed him an apology, but how could she do that when he was being so arrogant as to follow her to her chalet and mock her with his stupid jokes?

Mikael took a step closer to her, and Kat could smell the scent of his cologne. It was musky, masculine, and completely irritating.

'Are you sure? I think you have me all wrong.'

Kat took a step back, her heart racing. She hated the effect Mikael was having on her, hated the way her body responded to his proximity. She was determined not to let him get the upper hand.

'I'm sure,' she said firmly. 'Now if you'll excuse me, I'm going to bed.'

As she twisted the key and pushed the door open, Mikael remained on the path.

'Of course,' he said, 'but I would like to talk to you properly some time. I'm not the person you are making me out to be.'

His words sounded sincere; Kat could feel her resolve slipping.

They stood facing each other for what felt like minutes.

'I'm sorry, Mikael, I'm tired,' she said firmly and took a step back.

Mikael looked disappointed, but he didn't argue.

'Okay, see you tomorrow by the lifts.'

With that, he turned and walked away, leaving Kat standing alone in the doorway of her chalet. She watched him go with a mix of emotions.

It was clear that Mikael was interested in her, something that had surprised her after their heated argument yesterday and the cold shoulder he given her on the slopes all day today. He could have come to talk to her in the bar too, but he seemed intent on not being anywhere near her. Which was more than fine by her.

She'd have to be careful around him if she wanted to avoid any further complications or arguments. But even as she closed the door and locked it behind her, she couldn't help but wonder what might have happened if she had let him inside her chalet.

Chapter Fifteen

Mikael lay in bed thinking about Kat. Why had he followed her to her chalet tonight? He had acted without thinking. It was a stupid move that bordered on stalking.

Laughing and dancing all evening, she had shown him a different side. At one point, when she'd been sitting down talking to Pat and their eyes had briefly locked, he'd considered asking her to dance. But he hadn't wanted to take the risk of being turned down in front of his instructor mates. Besides, he never got involved with pupils, even if many of his friends did. His brother did enough womanising for the entire family. Mikael didn't want to be like Victor.

So why had he accosted Kat afterwards?

He already knew the truth. What she'd said to him the previous night had hurt him deeply.

So what if he was from a well-to-do family? At school, he'd known that his father ran a large and important mining company. He was not the only kid to have rich parents at the *Norsen* Swedish language school, but his were not only wealthy but also famous. His father was interviewed by the press often, and his views on the economy were sought out by government ministers.

Another reason why Mikael could not afford to step out of line.

Although Victor had no such qualms. Mikael earning his living as a skiing instructor was bad enough for his father; he didn't need to add #MeToo behaviour to his list of wrongdoings.

How the playboy Victor managed to keep his record clean and his father's approval ratings sky high was a mystery to Mikael. His brother was lazy, incompetent, and just using their father to get a free ride in the company. But it had always been like that. Victor could do no wrong.

Perhaps Mikael was simply jealous of his brother and afraid that if he did join the family firm, he'd be constantly compared to Victor. No, being like Victor made him sick to the stomach. As did joining the family firm.

What he wanted was to live here in Lapland and help as many people conquer the mountains as he could. He felt such a connection to the land, a real kinship to its people. Not to mention the pleasure he got from skiing. Whenever he wasn't teaching, he'd go off piste and revel in the quiet and magnificent beauty of the unspoilt nature.

But was that selfish of him to live his dream? His

mother's reaction after he'd told her it was her ancestry that kept pulling him back to Lapland made him incredibly sad.

His father would silence Ulla whenever she began talking about her parents, in particular her own mother, who had Sami blood in her. Thinking about it now, it all made perfect sense. How could Mikael have missed his father denying such an important part of Ulla's heritage?

Anger surged inside him over how his father had and continued to treat his mum.

Growing up, both he and Victor had sneered at their father's old-fashioned ideas about marriage. They'd thought it odd that Ulla did not have permission to work; Erik would cite the excuse of the boys being too young. She was needed at home, Erik would say, even when Mikael and Victor were teenagers. And when Victor left home at eighteen to do his military duty as a conscript, Ulla had continued in her role as a homemaker. And after Victor chose to get his own place while he studied engineering at Aalto University, Ulla's role never once changed.

When it was Mikael's turn to enter the army, Ulla had cried, until Erik told her to stop.

'The army will make a man of him, just as it did with Victor. Just as it did with me.'

Mikael had no idea how his mother had filled her time after both her sons had flown the nest.

It was obvious to him that Kat had grown up in a different kind of household. Perhaps that was why

Mikael was so drawn to her? But it was clear his feelings were not reciprocated.

He tossed in bed, trying to stop his thoughts from wandering. But he couldn't block out the image of Kat having fun on the dance floor. She'd been wearing a short black skirt and a tight-fitting jumper, showing off her sexy figure. She'd been laughing as her head bobbed to the music, and her eyes had sparkled.

Mikael had been transfixed by the sensual nape of her neck, visible due to her short-cropped hair. It had looked so sexy and kissable. Mikael had wanted to slow dance with her, to pull her body close to his and to stroke that lovely neck.

Stop it!

He shook the thought from his head and got out of bed, to get a glass of water.

The girl didn't even like him. In fact, she despised him. Once again, his family – or more correctly, his father was spoiling everything for him.

Chapter Sixteen

London, before

'But *chérie*, you are overreacting. Nothing happened.'

Jacques yawned and poured himself a glass of the red Bordeaux Kat had opened.

He took a sip and grimaced, then went over to the sink and spat out the liquid.

'*Qu'est-ce que c'est?*'

Jacques peered first at the bottle label, then at Kat.

'I picked it up from Tesco Express on Heath Street,' Kat replied. She felt the usual dread in the pit of her stomach. She was useless at choosing wines, whereas Jacques was the expert. The bottle had been the most expensive the store stocked, so she had felt sure it would pass muster.

'How many times have I told you? That place is no good. You need to go to Jeroboams!'

That evening, in their Hampstead apartment – or more correctly, Jacques' three-bedroom penthouse – overlooking the Heath, Kat was once again chopping vegetables.

It was their daily routine. Kat would leave the studio as soon as she'd finished clearing up the prep kitchen with the two assistants and the occasional intern while Jacques would stay on to discuss the day's filming and plan the following day with the production manager, Richard.

Kat usually went home via the shops, making up a menu in her head as she browsed the vegetables in her favourite greengrocers on Heath Street.

Jacques had told her that since she didn't eat meat or dairy, it was up to her to prepare their meals. It made sense. As the celebrity on the show, he worked much longer hours and had so much more responsibility than her. And Kat didn't pay rent on the flat, which was just as well, since her salary was a fraction of Jacques'.

Jacques often wanted their evening meals at home to pass in silence. He would say he needed calm to collect his thoughts after dealing with the busy and noisy studio.

But tonight was different. After witnessing what had passed between Jacques and the pretty intern, she had challenged Jacques as soon as he stepped inside the door.

'You are tired, *chérie*, and you are seeing things where there is nothing.'

Kat angrily stirred in a cupful of apple vinegar into a red-pepper goulash at the stove. She just couldn't contain her fury.

Jacques came over to her. 'It was nothing. *Rien!*'

Kat was no longer sure; perhaps what she had seen

was nothing after all. Jacques began to rub the nape of her neck with small, circular movements. The sensation was wonderful. Jacques knew exactly how to touch her.

'I'm here with you, not anyone else, Katherine. *Je t'aime.*'

His words relaxed her. She leaned back into Jacques arms, but as soon as she did, she felt his body tense. Jacques stretched over her shoulder to take in the aromas of the meal she was preparing.

'*Mon Dieu*, what are you making?'

Her vegan diet had been the cause of many arguments between them. Kat had tried repeatedly to convince Jacques that the environmental reasons alone were enough to stop eating meat and dairy. Added to that the health benefits of cutting down on animal produce, and a change in diet was indisputable.

She found herself explaining to Jacques that the goulash would taste wonderful once the vinegar had cooked off, but Jacques only huffed.

'Not only are you accusing me of all sorts, Kat, but now you are going to poison me with your – your, silly, dishes!'

His hands were no longer touching her. He gesticulated wildly at her and the pot she was stirring.

This was the point Kat where would normally apologise, because she knew that no one should be told how to live their life, or what food to eat. But tonight, something else stirred in her. She began to argue her case.

'I'm always the one who shops for and cooks the meals. You never lift a finger! And now you are flirting, and goodness knows what else, with young interns during the show – *our* show.'

For a moment, Jacques stood in front of her, speechless.

Then, he crossed his arms over his broad chest and, lifting his chin up, said, 'If I am so *horrible* to live with, perhaps I should leave you to your disgusting red-pepper mush.'

With these words, he stormed into the hallway, put on his coat, and left the apartment.

Kat was stunned. She wanted to cry, alone in the middle of the beautiful kitchen with a wooden spoon in her hand, but no tears appeared.

It wasn't the first time Jacques had stormed out in the middle of a fight, but usually it was after a far more serious argument.

Kat had seen him once having lunch with a female producer. Their heads were close together and her lips were a little swollen, she could have sworn they had just kissed. But Jacques had told her she was imagining it. Kat had no proof, and the producer then moved out of London a few weeks later, so Kat had surmised that was the end of it. If it had been anything at all in the first place.

She could be insecure when it came to men. One former boyfriend had accused her of having 'father issues', to which Kat had scoffed. The relationship had ended soon after. It was true that Kat's father had abandoned his pregnant wife and two children when Kat was a child, but she was over that disappointment now.

In a way, life had been calmer since her had dad left. There were no more arguments waking Kat and her little sister up in the middle of the night, and her mother cried a lot less than she had when her father was still around.

Kat was glad she didn't have anything to do with him anymore.

Jacques had been different from any of Kat's other boyfriends. For one, he was fifteen years older than her. He had seemed so wise when they'd met, and Kat had been swept off her feet with the romantic gestures. He had treated her to red roses sent to her flat share, dinners in private corners in the best restaurants in town, and late-night walks along the Thames.

He'd also made Kat feel safe and loved. When he was in the mood to do so. Which he seemed to be less and less interested in these days.

She waited until nine o'clock for Jacques to return before reluctantly tidying away his place-setting. She sat at the table and began to pick at the now-cold goulash.

Jacques had several friends in the restaurant business, many of whom he had trained.

He was probably out enjoying a meal in one of their fancy eateries all over London, so that he didn't have to suffer Kat's 'mush'.

Chapter Seventeen

When Kat woke up the next morning, after a disturbed night of dreaming of her dad of all people, there was still no sign of Jacques. She reached across the bed made up with silk sheets, but his side was exactly as it had been the night before.

Kat sat up in bed and heard the shower running.

Had Jacques been out all night?

She slid out of bed and carefully opened the door to the bathroom.

'Hello *chérie*. Did you sleep well?' a familiar voice said.

Jacques was standing in front of the mirror, drying his muscular body with a large, white towel.

Kat studied his face, but saw nothing unusual in his expression. It was as if last night's argument hadn't happened.

'When did you come in?' she asked.

Jacques switched to brushing his teeth with an electric toothbrush, the noise of which drowned out Kat's words.

Facing the mirror, he lifted his eyebrows questioningly. '*Quoi?*'

'I just wondered what time you got in last night?' she repeated, wringing her hands, suddenly uncertain whether she should be questioning Jacques' movements. He absolutely hated her doing it.

His response was his usual Gallic shrug, one that Jacques had perfected.

'You were asleep, *chérie*. Anyway, I'm running late. I have a meeting with Richard at eight.'

He gave her a light kiss on her cheek and left her alone in the steamed-up bathroom. Richard was the series producer, and effectively both her and Jacques' boss, although nobody on set was unaware of who held the real power.

When Kat returned to the bedroom, she sat down on the untouched side of the bed. She brushed the perfectly tidied corner of the light-grey quilt, wondering if Jacques had slept in the bed at all, or if he had been lying to her. What if he hadn't come home last night but this morning?

He hadn't *actually* told her when he'd returned.

Kat shook her head to banish the thoughts. They were in the middle of filming a high-rated cookery show, and that must be the priority. She needed to get going too – she had million things to do that day.

· · ·

The days on the set always got more hectic as they neared the end of filming. On the last day, Kat was counting down the hours of her final shift in the test kitchen. She hadn't slept properly for the past four nights.

On the morning of their big fight, Jacques had behaved as if nothing had happened. But in the days since then, Jacques was sulking more. As much as Kat wanted to tell him she loved him, this time she couldn't forget what she'd seen pass between him and the young intern.

Usually, after a disagreement and to ease her guilt, Kat liked to prepare something intricate and delicious Jacques liked, as her apology. They would share a bottle of wine that she'd taken the trouble to go to the best wine shop for. She'd drop Jacques' name and get a recommendation for something that complimented the meal she had planned.

But today, when she entered the kitchen and was told that her helper for the day would be the very same intern who'd been flirting with Jacques, Kat's blood began to boil again.

Surely this was some kind of hell that she was being put through?

But always the consummate professional, due to her two years working for the same TV company, Kat began prepping for the three remaining contestants. The final challenge was to prepare a five-star meal for a guest celebrity judge and Jacques. Hence, Jacques wasn't on set yet.

That morning, she had left him snoring in their

super-king bed. Giving him a last glance as she tiptoed out of the room, she remarked privately how handsome he was, stark naked in bed, lying on his tummy, with the sheet covering just a third of his body. Kat took in his muscular arms and back, his well-toned thighs and calves. She wanted to run her fingers down the backs of his legs and over the half buttock on show, and press her lips to his skin, to wake him up.

Jacques loved being woken up for sex – it was the other guaranteed way she would be forgiven for what he called her frequent bouts of jealousy.

But this time felt different. Kat was in the right. She'd seen with her own eyes what Jacques had been up to. That morning, she'd fought every molecule in her body not to wake him up. So, she'd turned on her heels and left him to sleep.

Now, she ordered the pretty intern to start preparing the globe artichokes one of the contestants was going to be using in his final dish. Kat began slicing radishes for another contestant who wanted them as thin as paper. But the small, round vegetables were hard to grip. Suddenly, her hand slipped; her thumb went through the sharp edge of the mandolin.

A scream escaped from her mouth and then everything went blank.

Kat woke up surrounded by people. She was lying on a couch in the reception area of the film studios.

'Are you OK, dear?' One of the older members of the

production team who oversaw the washing up, Carol, was standing over her.

'Yeah,' Kat said uncertainly. She tried to sit up but was stopped by a hand on her shoulder.

'Take it easy, girl.'

'But the show ...'

'Don't worry about that. Sheree, the new intern, took over and she's doing quite a good job, actually. Your instructions were excellent, which helped.'

Carol gave her a kind smile.

Kat lay back down and closed her eyes. Had Carol noticed that Jacques had been flirting with the intern? But before she could think any more about it, she touched her thumb and winced. The sharp physical pain overrode the emotional one that she'd been suffering since the beginning of the week.

'Now, you know I'm the first aider, right?' Carol said. 'So, you can rest assured I know what I'm doing. I've bandaged your cut. It's quite nasty, but I don't think you need stitches. You just need to keep the dressing dry and perhaps go and see your GP if it gets too painful.'

Kat stared at Carol.

She added. 'I'm just going to take your pulse now because you fainted.'

The older woman placed two fingers on Kat's wrist while gazing at her watch.

A short moment later, she said, 'All good. Just rest a while. I'll bring you a cup of tea.'

Kat closed her eyes. She couldn't believe that she'd fainted. It had only happened once before during a school concert, when she was sixteen and her period had been particularly heavy and painful.

She was grateful that Jacques wasn't on set yet because he would have thought her a lightweight. It was not the first time she had cut herself during her time working in TV. Once, when she had complained about how much it hurt, Jacques had told her not to be such a baby. He'd given her a bright-blue plaster and told her to carry on prepping the food.

'The show must go on,' he'd said.

What would he have said now if he'd seen her faint? Especially that they were on the war path with each other. Kat couldn't be certain he wouldn't have laughed out loud at her feeble reaction to a small cut on her thumb.

She draped her left – healthy – hand across her eyes and took a breath in and out to prevent the tears she could feel welling from falling.

Stupid, stupid Kat.

Chapter Eighteen

Despite her protests, Carol insisted Kat go home.

'It's a nasty wound – and painful, I bet. It's the last day of filming and we will manage.'

She also made Kat wear a sling.

Standing outside the studios, still a little wobbly, Kat decided to treat herself to an Uber. Getting on a bus with the sling and a painful thumb didn't appeal to her.

When she got inside the car, instead of Jacques' address, she gave the cabby a different one. She decided to surprise her mum, who lived close to the studios in Camden. While she wouldn't be able to complain about Jacques' behaviour, because her mum worshipped the ground he walked on and never wanted to hear any criticism levelled against him, she would at least let Kat rest and might even fuss over her a bit.

· · ·

'Mum?'

Kat let herself into her mum's one-bedroom apartment. She was surprised not to see her sitting at her desk as usual. Working as a freelance translator, Simona was often at home during the middle of the day.

She spotted her mum's red winter coat and her trusted Louis Vuitton handbag in the small hall next to the floor-length mirror, so reasoned she must be in. As her eyes caught her reflection, Kat saw the door to her mum's bedroom just off the open-plan kitchen was ajar. Through it, she could see a set of feet.

Fixated by the image through the glass, she worked out they weren't her mum's.

She turned away from the mirror and, as if on autopilot, she made her way towards her mum's bedroom.

But what Kat saw froze her in the doorway. She stared in shock at the sight before her.

Simona was lying naked on the bed, her legs spread wide, with a familiar body lodged between them. The pair were moving rhythmically and moaning while the bed creaked.

A wave of nausea hit her as she looked at Jacques. The man she loved, the man who she thought she was going to spend the rest of her life with, was having sex with her mother.

Simona shrieked suddenly when she spotted Kat standing in the doorway.

Kat stared at them, her eyes flicking between her mother and her boyfriend. She felt numb, as if she was floating above the room, watching the two of them tangled in her mum's satin sheets.

What was happening?

'Kat, I'm sorry...' Jacques climbed off the bed, found his trousers, and pulled them up. She stared at his strong body but couldn't comprehend what he was doing here.

Naked. In. Her. Mum's. Bed.

Jacques took a step towards her and placed his hands on her good arm.

'It's not what you think.'

It is precisely what I think.

Kat couldn't believe it.

'Kat,' Jacques said again. When she didn't respond, he whispered in her ear, 'I adore you, only you. This was a mistake.'

She couldn't speak. He reasoned her brain must be paralysed by shock.

Simona sat up on the bed and wrapped the sheet around her. Then she shuffled across the bed and out of the room without looking at Kat or Jacques.

Kat watched her disappear and then moved her eyes slowly back to her boyfriend, who was still in front of her.

'Kat, please, say something,' Jacques whispered, moving his fingers down her arm. He stopped and frowned. 'What happened to your hand?'

Her body was shaking, she noticed, as she watched herself during her out-of-body experience.

'Why?' Her reply was so faint, she wondered if Jacques had heard it.

It seemed he had.

Remorse and regret appeared on Jacques' face.

Suddenly, she was back on earth. Back in this room – her mother's bedroom, clearly.

As if a veil had been lifted from her eyes, Kat also saw Jacques clearly too. Saw who he really was.

She tugged her arm out of his grip.

You are a liar. And a womaniser.

She wasn't a fool. She knew now he was acting. Had he been pretending to love her for years? Of course, he had.

How can I have been so stupid?

'You disgust me,' she spat.

Despite her anger, or perhaps because of it, her eyes filled with tears. She felt the outrage flare inside her, but she didn't know what to do with it. She wanted to scream, but her lungs were empty. Instead, she began to gasp for air.

He frowned. 'Are you OK?'

When she didn't reply, Jacques gazed at her for a moment then looked away.

Her mother returned, dressed in a bright-coloured kaftan. She ignored Kat, giving Jacques a look that Kat could only interpret as a glacial stare.

Jacques turned away from Kat and mouthed something to Simona.

'I'm sorry,' he whispered again, giving Kat all his attention again. He placed his hand on her cheek.

She wanted to slap his hand away, but was so upset that all she could do was burst into tears.

'Please don't cry, *chérie*. This was a mistake,' he said,

taking hold of Kat's good arm again.

'Don't touch me.' Kat took a step back forcing his hand to drop.

Her eyes flitted across his face. She gazed at his mouth, knowing what it felt like to kiss him. Knowing how he had looked at her whenever they made love.

She shook her head as tears fell onto her cheeks. She wiped them away with the back of her good hand and lifted her head.

'Don't do this to me,' she said. It was a plea more than a statement.

Jacques took a step towards her, but Kat backed away from him.

'No, no, no!' she said, holding her hand up to stop him from coming closer. Her back hit the wall behind her.

Jacques stretched out both hands for her. Kat shook her head again and that made him stop.

'You need to go,' she said, turning her back to him. She felt her mother's proximity before she saw her.

Simona came up next to her and put a hand on her back.

'Don't worry, Kat. We'll sort this out,' she said soothingly.

Kat half turned to her mum.

'No, we won't. What you have done here is –'

Her voice cracked with the pain. She couldn't find the words to describe what she had seen.

Simona turned to Jacques and muttered, 'We'll talk later.'

'Goodbye, Kat,' Jacques said and left.

Kat didn't reply. She was too busy trying to pull herself together.

She heard the front door open and Jacques' footsteps echo outside as he made his way out of the apartment and out of her life.

Chapter Nineteen

Her head was spinning. She felt sick.

'Come and sit down.'

Simona brought her into the lounge, a place so familiar to Kat from her childhood. She was too exhausted to resist and followed her mum to the old leather sofa, worn from years of use.

Simona settled next to Kat, who stared at her mum's face.

Simona's makeup had smudged underneath her eyes. Her hair was mussed up. Her lips were swollen from kissing Jacques.

She shuddered, suddenly very cold. And her finger was throbbing.

'I don't understand how ...' The tears were again threatening to fall, but Kat held them back. She swallowed hard and continued. 'How you could do this to me? With him? We've been together for two years! I thought, I thought, he was going to ...'

She stopped talking as her words fell away. Her mum was too calm.

A realisation dawned on Kat.

'This wasn't just a one-off mistake, but something else?'

She stared at her mum. She wanted answers.

'We've been in love for a while.' Simona took Kat's good hand into hers.

'What?'

Her mum touched Kat's sling. 'What happened to you?'

Kat looked down at her mum's hand then up at her face again. 'Don't even try to act normal. As if you care what happened to my thumb, or what happens to me at all. Look what you have done!'

Simona pulled her hand away and said desperately, 'Oh, God, what a mess!'

Kat simply gazed at her mum in disbelief.

Simona said, 'All those times he told me he adored me, it was a lie. It was all a lie.'

She threw her head back and laughed, but stopped as abruptly as she began.

'How could you?' Kat said, not able to give words to the betrayal she felt at that moment. 'All those things he said to me, all those things he said to you –' She stopped when her breath came in short gasps.

She composed herself and stared at her mum, seeing her with new eyes. 'How could you do this to me?'

The anger within Kat was so acute, she could see white spots in front of her eyes. She stood up and began pacing the room, coming to a stop in front of her mum.

'Well?'

Simona was looking at the floor and hugging herself.

'I know, I know. I'm sorry, Kat. I've been a terrible mother. You mean everything to me. You always have. As much as I love Jacques, you're my daughter.'

Kat's anger flared hot red as her mum tried to defend her actions.

'You betrayed me! My relationship is over... And what about you? Look me in the eye and explain this to me.'

Simona met her eyes but said nothing.

Kat felt as if someone was pulling the ground from under her feet. She stepped away from her mum.

'Kat, Jacques and I love each other,' her mum finally said, her voice thick with emotion.

Chapter Twenty

Present day

On the third day of her holiday when Kat was not only mastering the skiing but also enjoying it, she got a message from her younger sister, Lily.

Phone me!

Kat was five years older than her. Simona had told Kat later that the marriage to their father was already on the rocks then. A year later, her mum had another baby, Daniel.

Because Kat had been so much older than her siblings, and with her father gone, she had become a second mother to them.

Even now, with Lily twenty-two and Daniel twenty-one, Kat often got impatient messages from the pair demanding an immediate response or assistance of some kind.

When they were all growing up, Kat had liked how her two younger siblings had treated her as an adult.

When she'd picked Daniel up from school her younger brother would run to Kat, telling her what had happened that day. When her little sister was being teased for having flame-red hair, again it had been Kat who had told the bullies to shut their mouths.

She considered replying immediately, but decided to ignore the urgent request to call Lily back. It usually wasn't as important as her little sister made it out to be. Lily could wait, she decided. Instead, she was going to enjoy the snow and skiing.

She didn't pick up the phone to call Lily until she was back at the chalet.

'You have to make it up with mum!' Lily demanded. She sounded close to tears.

Kat's heart hardened. This was not the conversation she wanted to have right now.

She took a deep breath and tried to keep her voice calm. 'What's happened? Why do I have to make it up with mum?'

Kat prayed that Simona hadn't told Lily anything. She didn't want her little sister to get involved, or to learn about the disgusting entanglement of her mother and Jacques. Kat abhorred her own involuntary part in it all. She imagined how it would look from the outside to her sister and brother. How they would turn on their mum and pity Kat. No, she would never talk about the affair to either of them. It was a secret she was willing to keep forever.

'She's been really upset since she spoke to you last.

She feels like you don't care about her anymore,' Lily reported.

There was deep emotion in her sister's voice; Kat tried to ignore the pang of guilt filling her chest. Simona had called her a few days before she'd left for her skiing trip, and Kat had been short with her. At the time, she'd felt gracious for even agreeing to speak with her mother after what she had done.

'But you haven't talked to her in days, Kat. She's our mum. You need to make things right with her. Please?'

'Lily, don't get involved in this. It has nothing to do with you.'

There was silence at the other end of the line.

Lily spoke. 'But she was *crying* when I spoke to her. And I'm up here in Edinburgh and can't do anything about it. I'm sure if you just called her and sorted out whatever it is you've fallen out over, it would all be OK.'

Kat sighed. Her mum wasn't a stranger to histrionics, and the worst was generally preserved for Kat. At least Lily hadn't been told what had happened between Simona and Jacques.

'Please Lily. It's nothing. Mum is just using you. Don't let her.'

'Gosh, Kat, you sound so cold. What *did* happen between the two of you?'

'Don't worry. It's my business and mine alone. Please stay out of it. I'll sort it out when I'm back in London.'

Lily tried to prise the truth out of Kat a few more times, but Kat remained firm. It was too raw, too horrible for her to think about, let alone talk about.

Chapter Twenty-One

The next morning, as Kat was having breakfast with the rest of the skiing group, there was another message, this time from Daniel.

What's up, big sis? Got a call from mum in hysterics, saying you have abandoned her.

Kat sighed.

She could see what Simona was trying to do, but she was surprised that she would go as far as to phone Daniel, who was studying engineering at Birmingham University. Her brother never got involved in any of the family arguments, and her mum, who usually started them, rarely included Daniel in her rants. He was her mum's golden boy.

It's nothing. Usual mum stuff. I'll deal with her when I get back from Lapland.

The reply, just a 'K' arrived swiftly.

This made Kat smile. Her brother was a man of few words. She was certain he didn't know that Kat was away or where, yet he didn't ask why she was in Lapland. Some might have mistaken Daniel's lack of interest in other people's affairs for arrogance, or coldness, but they'd be wrong. Kat didn't know anyone as warm and generous of spirit as her little brother.

Kat grinned.

Daniel wasn't so little anymore. Six feet four and sporty with broad shoulders, he towered above the women in the family. He had inherited the blond hair and bright-blue eyes of their Finnish grandmother, and the height from their father.

Kat remembered when she had been in the sixth form and Daniel was still only thirteen. Even then, girls in her year had thrown admiring glances at her brother as he sauntered past in his rugby shirt and shorts. In his own final year, he had been voted the heartthrob of the year, something that had made Daniel laugh with embarrassment when Simona, Kat and Lily had found the description next to his photo in the yearbook.

Kat hoped that her mum would leave Daniel alone to concentrate on his studies. She didn't want to talk to her. She would have to at some point, but now it felt as if she didn't want to see her ever again. It was as if she didn't have a mother at all.

'Ready for the slopes?'

Mikael's question shook Kat out of her thoughts. He was standing at their table, smiling down at her.

Kat didn't reply, nor did she return the smile. She really didn't want to encourage the guy. Instead, she snapped, 'Just finishing my breakfast.'

Mikael, startled by her answer, lifted his hands up in surrender.

He gave a nervous laugh and looked at the other members of his group in the small breakfast room.

Addressing Reg and Pat instead, who were sipping their coffees at the same table, he said, 'No rush, except we'll be meeting by the lifts in ten.'

'Right you are,' Reg said and gave Pat a nudge. 'Better get going, dear.'

Kat swallowed the last of her orange juice and got up to get the rest of her kit from the chalet.

As she was walking through the snow-covered path, she thought about how different two guys could be. Here was Mikael, the embodiment of an entitled rich boy with the diplomacy of a charging bull, while her dear little brother was warm and loving.

Charm personified.

Why couldn't she find someone like Daniel?

Of course, she thought she had found someone exactly like him in Jacques.

Arriving back to her chalet and sitting on her bed, Kat shook her head.

No more moping about what has happened or what could have been.

Chapter Twenty-Two

The next morning, as Kat trudged with her skis and boots from her chalet to the meeting point of a new lift, the sun was blinding her. It was a beautiful February day, and the temperature had soared to nearly oC. The better conditions and sun were a relief from the chilly, overcast weather the day before.

Before leaving her chalet, Kat had stuck a pair of wraparound sunglasses into the pocket of her old ski jacket. As she fished them out and put them on, she noticed Mikael was sporting a fancy pair of dark-purple, mirrored goggles on top of his helmet. When she arrived, he told the group they would be going to the highest point of the mountain. Before he led them to the car that would take them all the way to the top, he glanced around at everyone.

'I'm glad to see you're all wearing goggles. The sun and its reflection on the snow will be blinding today. Kat, you may want to go to the shop and get a proper pair. You can do that after the first run or during lunch.'

'I'm OK,' Kat said.

Mikael shrugged his shoulders. 'Whatever. I'm merely giving you advice as your ski instructor, but naturally, you can ignore it.'

Kat ignored his snippy reply. She wasn't about to waste money and precious resources on a new pair of goggles just so that she could look the part on the slopes. The glasses she wore were from Oxfam, and she used them often while running in the park in the summer. She couldn't see why they wouldn't be good enough now.

Mikael stared at her for a moment longer but when Kat gave him no reaction, he told the group to follow him, and they all piled into the bubble car. With a jolt it took them upwards, towards the top of Ylläs Fell.

A few moments later, Kat skied down the mountain, feeling alive. The wind rushed past her face. The sun blurred her vision, but she didn't care. She felt free. Pride in her accomplishment grew when she saw that she had left Pat and Reg behind. Even Mikael, who was leading the group, was now a few metres behind her.

Suddenly, she caught a glimpse of someone skiing beside her. She turned her head slightly and saw that it was Mikael. He moved effortlessly, his body shifting in perfect harmony with the skis. Kat had a pang of jealousy. Why hadn't she learnt to ski when she was younger? Why hadn't her mother made an effort to take her children more often to Finland, her homeland?

Of course, Simona had had no money for such trips. Unlike Mikael, whose family she was certain took him on the most luxurious holidays.

Kat blushed out of shame for having such thoughts. She wasn't jealous of Mikael's childhood. She knew nothing about it. And she wasn't interested.

At least she was making something of herself. She had a career in TV, which she was very proud of. And now, here in the beautiful Lappish landscape, she was learning a new skill, while trying to heal her broken heart. She would find happiness again.

You can be happy on your own. You don't need a man.

This was becoming a mantra to Kat. Perhaps if she said it often enough, she would finally believe it herself.

Mikael skied past Kat and stopped skilfully at the edge of the piste a few metres along, his skis spraying white powder. He waved at Kat to join him.

She took a deep intake of breath and moved her skis into a plough position, which made her slow down. She didn't manage to stop right by Mikael, but a few ski widths below him. At least she had managed a parallel stop.

Mikael walked downhill towards her and, as if sensing her jealousy, said, 'You're a good skier, Kat. Don't compare yourself to me, or anyone else for that matter. Just enjoy the moment. You've only just learnt and look at you now!'

Kat was taken aback by his words. Was this a truce between them? He was actually being kind to her.

'Thank you,' she said.

'Go on, I'll follow you.'

Mikael lifted his pole, pointing it downhill. Kat nodded but took a moment to admire the incredible vista in front of her. Sunlight bathed the slopes, creating a winter wonderland where the sky met the earth in a brilliant blue embrace, only broken by the dark pine trees bordering the snowy mountains.

With a smile on her face, she pushed off and began gliding down the piste. She glanced back to see if Mikael was following her, but when she faced the front, she was blinded by the sun reflecting off the snow. She squinted, trying to see through the glare, but it was no use. She couldn't make out anything in front of her.

Panic set in as she picked up speed. Cursing her useless glasses, she tried to see where she was going. Her heart raced and her stomach churned.

Just as she was about to lose her balance, a strong arm wrapped around her waist, pulling her to a stop. She looked up to see Mikael's concerned face.

'Are you alright?' He asked, his voice soft.

Kat nodded, still a little shaky.

'Thank you,' she whispered.

Mikael smiled at her, his hand still on her waist. In that moment, she felt a jolt of attraction towards him. Mikael seemed to sense her thoughts and leaned in closer, his lips dangerously close to hers. Kat's heart pounded in her chest, unsure of what was happening.

But then, Mikael pulled away, his hand dropping from her waist.

'We should continue down the mountain,' he said, his voice low and husky.

Kat nodded, the heat of his touch still burning through her snowsuit. As they continued to ski down the slope towards the lifts at the bottom, Kat couldn't help but steal glances at her instructor. She felt something stirring inside her, something she recognised but had promised never to feel again.

Especially not with Mikael.

As they reached the bottom of the slope, he turned to her, a small smile playing on his lips.

'You're a natural, Kat, as I said up there. I knew it from the beginning.'

Warmth spread through her chest at his praise, but she pressed down the sensation.

'Thank you,' she said as coldly as she could muster.

Mikael grinned at her, as if he could sense she was trying to resist his charms.

'Don't forget to nip into the ski store to get a pair of goggles.' He pushed himself towards his group of students who had gathered farther down the slope. Had they seen her near-fall and how Mikael had gathered her up and rescued her?

She felt her cheeks flush at the thought and turned towards the low buildings scattered at the bottom of the fell. As infuriating as he was, Mikael had been right about one thing: she did need a new pair of goggles.

Chapter Twenty-Three

'I have some bad news for you,' Mikael said at their breakfast table the next morning.

Kat was sitting with Pat and Reg in the main hotel building when Mikael stomped across the reception and headed for their table.

'There's an avalanche warning. It doesn't really concern us since we'll only be using the prepared pistes, but if you want to skip today's lesson, you can.'

Kat's heart sank at the news. She had been looking forward to today's lesson, eager to improve her skills. She only had three days left at the resort and the day before had been such a good one. But the thought of the potential danger made her uneasy.

'We're going to skip it and take it easy today,' Pat said. Reg nodded, both looking clearly relieved at the option to skip.

But Kat didn't want to miss out on the opportunity to learn from Mikael, even if it meant facing a potential risk.

'I'll still come,' she said, her voice firm.

Mikael raised an eyebrow, clearly surprised by her response.

'Are you sure?'

Kat nodded. 'I want to learn. And if it means taking a little risk, then I'm willing to do it.'

Mikael smiled at her, a hint of pride in his eyes.

'Alright then. But we'll need to be careful. Stick close to me and follow my instructions.'

Kat nodded. Excitement mixed with fear grew inside her. It turned out she was the only one from her group willing to take to the mountains that day. It was understandable; many of the others were a lot older than Kat. Still, it didn't make her feel any less uneasy about the day.

She had come to Lapland to challenge herself, as well as try to come to terms with Jacques' betrayal. What could be better than to return with having learnt a new skill – even under difficult weather conditions?

Stepping out of her chalet, Kat saw Mikael was already waiting for her outside the hotel entrance. He was holding something in his gloved hands and as Kat got closer, she could see it was a pair of new goggles.

When she reached him, Mikael handed them over to her.

'These were in the lost and found. No one has claimed them so I thought you might as well borrow them. Saves you buying a new pair.'

His smile was lopsided and there was mischief in his expression.

Kat felt embarrassed by his gesture. 'It's not that I don't want to spend the money –'

Mikael cut her off. 'I know, you're saving the world's resources. C'mon, let's go before the light fades.'

He turned his back on her and they trudged towards the first lift.

As they stood inside the bubble lift to reach the highest peak, Kat felt another rush of adrenaline. The sky was cloudy, and the air felt heavy with inclement weather, but the snow was perfect. It was a perfect day to ski.

When they approached the top of the mountain, Mikael turned to her and said, 'We'll be taking a different route today. It's a bit more challenging, but I think you're up for it.'

Kat nodded eagerly. She wanted to prove to Mikael that she was capable of handling anything.

If only her mother could see her now. Simona had vocalised her no confidence in Kat's abilities to learn slalom many times before. Just because Kat hadn't gelled with ballet, her mother had suddenly decided she had no grace or balance; hence, there was no point in taking her to her native Lapland on a skiing holiday. Not that they had been able to afford it anyway.

Now, she and Mikael stood at the top, her instructor pointed out the different landmarks, explaining the terrain and the possible dangers. Kat listened intently, taking in every detail. It was true that she had reservations about his lifestyle and beliefs, but at the same time she trusted Mikael. His knowledge and expertise when it came to skiing in Ylläs were bar none, she was certain of it.

Still, Kat was surprised by her reaction, previously she'd seen nothing good in him. But he *had* rescued her yesterday from what would have been a painful fall. She might have broken a few bones too, or hit her head.

And today, he had thoughtfully found her a used pair of goggles.

So, yes, Kat did now have a certain degree of respect for Mikael. Or at least for Mikael, the ski instructor.

Chapter Twenty-Four

At the top of the mountain, Kat and Mikael started the descent. The first part of the run was easy, with wide-open spaces and gentle slopes. Kat felt a surge of confidence, as she enjoyed the speed and exhilaration of being in control. But as they approached the middle section of the run, the terrain became steeper and more challenging. Kat's heart rate increased, and she could feel the adrenaline pumping through her veins. Her legs began to shake.

Determined not to show him her fear, she followed Mikael's instructions closely, trying to mirror his movements.

Suddenly, there was a loud rumble, and Kat felt the ground shake beneath her feet. She looked up to see a wall of snow hurtling down towards them.

'Oh no,' she muttered.

Mikael turned to her, his face serious.

'Kat, we need to move quickly. Follow me,' he shouted.

She did as she was told, skiing as fast as she could towards the edge of the slope. The snow was getting closer, and she could hear the deafening roar of the avalanche. Panic rose inside her, but she forced herself to stay focused.

As they reached the edge of the slope, Mikael stuck his pole into the back of Kat's skis, freeing her from them. He did the same to his own, and then grabbed her hand and pulled her towards a small outcrop of rocks.

'Hurry!' he shouted over the noise.

They reached the rocks just as the avalanche hit. The snow surrounded them, engulfing them instantly in a white darkness. She couldn't see anything, couldn't hear anything except for the sound of the snow crashing around her. Mikael's hand tightened around hers, and she clung to him, safe in his strong grip.

For what felt like an eternity, they remained buried inside their small bubble in the snow. Kat could feel the weight of it pressing down on them. It was difficult to breathe.

Suddenly, a faint light shone on her face. Mikael was holding a small torch.

'Are you OK?' he whispered.

Kat nodded; she couldn't speak.

They were crouched next to each other, their backs pressed up against a large boulder. Mikael was still holding her mittened hand. She didn't want him to let go of her.

When he placed the torch between them, Kat could see Mikael's face.

'No loud noises, OK?' he said in a hushed tone. 'Just concentrate on your breathing. Slowly in and out.'

Kat followed his advice, watching as he demonstrated pulling air through his nose and pushing it slowly out of his mouth. She felt a tear run down her cheek.

Using the thumb of his mittened hand, Mikael gently wiped it away. With his other hand, he tightened his grip on her and gave her a smile.

'It'll be over soon, I promise.'

Kat gazed into his eyes.

'I've been a complete cow to you, haven't I?' she said quietly.

She registered the surprise on his face, but it was followed quickly by a smile.

'Yeah, a bit. But it's OK. Apology accepted. It's just a shame I had to take you inside an avalanche to get one out of you. Besides, I've been a bit of a prick too.'

Kat chuckled, then she started giggling.

'Shh, don't,' Mikael said, also beginning to chuckle.

A loud crash quietened them both, but after that, the thundering noise began to subside.

Mikael stirred first, digging a hole in the roof of their makeshift igloo. He freed himself from the snow and helped Kat to do the same. By the end, they were both covered in white powder, but miraculously unharmed.

Kat stared at Mikael in disbelief.

'How did you know what to do?' she asked, her voice shaking with emotion.

Mikael's eyes crinkled at the corners. 'I've been doing this for a long time. You just have to trust yourself and trust the snow.'

Kat nodded feeling a new awe and admiration for Mikael. He had saved her life, and for that she was grateful.

They made their way down the rest of the slope on foot, treading with difficulty along the harder edges of the piste – or what was left of it. The adrenaline was still pumping through her veins, and Kat couldn't help but steal glances at Mikael.

Something stirred inside her once more, something she had promised never to feel for another man. But this time felt different. It was a mixture of respect, admiration, and maybe even a little bit of attraction.

Later that same afternoon, when dusk had already settled over the landscape, they reached the hotel and told the others in their group of the incident. Mikael walked Kat back to her chalet. She didn't object to his company, but they hardly spoke to each other. Kat was shivering and, briefly, Mikael placed a hand around her, rubbing her arm.

'Are you OK?'

They reached the door to her chalet.

'I need a hot sauna and sleep, I think,' she replied, turning around to face him.

'I'll give you my number, just in case you need anything.'

Kat nodded and handed over her phone. Mikael tapped in his contact details.

'Thank you for today,' she said.

Mikael was looking at her with a confused expression, so she added, 'You saved my life.'

'Rubbish. You're my pupil. I was only doing my job.'

But the look he was giving her belied his words. It was so intense that Kat felt dizzy. She gave a little cough to break the spell.

'I'm grateful, and I really am sorry about what I said to you the other day. I was well out of order.'

The expression on Mikael's face changed. His eyes widened and he took a step back. He lowered his eyes to his boots and ran his hand through his hair.

'Water under the bridge. Isn't that what you English say?' Mikael looked up at her and gave a small laugh. His eyes were friendly again.

'Yes, that's what we say. But thank you again.' Kat gave a yawn. 'I'm so tired. I'm not sure what's come over me.'

'It's the adrenalin leaving your body. The best thing to do is rest, but please send me a message if you need anything.'

'Will do.'

She opened the chalet door and standing inside, she watched Mikael walk back to the hotel. He gave her a wave and smile before he turned a corner and disappeared from view.

Chapter Twenty-Five

Kat slept all afternoon and through the night. She'd been exhausted.

Early the next morning, she walked to the hotel lobby to get some breakfast. She found the place crowded with people.

There were reporters and cameras everywhere. Kat couldn't help but feel overwhelmed by the chaos. She felt panic rising in her chest as she tried to navigate her way through the crowd.

Then she heard someone calling her name. It was Mikael, waving to her from across the room. She felt relief as she made her way towards him.

'Good morning,' he said, a smile on his face.

Kat couldn't help but smile back. She was grateful for his calm demeanour that was helping to ease her nerves.

'What's going on?' she asked, gesturing towards the chaos in the lobby.

Mikael sighed. 'It seems that our little incident yesterday made the news. Everyone wants to talk to us.'

Dread crept up her spine. She didn't want to be in the spotlight, didn't want to be the centre of attention. That was why she was working behind the scenes in TV. The thought of doing what Jacques did in front of the camera filled her with terror.

'What are we going to do?' she asked him, unsure of what their next move should be.

Mikael thought for a moment before speaking.

'I think we should lay low for a while, let the media frenzy die down before we make an appearance. Unless you're keen to become famous now?'

'Please, no!'

'But I thought you worked in TV?'

She frowned. 'How did you know that?'

Mikael nodded at the breakfast room where the group of skiers were gathered.

'I'm sorry, Pat told me. I wasn't digging, honestly, it just came up in conversation.'

Mikael looked sincere, which made Kat smile.

She placed her hand on his arm, and said, 'Oh, don't worry. But to be honest, I'm relieved you don't want to talk to the reporters, either. I work in production, in the background by choice.'

'Ah, OK.'

'Which means I don't want to deal with the press attention. I just want to enjoy the rest of my holiday without any drama.'

Still holding his arm, Mikael put his hand on hers.

'Listen, I'm so sorry about yesterday. It was a bad idea to go skiing, but the warnings were not for the prepared slopes, only for off-piste skiing. It's highly unusual for an avalanche like that to hit where we were.'

Kat looked at Mikael. 'You saved my life, and you have nothing to apologise for. Besides, I decided to take the risk.'

Mikael nodded. 'Still, I am the expert, so I should have known.'

His face was soft, and she couldn't help but stare at his lips. She began to imagine what it would feel like to kiss him.

She stopped the thought, and said instead, 'You know an unusual weather phenomenon like that is most likely caused by climate change. In only thirty years' time, there will only be snowstorms and avalanches here. Normal snow fall will be a rarity, and when it does snow it'll melt away in a matter of days. The only snow you will be able ski on will be artificially produced. Unless we do something about it now.'

Mikael stared at her and removed his hand, letting it fall beside him. His mouth was in a straight line and his face strained. All the softness gone from his eyes, they narrowed as he spoke.

'Yes, I follow the news. I'm not a complete idiot.'

'But what exactly are you doing about it?'

Kat crossed her arms over her chest and stared at him, waiting for him to say something. But Mikael had no answer, which Kat didn't find in the least bit surprising.

Chapter Twenty-Six

Mikael left Kat standing alone in the middle of the lobby and walked into the breakfast room to speak with the rest of the skiing group. With his back to Kat, he stopped for a moment to take a couple of deep breaths, trying to calm himself before he faced the others.

Why did she think so little of him? Even after everything that had happened yesterday, Kat was still treating him like some rich, spoilt brat. Hadn't he shown he that he was nothing like that?

Mikael shook his head. Why did he even care what Kat thought? And why was her indignation and the assumption he had no consideration for the environment and people up here so hurtful to him? He hardly knew the girl, yet amidst all that danger yesterday, and earlier this morning, he thought they'd shared a moment. He noticed how she'd looked at him when he'd left her at the chalet. He'd wanted to kiss her, but it had felt like the wrong time. She had still been in shock after their narrow escape, and he hadn't wanted to take advantage of her.

Mikael opened the glass doors to the restaurant. His thoughts were interrupted by the sound of vigorous clapping. Everyone in his skiing group, and some of the others staying in the hotel who he didn't know were on their feet, applauding him.

'Our hero!' Pat cheered.

Her husband Reg slapped his back with such force, Mikael nearly lost his balance. He lifted his hands up in recognition of the tribute.

'Please, stop,' he said.

He was embarrassed by all the attention, but at the same time he wondered how it could be that the people now sitting down looking up to him as if waiting for a speech could appreciate him so well, while Kat thought so little of him.

Kat stood in the lobby for a moment, aghast at how Mikael had reacted to her words. What had she done wrong? She'd only been pointing out facts. How the weather patterns were changing so much that they would render sports like skiing obsolete, something that Mikael obviously loved above all else. A few years ago, she'd read in a brilliant book called 'Snow' all about the devastating effects the lack of snow would have on the world as soon as the 2050s.

Instead of getting all upset, why couldn't he have just agreed and lamented with the way the world was going?

Surely it was in his interest to try to stop the upward spiral of the globe's temperature? She would have told him what he could do to try to stop the development if he'd only asked for her advice. Perhaps he didn't believe in climate change? Was he one of those people who denied its existence?

Kat heard the clapping coming from the breakfast room and realised they were cheering Mikael. Of *course* he was their hero now.

When the noise had abated a little, she opened the doors to the restaurant. Mikael was sitting with her group at the head of the table. He turned his head and gave her a cursory glance.

He's really angry at me.

'Kat, are you OK?' someone said.

She was stirred from her thoughts by Pat, who was suddenly by her side and taking her hand.

She smiled at the older woman. 'Yeah, I'm fine.'

'You must be quite shaken up. Thank goodness Mikael was there and knew exactly what to do. He's been telling us all about it, although he claims he was just doing his job. He's a lovely young man, isn't he?'

Pat peered at Kat. Kat forced a smile.

'Come and join us. We're planning how to escape this circus.' Pat nodded at the floor-to- ceiling windows, beyond which the pack of reporters were huddled in the cold.

'I'm beginning to feel sorry for them,' Kat said. 'Still, I don't want them here.'

Pat nodded. 'Come on then.'

The group, in the middle of breakfast, ate and chatted about their plans for the day. Mikael suggested they take a break from skiing and explore the local town, maybe do some shopping.

Kat agreed, excited at the prospect of exploring the area, but wary of being in Mikael's company. She resolved to stay close to Pat and Reg and avoid her instructor as much as she could.

Chapter Twenty-Seven

Kat, with Pat and Reg and the rest of the ski group, spent the morning wandering around the local shops. She and Mikael hadn't exchanged one word, and she was glad that he was also keen to keep away from her.

After they'd visited a couple of artisan boutiques selling Lappish souvenirs, looked around the large spa hotel in the centre of the resort, and browsed in the ski shop, Mikael led the group to a café near the nursery slope, where they had coffee and cinnamon buns. To her delight, Kat found that they also made a vegan version of the buns, which were delicious.

Mikael, who was sitting at the far end of the table to Kat, spoke to all of them.

'I think we've exhausted the sights in this small town, but I could arrange a husky ride for this afternoon, if any of you are interested?'

The 'oldies', as Kat had named the rest of the group privately, muttered between themselves.

'That's very kind of you, Mikael,' Reg said, smiling, 'but I think my dear wife would like to try out the spa.' He had his arm around her shoulders and she was leaning into him.

'My aching joints could do with some TLC,' Pat joked, grinning at Kat.

The others muttered their agreement with Pat's sentiment and began to disperse. Suddenly it was Pat, Reg, Mikael and Kat sitting in the café.

Kat didn't know what to do. It would be rude to up and leave when Mikael was making such an effort to entertain them all, not to mention that he'd saved her life yesterday.

'Well, we'd better be going, love,' Reg said, helping Pat up from the table.

'You two can spend some quality time together.' Pat winked at Kat and Mikael.

Maybe Kat saw it wrong but had Mikael's cheeks just flushed? He got up abruptly, nearly knocking over the cups on the table.

Kat followed him out of the café and they stood outside in the biting cold. The ski resort was crazily quiet with all the pistes shut. Even the nursery slope where Kat had had her first lesson with Mikael – it felt like weeks ago – was empty.

A slight wind rushed over the landscape and swept snow over the slopes.

Being alone with him after Pat's suggestive comment made her feel self-conscious.

Mikael wasn't looking at her, but instead busying himself with putting his mittens on.

'Look, Mikael, it's very kind of you to arrange stuff for us to do today. The oldies are tired though, so ...'

Mikael lifted his eyes to Kat; she was taken aback by how blue they were.

'Sure. The husky ride was just an idea, but never mind.'

'Is the offer still open?'

Kat couldn't believe what she just said. She'd promised herself to keep away from this guy, but suddenly she felt sorry for him. He was trying so hard to be nice. Perhaps he wasn't that bad after all? Perhaps she could change his mind about climate change if she gave him the time of day and took things more gently?

'Yes, of course. I'd love you to come along,' he muttered, giving her a wary look.

Kat swallowed. 'So ...' she said, looking at Mikael, 'can you tell me more about what's involved?'

The idea of being pulled by a bunch of dogs that were probably mistreated and overworked didn't appeal. At the same time, she didn't want to make any assumptions. Perhaps it was time she stopped making assumption about people too.

Mikael's face brightened. 'It's a wonderful experience. You get closer to nature in a way you can't imagine.'

'And the dogs, where do they come from?'

'Oh, the huskies are locally reared. The owner is a

friend of mine, and he loves the dogs like his own children.'

Mikael sounded convincing enough, but she couldn't help having a sense of foreboding. She hoped she wouldn't find a bunch of starving animals forced to pull tourists along paths heavy with snow.

Kat nodded. 'Alright, that sounds great.'

She followed Mikael past a few wooden houses to a small shed where the owner was waiting with his huskies.

She couldn't have been more wrong. The dogs were beautiful, with thick, white-fur coats and bright, ice-blue eyes. They looked the picture of health and Kat gave a sigh of relief. They seemed friendly, wagging their tails as they sniffed around them.

The owner greeted them warmly and led the pair over to the sled. Mikael helped Kat onto the low-slung carriage, settling her in before taking the seat next to her.

'Here, put your legs inside the cover.'

They both moved a little awkwardly, getting their feet inside a fur-lined blanket that was fixed to the sides. Kat hadn't used animal products for over decade, but she decided not to make any comment. It was delicate enough sitting so close to Mikael; she didn't want to make things more awkward than they were.

A guy with straw-blond hair and a wide moustache stood at the back, while the dogs whined and barked with impatience.

'Are you OK to go?' the man asked Kat in heavily accented English.

Kat nodded.

Suddenly the man said something to Mikael in Finnish, and Mikael pulled a pair of mittens from the side of the sledge.

He handed Kat a pair. 'It can get chilly on the ride.'

She noticed the mittens were made of leather, but said nothing and dutifully put them on.

The guy took hold of the reins and commanded the huskies to get moving.

Kat held on tight, bracing herself against the jostling of the sled as they took off across the snow. The huskies pulled them quickly through winding trails, past snow-covered trees and rocks. The air was cold and crisp, making Kat's cheeks tingle with excitement. As they made their way up a steep hill, the driver urged his team of dogs onward with cries of encouragement. Soon enough, the sled had stopped and they were standing atop a frozen lake that stretched out for miles in all directions.

Kat took it all in with wonderment. With the sun peeking out from a set of clouds, lighting up the lake in shades of pink and orange, it truly felt like one of nature's greatest gifts. They took turns snapping pictures and enjoying this magical moment until eventually, the driver indicated that it was time to head back down the mountainside.

Again, they set off on their journey, this time heading home. Kat could feel her heart swell with joy. This husky ride had been a complete surprise and would be one of her fondest memories from this holiday.

'That was amazing, thank you!' Kat said to Mikael when they disembarked from the sled.

In her exhilaration over the experience, she had forgotten to ask about the animal products the husky riders were using. She was certain they could swap them for vegan products over time at little cost. She decided to send them an email once she got back to her chalet.

Mikael glanced at Kat as they walked towards the centre of the resort.

'Do you want to have a bite to eat? I know a great place. We deserve a good meal after all that.'

Kat hesitated for a moment. All this was beginning to feel like a date.

'Don't worry, Mikael. I can get something back at the hotel.'

Kat wasn't looking at Mikael but at the vegan Doc Martens on her feet that she had splurged on back in London when there had been a severe cold snap last year. The warm boots had served her well on this holiday, so she wasn't too worried that she had broken her 'nothing new' buying policy that one time.

Mikael stopped in the middle of his stride.

'Oh, OK. I just thought since we have a free day from skiing, it would be a good opportunity to introduce you to some great local cuisine.'

Kat couldn't but help smile at Mikael's choice of words. Who used words like "cuisine"? Even she didn't and she was a food producer on TV.

An involuntary snort escaped from her mouth. 'You

want to go to a Michelin starred restaurant for some local *cuisine?*'

Mikael looked offended, but when his eyes met Kat's, she saw the smile twitching his lips.

'English is my third language, so I'd appreciate it if you didn't laugh at my choice of words.'

'Sorry,' Kat replied, chastened.

What was it about this bloke that made her always say the wrong thing?

'Don't worry. Anyway, all I was thinking was that we could go to a place where they serve local food.' Mikael emphasised the last word and looked at Kat. 'It's in a *Lavvu*, a traditional Sami dwelling, and they cook everything over a fire in the middle. I thought this would be something you'd like to experience?'

'OK, that sounds great.'

Mikael was right; it was exactly what she'd like to experience.

Chapter Twenty-Eight

The restaurant was a short walk away from the hotel. While they made their way along a small road running through snow-laden woods, dusk had settled over the landscape. Mikael led Kat to the back of a low-slung building where a path, lit by several torches, led up to a large, tent-like structure.

'That's a *Lavvu*,' Mikael explained.

At the entrance, a man in a traditional Sami clothing of a colourful coat with a skirt-like hem and long, black leather boots stood with an iPad in his hand. The contrast between the traditional costume and the modern device was so stark that it made Kat smile.

The Sami man and Mikael conversed in Finnish. At first, the man shook his head and Kat wondered if they were fully booked, but after Mikael pointed at Kat and said something, the man nodded.

Turning to Kat he said, 'Please enter here.'

Inside the *Lavvu* they were greeted by a woman wearing a similarly colourful Sami dress.

'Please,' she said, and pointed to a large table at the back of the room. There were just two seats remaining, right at the end of one of the benches.

In the middle of a long fire, flickering flames were licking pieces of meat hanging from hooks placed above it. Kat could see sausages there, as well as different cuts on the grills.

She saw no vegetables.

'You do know I'm vegan, right?' Kat whispered to Mikael.

Mikael looked at her with panic in his eyes.

'Oh, no,' he exclaimed.

Kat felt the familiar dismay. How many times had she been in this situation where her veganism was treated like some kind of bizarre affliction? She'd been looking forward to a local feast, but now she realised that she wouldn't be able to eat anything.

'It's alright,' she said, trying to hide her disappointment. 'I'm sure they'll have some bread.'

The Sami woman brought over a basket of dark-rye rolls and a bowl of butter. Kat looked at the dish with dismay – she hadn't eaten dairy products in years.

'I'm sorry, I can't eat this either,' she said to Mikael.

Mikael nodded. In the darkness of the *Lavvu*, Kat couldn't tell if he was annoyed at her or just taken aback by the situation.

'I'll go see if there's something else for you.'

Kat watched as he approached the woman and spoke

to her in Finnish. She glanced at Kat before disappearing into the kitchen.

A few minutes later, she returned with a plate of roasted root vegetables and a bowl of mushroom soup. Kat's heart swelled with gratitude for Mikael for making sure she could enjoy this experience. The vegetables were perfectly cooked, and the soup was rich and flavourful.

'Are you vegan for the sake of the environment?' Mikael asked, as he was served a plateful of meat with similar relishes to the ones that were on Kat's plate.

Kat nodded. 'Did you know that animal industry is one of the top two significant contributors to the serious environmental problems?'

'Ah, yes, I see. This meat, however, is sustainable because it's reindeer.'

Kat cocked her head at Mikael. 'I don't think so.'

'Honestly, it is. I read a report on it recently.'

Kat didn't believe in research carried out by the food industry, which she suspected was the one Mikael had read. But she didn't want to argue. Once again, he had given her a wonderful experience.

Besides, she was pleasantly surprised that he knew of the harm people were causing the environment. It wasn't something Kat thought would ever feature in his thoughts, with how he had reacted to her comments about it, not to mention his interest in fancy designer gear and fast cars.

Mikael began chatting to a Canadian couple on the other side of the table. Giving him a sideways glance, she realised that not only had she been ungrateful – the man had saved her from a disaster twice now – but incredibly condescending.

What did she know about Mikael, really? Could it be that she'd got him completely wrong and that he wasn't the spoilt Eurotrash she thought he was after all? Had she been partly affected by Jacques' often expressed prejudices? Or blinded by his betrayal?

A blush warmed Kat's face as she recalled how she had acted towards Mikael since meeting at Helsinki airport. The guy had been nothing but friendly towards her from the very beginning.

Yes, he talked about his fast car, he wore expensive ski gear, a Rolex, a signet ring, and his family were obviously rich. But had he at any point showed anything but love for nature and the environment?

Except for the fact that he'd taken a flight rather than train to Lapland. But hadn't she done the same?

As they ate, they chatted more with the Canadians who were interested in the husky ride Mikael and Kat had taken that afternoon. Around the table there were people who'd come from all over the world to experience the Sami culture and cuisine. The glow from the firelight danced on their faces and the smell of wood smoke filled the air.

After dinner, she and Mikael stepped out into the cold night air. The sky was clear, and the stars twinkled overhead. The torch-lit path looked even more enchanting.

When she walked home beside him, contentment washed over Kat. She was grateful for this unexpected adventure, for the kindness of strangers, and for the chance to share such a beautiful moment with Mikael.

The last thought surprised her, but she allowed herself to enjoy the moment. Perhaps it was the wine, or the warm, magical atmosphere inside the *Lavvu*, or the star-filled sky that prompted her to take Mikael's hand.

Mikael looked at her, surprised, yet pleased. He firmed his grip of her mitten and drew her closer, his breath visible in the cold air. Matching each other's steps, they walked back to the hotel, neither speaking.

When they arrived at the hotel entrance, which, thankfully, was now free of reporters, Mikael turned to Kat and took both her hands in his. They were standing so close to each other that Kat could feel the warmth emanating from Mikael's body. It was another cold, clear night, and the stars were out in full force.

'I'm glad I met you,' he said quietly. 'It's been a wonderful night.'

'So am I,' she replied, surprising herself. She added, 'I really enjoyed today. This place is beyond magical. Thank you for going to such trouble for my sake.'

Mikael's blue eyes peered down at her, and Kat could see he was about to bend down and kiss her. She wasn't sure she wanted that, yet she found herself staring at the curve of his lips and imagining what they would taste like.

'May I kiss you?' Mikael asked hoarsely.

Chapter Twenty-Nine

Kat didn't have time to reply to Mikael's question because, at that moment, the door to the hotel opened behind them. She heard a familiar voice call out.

'Kat!'

Mikael let go of her hand and turned round to the person calling her name.

Kat froze and stared at the man running towards her. She couldn't believe her eyes.

Jacques was standing in front of her. Jacques, her ex-boyfriend, who she had vowed never to lay eyes on again.

He was panting, out of breath.

'What are you doing here?' Kat asked in a whisper. Her lungs had emptied of all air, amid the mix of shock and confusion she felt.

Jacques gazed at her, his eyes wide.

'I came to find you. I saw in the news that there had been an avalanche and that you were hurt!'

As she stared at him, the wave of anger that she had all but forgotten washed over her. She couldn't believe that he would come all this way, after he had betrayed her in the most venal way.

'You can't just show up like this,' she said, her voice low and angry. 'You can't be here.'

Mikael flicked his eyes from Kat to Jacques and back again.

Jacques ignored Mikael and gazed at Kat, his face full of remorse.

'I know I messed up,' he said, 'but I had to come and see that you are OK. I got on the plane as soon as I heard what happened. I came for you. I've missed you, *chérie.*'

Kat's fury made her heart beat so hard, she thought she might faint. She curled her fingers into fists, pushing her nails into her palms inside her mittens. The pain allowed her to calm down and concentrate on her words.

But before she could speak, Mikael spoke.

'Who are you?'

Jacques turned to him and spat out, 'More to the point, who are you?'

He was squaring up to Mikael, who was a head taller than her ex.

Kat fumed. Jacques' arrogance was preposterous. Who did he think he was?

'He is a friend. Mikael, this is Jacques. He is ... a former friend,' Kat said as coolly as she could.

'Ah,' Mikael said. He stretched out his hand.

Jacques ignored his gesture, and instead took hold of

Kat's arm, pulling her away from Mikael and the hotel reception.

'C'mon Kat. They told me our chalet is this way.'

Kat removed her arm from his grip.

'It's not "our chalet" it's *my chalet*, and you are not going anywhere near it.

'Please, let me talk to you. I promise I'll leave afterwards,' Jacques pleaded with her, his face filled with pain.

She hesitated, her mind racing. She didn't want to be alone with Jacques, but she also didn't want to make a scene in front of Mikael and the hotel staff.

Mikael stepped forward, placing a hand on Kat's shoulder.

'Is everything alright?' he asked, looking at Jacques with suspicion.

Jacques glared at Mikael. 'Everything is fine.'

Kat sighed. 'It's OK, Mikael.'

She walked away towards her chalet. Jacques followed.

'And how is my dear mother?' she said to Jacques over her shoulder, her voice full of malice. She had wanted to sound calm and controlled, but the words came out quivering.

Jacques trudged through the snow-covered path in a pair of city shoes. If she wasn't so angry, she would have found it funny how the Frenchman was so ill-prepared for winter in Lapland. Surely, he must have known what to wear to a ski resort? Or had all his stories of skiing in the Alps been lies too?

'I haven't seen her for weeks. It's over, Kat.'

Kat stopped and turned around. She gave a sarcastic chortle.

'You know that doesn't change anything.'

Jacques stepped forward and put his arms around Kat. She stood rigidly. His touch on her, even through the layers of her warm clothing, made her skin crawl. How did this man think that after what he had done, she would forgive him and go back to the way things used to be? He must have been out of his mind.

'Please, let's just get inside and talk,' Jacques said. 'I will explain everything, I promise. It's so cold out here. I'm freezing and can hardly think!'

They were at the chalet door and Kat saw he was chilled to the core in his London overcoat and jeans. He was obviously not prepared for the climate here. She tried to fight the sympathy she felt for him.

But she had to make something clear before she let him inside the warmth of the chalet.

With the chunky key in her hand, she lifted her eyes toward Jacques.

'You can come in to warm up while you find yourself a flight home, or another room.'

Jacques nodded.

He is meek as a lamb now, Kat thought, and opened the door.

Chapter Thirty

Kat was watching Jacques remove his inadequate wool overcoat and shoes when her phone pinged with a message.

How are you, darling? I hope Jacques has arrived by now. We are both very worried about you. Love, mum xx.

Kat stared at the screen and her anger rose. So much for Jacques not seeing Simona anymore. Not that it would have made any difference to her.

The hurt she had felt finding Jacques in her mother's bed bubbled up again. She realised that the skiing, the friendships she had forged with Pat and Reg – and yes, Mikael – had almost made her forget about the horrific events in London and the pain she had felt since her mother's terrible revelation.

She turned to face Jacques.

'I'll get you a warm drink, but then you need to find

yourself another room for tonight and a flight back to London tomorrow.'

Jacques took a deep breath and gazed at her, his eyes filled with regret.

'You know I love you, Kat, even with your beautiful hair cut off,' he said. 'And I never wanted to hurt you.'

'But you did,' Kat snapped, touching her cropped head. One of the things Jacques had loved about her – or had said he loved about her – was her long, chestnut-brown hair. That was probably why she had cut it off after witnessing the horrible scene in her mum's bed.

'I know,' Jacques said. 'And I'm sorry. I messed up, but I was confused. I didn't know what I wanted.'

'You didn't know what you wanted?' Kat repeated, incredulous. 'So, you thought it was OK to cheat on me with my mother?'

Jacques winced at the mention of Simona.

'I knew it was wrong,' he said. 'I was in a bad place. And I've been trying to understand what's going on with me, but I needed your help. Please, Kat.'

Jacques dropped to his knees and took hold of Kat's hands.

Kat pulled out of his grip, and stepped back, shaking her head.

'Get up,' she said, her voice laced with venom. 'You don't get to touch me like that after what you did.'

Jacques looked up at her, his eyes pleading.

'Please,' he begged. 'I just need you to hear me out. I am seeing a therapist and I've been trying to work through my issues. I know I messed up, but I'm willing to do whatever it takes to make things right.'

Kat stared down at him still on one knee with a mix of emotions. A very, very small part of her wanted to believe him, to give him another chance. But she brushed the feeling away. She was filled with too much anger and hurt to forgive him for what he had done.

'I can't help you,' she said. 'I can't fix this. You made a choice, and you must live with the consequences.'

Jacques stood, his eyes filled with tears.

'Please,' he said again, his voice cracking.

'No, Jacques. You don't get to say that you love me and then cheat on me with my mother. You must be crazy if you think you can just come back into my life and expect me to forgive you. I deserve better than that.'

Jacques nodded. 'I understand. I'll get another room for tonight and go tomorrow. I'm sorry, Kat. I truly am.'

Jacques was sitting by the fire which Kat had lit after their row, in an attempt to calm herself. She was making them two mugs of hot cocoa with oat milk in the small kitchenette on the far side of the chalet while he was on the phone arranging another room for himself.

He ended the call and joined her. 'The hotel is fully booked.'

'What?'

Kat put down the two mugs on the table by the fire. She couldn't believe her ears.

'I'm sorry, *chérie,* we have no choice.'

Jacques' eyes moved from the bed in the middle of the room back to her. He was pleading with her, but she could also see a glimmer of something else, a sudden spur of hope.

'No, Jacques, you are not staying here.'

He got up and took her hands into his.

'Please, I promise I won't do anything. Could I just hold you?'

Kat tore her hands out of his grip and stepped back towards the kitchenette. She was trembling with indignation.

'Have you lost your mind? I don't want to see you, talk to you, let alone be touched by you. Why you think I'd want to sleep in the same bed after what you did is frankly inconceivable. Being in the same room as you is making me feel sick!'

Jacques hung his head. 'OK, if you insist, I will sleep on the floor.'

Kat glared at him. This was too much for her. She could not bear to be in his presence any longer.

Gathering her coat and Docs, she left without another word. The snow crunched beneath her feet as she walked away. She stared up at a sky filled with stars that were even brighter now that night had fallen. The beauty of the landscape was in sharp contrast to the terrible mess that she was a part of.

Chapter Thirty-One

The farther away from Jacques and the chalet she got, the better she felt.

For the past two days, she'd begun to feel free from the events in London, as if her heart was finally beginning to melt from the frozen grip of the betrayal. For the last twenty-four hours she hadn't thought of Jacques once, not until he turned up tonight. Seeing him in the flesh had reminded her how she now abhorred him. Having him close made her skin crawl in a way that she had never experienced with anyone else.

Thoughts raced through Kat's mind. How could she ever return to London if even here, thousands of miles away, the person who used to be the centre of her world could rouse such intense anger and repulsion? Back in London, surely it would be impossible to work with him day in day out?

Her thoughts were suddenly interrupted by Mikael's appearance at the hotel entrance.

'Are you OK?' Mikael asked, concern etched on his face.

Seeing him made Kat's eyes fill with tears, but she fought them back. Jacques wasn't worth it.

'No,' she replied. 'I'm not.'

Mikael stepped forward and wrapped his arms around her.

'Come on,' he said softly. 'Let's go back to my chalet and talk.'

Kat nodded, her body shaking. She felt so cold.

As they walked to Mikael's chalet, she couldn't help but feel grateful for his presence. He'd been a stranger a few days ago, but now he felt like the only person she could trust.

Inside the chalet, Mikael led her to the couch, sitting down beside her.

'What happened?' he asked gently.

Kat took a deep breath, trying to calm herself.

'Jacques was...'

Tears which she had fought back welled up in Kat's eyes again. The thought of having to tell a stranger about her horrible tale was unimaginable. She was ashamed to be connected to such immoral people.

'He cheated on me with my mother,' she finally admitted, her voice breaking.

Mikael's eyes widened. 'With your mother?'

Kat nodded, tears streaming down her face.

Mikael put his arm around her, holding her close.

'I'm so sorry,' he said softly. 'That must have been incredibly difficult for you.'

Kat nodded, grateful for his comfort.

'It was just... How do I go back to my old life after this? How can I trust anyone again?'

Mikael looked at her, compassion in his eyes. 'You don't have to make any decisions right now. Just take some time to process everything. And if you need anything, I'm here for you.'

Kat nodded with a glimmer of hope in the darkness of her situation.

'Thank you,' she said, and added, 'The hotel is fully booked so now he wants to stay in my chalet. I just can't _'

Mikael interrupted her. 'You don't have to let him stay there if you don't want to,' he said firmly. 'It's your space, and you have every right to decide who you want in your chalet.'

'But where could he go?' she asked, feeling guilty for potentially leaving Jacques out in the cold, even if he wasn't her responsibility. Nor was it her fault he'd come all this way and not arranged somewhere to stay. His arrogance knew no bounds.

Mikael thought for a moment before answering.

'I have a spare room in my chalet. Each of us usually shares with another instructor, but my buddy is off sick,' he said. 'Your ex could stay here for the night.'

Kat couldn't believe his generosity. 'You can't do that!'

Mikael smiled at her, his eyes kind and filled with understanding. 'Of course, I can. I'll make them charge him for the room, though,' he added with a wicked expression on his face.

Kat gave a little chortle. Instantly, a weight lifted off her shoulders.

'Thank you. You don't know how much this means to me.'

Chapter Thirty-Two

When Mikael and Kat entered her chalet, they saw Jacques had fallen asleep in the chair by the fire.

For a moment, Kat stared at the man who, only a few weeks ago, she thought she'd wanted to spend the rest of her life with. He hadn't asked her to marry him, that was true, but he had told her that he loved her. And he had hinted at buying her a ring.

All the while, he'd betrayed her.

For the first time since she'd found out, Kat truly understood the full horror of their treachery. During the first two weeks after it had happened, she'd walked around in a daze. She'd continued working with him, but she hadn't been able to look in his direction. Luckily, they had been in post-production, which meant Jacques hadn't been required to be in the office every day.

She had been numb, unable to think about anything else but getting away from Jacques and her mother.

As she watched Jacques shift position on the chair, still fast asleep, she wondered how she could have ever loved him, or even liked him. He'd wooed her with romantic gestures like flowers and meals in fancy restaurants, but that was all superficial. None of it was real.

Why couldn't I see him for what he was?

Mikael shifted next to her, and suddenly Kat remembered she wasn't alone and the reason why Mikael was there. She couldn't wait to have the place to herself again.

'Jacques!'

Startled, he straightened his back and looked up at her.

'Oh, *chérie*, you're back.'

'Don't call me that. This is Mikael, who you met earlier. You can stay in his place. He has a spare room.'

'*Michel*, that's so very kind of you, but there's no need. Kat and I are – how would you put it – are already well acquainted, so I'm certain we could manage to sleep in the same bed for one night. Please, *ché*... Kat.'

Jacques got up and took hold of her shoulders and his eyes pleaded with her.

For the second time that night, Kat pulled away from him. This time she took more than a couple of steps back. Before she could reply to Jacques, Mikael had filled the space between them.

'I think it's best if you come with me, mate. We don't want any trouble here.'

Mikael's words were ice-cold, and his face was serious. Standing next to each other, Mikael was a lot bulkier than her ex-boyfriend.

If he wanted to, Mikael could beat the daylights out of the Frenchman.

Mikael isn't going to hurt Jacques, is he?

'I am not your *mate*. This is between me and my girlfriend, so butt out!'

Jacques spat the words at Mikael, but Mikael only stood taller. The two men were squaring off against each other.

'She isn't your girlfriend anymore, I believe.'

Jacques' eyes shifted from Mikael to Kat and back again.

'Ah, *je comprends*! You have found yourself a little holiday fling, have you?' Jacques sneered at Kat.

'Please, just go, Jacques,' she said, her voice trembling with fury.

'Don't worry, *chérie*, a fling is a fling. A little revenge sex, eh? I forgive you, but now we can get back together and forget all about our mutual indiscretions?'

Kat couldn't take it anymore. 'Are you drunk? Mikael is the ski instructor, and he has been very helpful. In fact, he saved my life yesterday in the avalanche. There's nothing going on between us.'

Kat didn't look at Mikael because she wasn't quite sure she was telling the truth. However, whatever may or may not be happening between them had nothing to do with Jacques.

'My name isn't *Michel*, but Mikael and I work at the hotel. I'm offering a room in my chalet, but if you'd rather take your chances with the other hotels in the resort, you're welcome. But Kat doesn't want you in her room. It's your choice.'

Later, as Kat lay down in her bed, and Jacques had gone with Mikael, she felt a peace settle over her. For the first time in weeks, she could breathe without the weight of Jacques and Simona's betrayal crushing her.

The road ahead would be difficult, but for now, she was grateful for the small moments of solace that she'd found with – of all people – Mikael.

Chapter Thirty-Three

The following day, the weather turned bad again. An intense snowstorm hit the resort and Mikael had to deliver the bad news during breakfast: skiing was off-limits once again. Pat and Reg – along with the rest of the group – let out a collective sigh of dismay. Mikael glanced over at Kat, who gave him a quick smile, before he spoke again.

'Unfortunately, the flights have also been cancelled for today.'

Mikael heard Kat take a sharp breath in.

He hadn't heard a peek out of the Frenchman's room when he had woken early, as he always did to check the weather forecast for the day. Last night, when they had arrived in his chalet, after the uncomfortable scenes in Kat's rooms, his unwelcome guest hadn't said more than a couple of words. Neither of them had been, 'Thank you'.

Mikael had managed to contain his frustration with the guy. He'd given him a towel and showed him his bed for the night, and where he could get washed in the small shower room.

'That means I have to stay another day in this hell-hole, does it?' someone said behind him.

Mikael turned around and came face-to-face with the Frenchman.

'Jacques!' Kat barked at him.

The group was silent, their eyes flickering between Kat, Jacques and Mikael.

'What?' the Frenchman exclaimed, stretching his arms wide. 'I'm only giving my honest opinion of this godforsaken resort. I mean, why are you guys all here? Not for skiing on those little hills that you call mountains, surely? They're like little girl's tits. Not like the majestic Mont Blanc!'

'That's enough, Jacques.' Kat said, rising from the table where she'd been having breakfast. 'You are being rude.'

'There is a bus service to Rovaniemi. There you will find a flight to London, I'm sure.' Mikael said.

He held his hands in tight fists either side of his body, trying to control himself. He wanted nothing more than to punch the arrogant Frenchman in his face, but that would achieve nothing.

Jacques snorted. 'I don't want to go on a wild goose chase to some other uncivilised town. I'm going to stay here until the weather improves.'

Mikael clenched his teeth, trying to keep his anger in check.

'I'm sorry, but that isn't an option,' he said. 'The hotel

is fully booked, and we can't accommodate you any longer.'

Jacques looked around the table, his eyes settling on Kat. 'Can't I stay with you, *chérie?*' he asked, a sly smile creeping across his face.

Kat recoiled, disgust etched on hers.

'No, Jacques. That isn't going to happen. And I told you not to call me that.'

Jacques laughed. 'You're still sore about your mother, aren't you? Don't worry, *mon amour*, I'll make it up to you.'

Mikael's anger rose. He squared up to the Frenchman. 'That's enough. You need to leave. *Now.*'

Jacques sneered at him. 'Who do you think you are, telling me what to do?' he said, taking a step closer to him.

Mikael stood his ground, his eyes fixed on Jacques.

'I'm someone who won't tolerate your disrespectful behaviour any longer,' he said firmly.

Jacques looked around the table, his eyes settling on Kat once again.

'You're just a ski instructor, *le bon-à-rien,*' he sneered. 'You have no authority over me.'

Kat clearly bristled at the insult, but Mikael was unruffled.

'It doesn't matter who I am or what I do,' he said to the Frenchman. 'What matters is that you leave.'

Jacques looked at Mikael with contempt.

'Fine,' he said. 'I'll leave. There's a hotel near the airport. But mark my words, Kat. You'll regret this.'

Kat stood up, her eyes flashing with hatred.

'Get out of my sight, Jacques,' she said, her voice cold and hard.

Jacques snorted and turned to leave, but not before he leaned in and whispered something in Kat's ear that made her recoil. Mikael saw the fear in her eyes and his blood boiled with fury.

The Frenchman added a parting shot at the group.

'You all should be grateful that I even graced this dump with my presence,' he said and stormed off.

Everyone let out a collective sigh of relief and Kat slumped into her chair.

'Are you OK?' Pat, who was sitting next to Kat, asked gently.

Kat looked up at her, tears filling her eyes.

'No,' she said, her voice shaking. 'I'm not, really.'

Mikael came over and sat next to Kat. He placed a hand over hers.

'It's going to be fine,' he said softly. 'I'm here for you.'

'As are we,' Reg said firmly. 'What an unpleasant fellow.'

Kat gave them all a grateful smile and turned to Mikael, 'Thank you,' she said, her voice soft.

Mikael gave her a small smile. 'Don't mention it. I won't let anyone treat you like that.'

Glancing out of the windows, Mikael saw that the snowstorm outside was showing no signs of abating. The weather report early that morning had forecast the same. There would definitely not be any skiing today.

'How about a day on the ice? I could organise an impromptu trip to the indoor ice rink for you all?' Mikael said, trying to lighten the mood of the group.

A joint cheer went up.

'I've not been on skates for years!' Pat exclaimed.

'And me never,' Reg said, smiling at his wife. 'There's a first time for everything!'

'Right then, you get ready, and I'll meet you in the lobby in half an hour, OK?'

Mikael was speaking to the whole group, but his eyes were on Kat.

She was now talking animatedly to Pat and Reg. They were laughing and smiling, so Mikael was certain she wasn't telling them what Jacques had done to her. Perhaps they already knew?

Kat seemed surprisingly OK, if a little shaken by yet another nasty encounter with her ex-boyfriend. Mikael wondered how a man like Jacques had gotten her to fall for him in the first place. Not only was he a lot older, but he was also a complete ass. Mikael looked out the floor-to-ceiling windows overlooking the hotel entrance.

The guy was standing outside, hoping from one foot to another. Just then he nearly fell over on the slippery surface.

Mikael couldn't help but grin. Wouldn't it be sweet if the guy fell right in front of everybody? Mikael hadn't met someone so infuriatingly bad mannered and full of himself in a long while.

And Kat had called him, Mikael, arrogant!

But that was days ago, and since then, he thought

they had formed a firm friendship, if not something more. Mikael certainly wanted to take things further with Kat, but he doubted she was ready for that. Mikael didn't want to be the rebound guy, that's for sure.

'Hey, penny for them?'

He was startled from his thoughts by Kat, who was gazing up at him, concern in her eyes.

Mikael smiled at her, trying to push away his tender thoughts about her.

'Just watching Jacques leave,' he said, gesturing at the window. 'Glad to see the back of him.'

Kat nodded, her eyes following Mikael's gaze.

The Frenchman was now getting into the back of a taxi. Luckily, he wasn't looking in their direction. When the car pulled away, she turned to Mikael.

'Me too,' she said softly. 'Thank you for standing up for me last night and today. I don't know what I would have done without you.'

Mikael shook his head. 'You don't have to thank me. I just hate seeing people being treated badly.'

'Still, I appreciate it,' Kat insisted, giving him a small smile.

The two of them fell into a comfortable silence, both lost in their own thoughts.

Mikael wondered if he should tell Kat how he felt about her, but decided against it. It was too soon, and he didn't want to scare her off.

'Ready for the ice?' he asked her instead.

Chapter Thirty-Four

The ice-skating had worn Kat out, but when Mikael suggested they all go for a drink after, she couldn't refuse. She didn't want the day to end.

She'd always adored ice-skating and it had been years since she'd last done it. It had been exhilarating to feel the cold air on her face and the ice beneath her feet. It was the perfect way to take her mind off the lurking dread she felt that Jacques might turn up at the hotel that night.

Now, as they sat in the bar, sipping on their drinks, Kat couldn't help but feel a flutter in her chest as she looked at Mikael. There was something about him that made her feel safe and happy.

And she couldn't deny that she was attracted to him.

Mikael was talking about the time he'd gone ice-skating with his younger sister, and Kat listened with interest. She loved hearing about his childhood in

Finland, and seeing how his eyes lit up when he talked about it.

Mikael ordered a round of shots for the group. He told them it was a special Finnish drink, vodka laced with liquorice. Kat balked at first, but Mikael insisted, saying they deserved a night of fun after the day they'd had.

Kat downed her shot, which burned in her throat. She looked at Mikael, who was grinning at her.

'I don't think I've ever seen you drunk,' she said, amused.

Mikael shrugged. 'I have an occasional beer after a day's skiing, but I don't often go all out.'

Kat laughed, her inhibitions slowly slipping away. She felt safe with Mikael, and safety was something she hadn't experienced in a long time.

As the night wore on, the group size dwindled until it was just Kat and Mikael.

While they chatted, Kat could feel the tension between them growing. She suspected Mikael had feelings for her, but she wasn't sure if she was ready for anything more than friendship just yet. But as they continued to talk and laugh, she found herself drawn to him.

She liked the way Mikael's eyes crinkled when he smiled, and tonight, he'd been doing a lot of that. They moved into a corner booth of the bar, the dim lighting and soft music adding to the cosy atmosphere.

Suddenly, Mikael leaned in, his breath warm against her ear.

'Kat,' he said, his voice low and husky. 'I don't want to

hide what I feel for you anymore. I know it's soon, but I can't help it.'

Kat's heart raced as she looked into Mikael's eyes with a mixture of nervousness and excitement.

'I don't know what to say,' she said.

Mikael took Kat's hand, his touch sending shivers down her spine.

'You don't have to say anything,' he said, his voice barely above a whisper. 'Just know that I care about you, and I want to be with you.'

Kat felt warmth spread through her body, and she realised that she felt the same way about Mikael.

She leaned in, touching him softly on the lips with her own. The kiss was gentle at first, but as the passion between them built, until it became urgent.

Their hands were everywhere, exploring, touching. Kat felt alive in a way she hadn't in a long time.

As they broke for air, Mikael looked at her with a mixture of desire and tenderness.

'Kat, I want to be with you, but only if you feel the same way. I don't want to pressure you into anything,' he said, his eyes searching hers for an answer.

Kat took a deep breath. Her heart was racing in her chest. She wanted to be with Mikael, but she feared getting hurt again. She had been through so much with Jacques. She didn't want that to happen to her again.

But as she looked into Mikael's eyes, she could tell that he was different. He was kind and caring. So different from the man she'd presumed he was.

She nodded, tears pricking at the corners of her eyes.

'I feel the same way,' she whispered.

Mikael smiled, relief flooding his features. He leaned in, kissed her again, and the passion between them reignited.

As they pulled away, Mikael took Kat's hand, his eyes locked on hers.

'Let's get out of here,' he said, a mischievous glint in his eye.

Kat nodded with excitement bubbling up inside her.

It was late, past midnight, and the reception was now quiet, but when they entered, the receptionist who had been whispering and laughing with Mikael on her first day waved him over. Looking serious, she said something to him, something Kat couldn't hear.

'OK,' he replied and walked back to Kat.

'My boss wants a word.'

'But it's late. Surely you should be off the clock by now?'

Kat tried not to sound desperate, but she couldn't understand why Mikael's boss would want to speak with him in the middle of the night.

He ran his hand across his blond hair, making the front of it stand up for a moment until it fell back down again to half cover his bright-blue eyes.

'Things work a bit differently out here. Apparently, she's been trying to contact me all night.'

'Ah.'

They'd both decided to turn off their phones, which

had been bleeping with news about the disaster on the mountains. Kat had had messages from her friends in London, as well as the one from her mum. She'd sent a message to Lily and Daniel telling them all was well before she'd gone offline. She'd also contacted Toni, her friend, to say she was OK.

Without thinking, Kat placed her hand on his arm and squeezed it. She could feel his muscles tense underneath his jacket. He lifted his eyes to Kat's, and they stood there staring at each other, saying nothing.

A cough from the girl behind the reception desk brought them back to reality, and Kat forgot what she was planning to say to him.

'Sorry about, you know ...' Mikael whispered in her ear. 'A rain check?' He gave her a quick peck on her lips.

'Of course. I'll see you tomorrow?'

'You will.'

She watched him walk past the reception desk and through a door at the back.

Chapter Thirty-Five

Petra Laukkanen was a woman in her forties with bright-red hair (coloured, Mikael presumed) secured in a tight ponytail.

Mikael wasn't surprised that the hotel manager was in her office gone midnight. She was known for working round the clock. Some of the staff had reported seeing her asleep on the couch in her office. Even though she had a beautiful villa only a short drive away from the resort, apparently she couldn't afford the time to go home for the night.

'Take a seat,' Petra told Mikael when he entered her office.

She indicated to the chair opposite her desk. But he didn't want to sit down.

'What's this about?' he asked.

Petra's face registered surprise.

'Surely you can guess? I need to talk about the

avalanche. We've given a statement to the press but now there's been a complaint. About you personally.'

'Really? Who...? Look Petra, I followed the advice given to the letter. The prepared pistes were supposed to be out of the danger area.'

'Is that what you would have told her family if the worst had happened? And what do you think would have happened to the reputation of this place – and the resort? As it is I'm forced to counter all sorts of negative reports. Goodness knows what this will do to the bookings for next season.'

'That's the real reason, isn't it?' Mikael uttered the words before thinking.

Petra gave him a sharp glare. 'For goodness' sake, do sit down! You're giving my neck a crick standing there.'

Mikael dropped his head and did as he was asked. He felt ashamed for his little outburst.

Petra continued, 'You know as well as me that if we have no bookings, you will not have a job. And I know you love your job.'

Mikael nodded. Petra had been the person who had hired him. She knew of his family's objections to his choice of career and understood what trouble his passion for the outdoors, Lapland, and skiing was costing him at home. He'd surprised himself with how much he had divulged to her during the interview. He rarely spoke to anyone about his family or his father's disappointment in him in general.

He kept his eyes on his hands, resting on his lap.

Petra sighed and continued. 'We've had a serious complaint from the woman's fiancé.'

'What?'

'Katherine Wootton's partner came in earlier this morning and made a complaint. Or rather, he issued a threat. If we don't investigate the incident, and particularly your part in it, he will sue us for negligence. I've looked him up. He's an influential man and famous chef in the UK. That means he has the money to carry out this threat.'

'He's not her fiancé,' Mikael corrected.

Once again, Petra raised an eyebrow. 'Be as it may, this is a serious situation. My hands are tied, Mikael. I am going to have to suspend you until we have this sorted out.'

As Mikael got up the manager added, 'One more thing. It might be best if you don't spend any more time with the Wootton woman. I hear you've gotten quite close.'

'Who told you that?'

The hotel manager gave a short laugh. 'Come on, Mikael, the staff talk. You know that.'

He thought of Salla in reception. She was always friendly with him, and they often joked with each other. Had she gossiped to Petra about him and Kat?

Petra continued. 'It wouldn't look good if it turned out that you took her to the mountain alone just so you could be with her. And then what happened, happened. Besides, she is engaged to be married, isn't she?'

'No, actually that's a lie.'

'Oh? Are you sure?'

Mikael nodded, but suddenly he wasn't sure of anything. Perhaps Kat had been engaged to the Frenchman.

But surely, she had broken it off?

'Well, whatever their relationship is, we cannot ignore such a serious complaint, I'm sure you can see that. Plus, the news reports of the incident are all over the media. This is very bad PR for us, so we need to show that we are doing everything we can to mitigate it. We need to come out of this whiter than the snow on the mountain.'

Chapter Thirty-Six

Mikael dragged his feet walking back to his chalet. He wanted to talk to Kat, but was afraid that he would just make things worse for the hotel, her, and himself.

What a snake Jacques turned out to be!

He still couldn't understand what Kat had seen in him, but that was the least of his worries.

Petra had told him that, as a special concession, she would let Mikael stay in the chalet. There would be an internal inquiry, which she said she hoped would satisfy the Frenchman.

'And if that's not enough?' he'd asked her.

Mikael had guessed what the alternative was: his dismissal.

He could only imagine what his father would make of that. Going back home after having failed as a ski bum would make his day.

But what alternative did he have?

Petra had assured him that she would do everything in her power to try to sort it out so that he could have his job back.

'Not that you have lost your job – yet,' she'd added dryly.

Starting later that morning, another ski instructor would take over Mikael's group for the final two days of their holiday.

The thought of not being able to teach made Mikael's heart ache.

And how was he going to explain to Kat he couldn't see her anymore? What on earth was he going to do?

When he stepped inside his chalet, he heard a ping on his phone. It was a message from Kat.

How are you? What did your manager say?

He read the words, wondering whether he should follow Petra's advice. Or had it been an order? He wasn't sure.

He dialled her number.

'Hello?' Kat answered immediately.

Just hearing her voice made Mikael feel better.

'I'm suspended. She wasn't happy that I took a pupil up to the mountain when there was an avalanche warning in place. Even though the warning specifically said that you could use the prepared routes.'

'You'll be OK, won't you? If you want me to talk to her ...'

Mikael shook his head vigorously, even though Kay couldn't see it.

'No, no. I'm fine.'

'Are you sure? Do you want me to come over?'

The temptation to hold Kat in his arms was almost too much to bear. But Petra's warning rang in his ears.

He wanted to tell Kat everything, but he didn't know how. He worried he might start interrogating her on her relationship with Jacques and find out that they were engaged. It wasn't anything to do with him. And he didn't want her to feel guilty for his misfortune. After all, it was he who had decided to take her up the mountain with an avalanche warning in place. He could see how foolish he'd been now. But Kat had been so enthusiastic, and he'd wanted to share his passion for the sport and Lapland with her.

What have I done?

'No, it's late and I'm not very good company at the moment,' he replied.

'OK.'

Mikael could hear the disappointment in her voice. How he wanted to take her into his arms and look into her eyes and kiss those lips. He wished he could hold her and hear her tell him everything would be alright.

But he had messed everything up. He didn't deserve her love.

'Goodnight,' he said and ended the call.

Chapter Thirty-Seven

Mikael woke after a restless night, during which he had decided that Petra had no right to tell him who he should spend his time with. He was now effectively no longer employed by the hotel, even if he was still staying in his work accommodation. Neither the manager nor anyone else could dictate how he spent his free time.

He wasn't in the army or a police officer, for goodness' sake. Most of the ski instructors had flings with their pupils. Some thought it a perk of the job. He'd never done that though. Not that there hadn't been opportunities for it. Mikael just wasn't a guy who went for meaningless sex.

Sometimes he wished he was.

But he couldn't give Kat up. Not when they had formed such a good connection. He wanted to explore it, to see where it might take them. He'd never felt like this about anyone else in his past, so he owed it to himself to follow his instincts. Most of all, he needed to know if Kat felt the same about him as he did about her.

Last night before Salla had interrupted with an order to the manager's office, he was certain they would have ended up in bed together. He was hungry to know what that might be like. He'd dreamt about her last night, the images in his mind so real that he'd woken up with a desire to see her as soon as he could. He would take her for breakfast somewhere away from the hotel and the staff's prying eyes.

He called her and suggested they head to the café where his beginners' group had enjoyed cinnamon buns earlier in the week, and where Kat had relaxed for the first time since he'd met her. What's more, they offered a daily breakfast buffet with a large section for vegans.

Upon arrival, Kat was surprised by the selection, but Mikael explained that there were a lot of vegans in Southern Finland and as a tourist resort, Ylläs needed to cater for all diets.

'Hmm,' Kat said. 'It's not really a dietary choice. It's just one of the ways an individual can act to halt global warming. You should try it.'

Mikael smiled at Kat's persistence to change his habits. Her talk of environmental issues at every opportunity, which in the beginning had mildly amused him, was now endearing.

'OK,' he agreed, and selected from the vegan buffet.

Once their plates were filled with food, they sat at a table by the window of the small café. Outside, it was still windy and too dangerous for skiing.

At least I'm not missing out on a day up on the mountain today, Mikael thought absentmindedly.

Kat put a forkful of tofu 'scrambled egg', as she described it to Mikael, into her mouth and smiled.

'This is really good, you know.'

Mikael nodded. He hadn't yet dared to try the stuff that, frankly, looked as appetising as porridge. He hated porridge.

'Listen, I need to tell you something.'

Kat lifted her eyes to his. Her expression was serious, mirroring his own.

She stretched out her hand and placed it over his. 'Go on.'

Mikael recounted the main points of his meeting with Petra.

He finished with, 'Your fiancé is threatening to sue the hotel if I'm not dismissed.'

The rage in Kat's eyes was visible. 'He's not my fiancé!'

'I didn't think he was, especially after what he did to you, but –'

Kat interrupted Mikael. 'He never was!'

She spoke so loudly, her voice rang around the café, causing several of the other customers and the young woman at the till to glance in their direction.

Kat leaned closer to Mikael and said, 'Look, you should just ignore him. He has nothing to do with me. I'm certain he won't do anything. It's an empty threat. He just wants to get you into trouble with your boss.'

Mikael stared at Kat. Why hadn't he thought of that?

She added, smiling playfully, 'And I'm certainly not complaining about my skiing instructor.'

Mikael remembered his dream from the night before and felt that same desire creeping up his body.

'Well, that's alright then,' he said, returning Kat's smile.

The crisp arctic snow stung Kat's cheeks as she and Mikael trudged through the storm back to the hotel. The more she thought about what Jacques had done, the angrier she got.

How could he do this to Mikael? Why had he turned up here in the first place? The betrayal – with her mother, no less – cut deep, a jagged wound that threatened to split her in two.

And now Jacques was trying to get Mikael sacked from his job. Mikael loved skiing; it was the one thing that mattered to him. How could Jacques be so vindictive?

Was he jealous?

He had no right to be. Besides, nothing had happened between her and Mikael.

She blinked back angry tears as her boots crunched the icy terrain.

Guilt and shame twisted her gut. Poor Mikael didn't deserve to be dragged into her personal drama. She glanced at him.

Kat was hopeful that Mikael's future would be saved, yet she had been the cause of the drama. She should leave Lapland immediately, but the thought of returning early to her lonely London flat made her chest ache. She still had two days left of her holiday.

Maybe she could stay a little longer, if only to thank Mikael for his kindness? But hadn't she caused enough trouble for him?

When they arrived back at the hotel, a woman she presumed was Mikael's boss was in the lobby, speaking with some of the guests. As Mikael and Kat entered together, she walked over to them.

'Miss Wootton, I hope you are well and not too traumatised by your experience up on the mountain?' she enquired politely.

'Not at all, thanks to Mikael,' Kat replied. She gave him a glance.

Petra flashed a smile at Kat and then turning to Mikael, said, 'Could I talk to you for a moment?'

'Of course,' Mikael replied and followed the manager into the hotel offices.

Kat wanted to say something more to the manager, or to Mikael, but just then, Pat and Reg walked through the hotel doors.

'We missed you two at breakfast,' Pat said cheerfully, but seeing her dour expression, she added, 'What's happened?'

'Oh, it's a long story, but I think I got Mikael into trouble with the hotel.'

Chapter Thirty-Eight

For the second time that day, Mikael followed Petra into her office. Once inside, he slumped into the chair opposite her desk.

'Look, I know you said I shouldn't spend time with Kat – Ms Wootton – but it's ridiculous, because she's got nothing to do with the Frenchman anymore. He has no right raising any questions about her safety. And you heard what she said out there. She's not going to be a problem for the hotel.'

Petra regarded Mikael. 'OK, fine. Look, I wanted to talk to you because I reviewed the warnings, and you were right. It didn't say anything about the prepared pistes. Everyone agrees that it was a freak weather incident. I also spoke with the hotel owners. They do, however, want to carry out a short review.'

'Right,' Mikael said. 'Does that mean that I'm still suspended?'

'I'm afraid so, but I'm sure it won't be for long. Look,

why don't you take a couple of days off? Spend some time in the chalet in the national park. Apparently the weather is due to clear up soon. The skies could be on fire over the next few days. The Northern Lights are much more spectacular out there, and the place will get your mind off things here. Mikael, don't worry. If anything negative comes up here, I've got your back.'

Petra's eyes were full of kindness. A surge of relief flooded through him. As he left the office and walked back to the lobby, hoping to find Kat still there, he began to form a plan.

Kat told Pat and Reg the outline of what Jacques had done to Mikael. She wasn't yet strong enough to recount the whole sorry tale of her history with the Frenchman. To her relief, the older people appeared to recognise that Jacques wasn't exactly a nice person.

'He's quite an arrogant chap, isn't he?' Reg said, his wise eyes on Kat's.

'Yes. It's totally over between us.'

Kat was embarrassed about the situation, and didn't want to talk about it anymore, nor answer any questions Pat might have.

'Look, I need to go,' Kat said. 'See you two later?'

She was turning to go when Mikael walked into the lobby.

'Hello,' he said, taking Kat's hand in his.

Apparently, he didn't care if Pat and Reg saw that they had grown close. Kat's fury at Jacques had dissipated while she'd been talking about it to the older couple, and she was glad that Mikael was open about their budding relationship.

She was fed up with secrets.

'Everything OK, Mikael?' Pat asked, her eyes on their intertwined fingers.

'I'm sorry, I told them about your boss and Jacques,' Kat said, squeezing his hand while looking up at Mikael.

'That's fine. And it's all good. The hotel is still going to carry out an internal investigation, but Petra assures me I'll be fine.' Mikael smiled at Kat. 'I was wondering if you'd like to spend a night in a cabin in the wilderness. I'll get you back here in time for one last day of skiing if you want. There's a chance we could see the Northern Lights. The lack of light pollution makes the event even more magnificent out there.'

'Oh, how exciting. You must go!' Pat said.

Kat smiled at the older woman's enthusiasm. She'd almost forgotten Pat and Reg were still there. She'd been too busy gazing into Mikael's eyes.

Pat nudged her. 'Take a chance, Kat.'

Reg said, 'Let the youngsters sort themselves out. I'm sorry, she does like to interfere ...' He gazed fondly at his wife.

Pat waved her hand in the air. 'Shh, Reg, everyone needs a little push sometimes. I know love when I see it.'

Kat couldn't help but smile at the pair, despite her blush. Mikael also looked embarrassed by Pat's words.

Reg gripped Pat's shoulders and guided her gently out of the lobby.

'We'll leave you in peace. See you later,' he said, waving at Kat and Mikael.

Mikael stood stock still. He was still holding her hand. His eyes were wide, waiting for her response. Kat could see the darker inner part of his pupils and the tiny yellow specks at the edges.

'Well, I'd hate to miss out on the Northern Lights,' Kat said with a smile.

Back in her chalet, Kat grabbed her suitcase and placed it on the bed. She stared at the interior, which she needed to fill with her clothes now, if she was going to spend a night away. There would be too little time to do it if she wanted to ski on her last day. But the task was so unpleasant, she couldn't get on with it.

She sat on the bed next to the empty case and stared out of the window. The wind had abated a little and the sun was trying to peer through thick clouds, creating shadows on the snowy banks outside.

How could she leave this beautiful place where she had felt happier than she had in years? And what about Mikael?

She wanted to touch him, wanted his arms around her, and his naked body close to hers. Spending a night with him in a cabin somewhere in the middle of this wondrous landscape sounded so thrilling that just the thought of it made her breathless.

What had Pat said?

Take a chance.

She phoned reception and booked another week in her chalet, which was, to her amazement, free for another seven days. Then she cancelled her flight, a bold move that made her heart leap.

She didn't book a new return.

Chapter Thirty-Nine

An hour later, Mikael was standing outside Kat's door.

'I got this for you.' He was carrying padded overalls and gloves.

'Come in.'

Kat was so excited about her decision to stay that she wanted to tell Mikael straight away. At the same time, she wanted to surprise him. But he was so enthusiastic about their trip to the cabin that she decided to save her news till later.

'Where we're going we need to take snowmobiles, because there are no roads,' Mikael said. 'The place is in the national park and there are no cars allowed.' He glanced carefully at Kat. 'If that's OK? I know they're not particularly environmentally friendly, but the scenery really is amazing this time of year.'

'That sounds fine.'

Kat put aside her reservations about using such gas

guzzlers for a trip, especially as it was the only way to get to the deserted cottage.

'The cabin is by a lake, and it is quite small with just one room. But I promise to behave like a gentleman.'

Mikael was serious. She was surprised by his sudden reticence. She'd hoped he wouldn't hold back, but she didn't want to tell him that. What if Mikael didn't have the same deep feelings for her as she had developed for him? Perhaps she was just another tourist that he was enjoying sharing his passion for skiing and Lapland with.

Disappointed, Kat lowered her eyes and said, 'Sure.'

Her instincts were probably out of kilter after her experience with Jacques. Just as well she hadn't divulged that she was staying another week. How embarrassing would it be if he thought she'd postponed her return for his sake?

While he waited for her to get her overnight bag together, Kat stole glances at him. She wanted details about what the hotel manager had said to him. She wanted to ask him how he felt now that the threat to his career as a skiing instructor in the resort was over. She wondered if he'd ever considered doing anything else.

But it seemed Mikael didn't want to talk about his work situation. He was full of stories about how wonderful the place they were going to was, and how he'd heard from the hotel manager that the skies were going to be clear tonight, increasing the chances of seeing the Aurora Borealis.

.   .   .

They spent the next two hours zipping across snowy fields and through dense pine forests, accompanied by the crunch of snow beneath their snowmobile, and the gentle rustle of wind hitting pine needles. Mikael drove while Kat rode in the back, holding tightly onto his waist. Along the way, they stopped for hot cocoa – made with oat milk, Mikael informed her – and waffles with cloud-berry jam. Mikael pointed out arctic hares and reindeer as they went, regaling Kat with folklore about mythical creatures lurking in the woods.

By the afternoon, they had reached a remote lake reflecting the pale-blue sky. The cabin stood by the shore.

'This is my favourite place,' Mikael said. 'My father used to bring me ice fishing here when I was a boy.' Suddenly his expression darkened. 'Of course, now he barely talks to me.'

'Mikael, I'm so sorry.'

'It's OK. My grandparents on my mother's side were from Lapland. That's why we came here so much when my brother and I were younger.'

'Your childhood sounds idyllic,' Kat said. She hoped her voice didn't betray the tiny bit of jealousy she felt that hers wasn't. How she wished she too had spent her winter holidays in Finland.

Mikael kicked the ground with his boot but didn't look at her. 'It wasn't.'

When he didn't elaborate, Kat didn't ask him anything more about his childhood. She knew well enough how painful that could be. Instead, Kat looked around, struck by the serenity of the frozen landscape.

The skies had cleared during their journey, and the snow was sparkling under its rays. It created a glittering winter wonderland, with crystalline trees stretching over vast fields, like shimmering white lace. It was spellbinding.

'It's beautiful here,' she breathed. 'Thank you for taking me to see this magical place.'

Mikael squeezed her mittened hand.

'The landscape has nothing on your smile.'

Kat ducked her head to hide her blush, and her heart skipped a beat.

Perhaps he cared for her, after all? He certainly had a way of rendering her speechless with his candid charm.

Chapter Forty

The cabin was charming, but tiny. It consisted of one room and, Kat was relieved to see, a separate, indoor bathroom with a sauna. There was only one bed, but Mikael pointed out that he could sleep on the sofa across from the open fire.

'Right,' Kat said.

She couldn't read Mikael's mood. At times, he'd throw glances at Kat, which made her heart leap, but in the next moment he'd be all business-like. As if they were just good friends on an excursion.

The air inside the cabin was freezing, but warmed up quickly when Mikael got the open fire going. As dusk fell, they huddled around it, roasting vegan sausages that Mikael had pulled out of his backpack.

They ate in silence, the fire crackling between them, Kat acutely aware of how close they were sitting.

When Mikael pressed his hand on Kat's knee, she touched the signet ring on his left pinkie.

'What's this?'

He spread his fingers and smiled, gazing at the lilac stone which sparkled in the light of the open flames.

'This,' he said, 'belonged to my great-grandfather on my mother's side. According to ancient Sami folklore, it's supposed to bring happiness.'

Kat stroked the smooth stone with her finger. She'd even got this part of Mikael wrong. She'd thought it was some kind of status symbol when all it had been was an heirloom connected to his mother's Sámi heritage. She really needed to be less judgmental.

'It's beautiful,' she said, looking at Mikael.

Suddenly, he leaned in and pressed his lips to hers. She let herself kiss him back. All thoughts about Jacques and her doubts about Mikael's sincerity vanished as her hands explored his chest. Their kiss deepened, and the last of her hesitation slipped away.

Mikael pushed further, exploring her mouth with his tongue until she was breathless and trembling. When at last he pulled back, his eyes were dark with desire.

'I really like you,' he said, his voice low.

'I really like you back.'

Mikael took her head into his hands and kissed her mouth, moving to just below her earlobe, then her neck, then doing the same on the other side.

Kat's body was on fire, and she pushed herself against him. This felt so right, being here with Mikael. She wanted to rip their clothes off, and press her naked skin against his.

Mikael placed his hands on her waist and pushed her gently away, looking deeply into her eyes. 'Are you sure?'

Kat smiled, running her hands down his chest and playing with the buttons on his shirt.

'I have never been surer of anything in my life.'

'Then we should continue this discussion in bed before I take you where we sit.'

Mikael scooped her into his arms, carrying her across the cabin as if they were newlyweds.

Laughter bubbled up in Kat's chest at his enthusiasm.

'So impatient,' she teased, twining her arms around his neck and giving him a searing kiss.

'When it comes to you, Kat, I have no patience left.'

He set her down beside the bed, his hands roaming over her body, as if he couldn't get enough of her.

'I've been waiting for this for so long,' he whispered.

'Me too. I want to see you,' Kat whispered, tugging his shirt free of his trousers. She ran her hands over his skin.

'Really?' he asked hoarsely, peeling her out of her clothes with shaking hands.

'Yes.'

She tangled her fingers in his hair, holding his gaze with hers.

He began by slowly peeling away the layers of clothing covering Kat's body. He tried to rush, but was met with layer after layer. They laughed at the task.

'Let me,' Kat said, and pulled off the last long-sleeve top and a sleeveless vest she had under that. Standing in her bra and knickers, she watched as Mikael shed his own clothing, revealing a toned, strong chest and muscular arms.

He pulled her towards him and kissed her face, her neck, and her collarbone.

She wound her hands into his hair then let them trail down his back towards his bottom, still covered by boxer shorts.

'Take them off,' she whispered.

She took a step back as he revealed his penis, hard and ready for her.

Watching him, she took off her bra and slipped out of her knickers.

Unable to contain themselves, they clung to each other, skin to skin. Mikael made a sound of raw longing, as he crushed her against him and claimed her mouth again. In a flurry of restlessness, they fell onto the bed together, hands and lips exploring each other with tender urgency.

When at last he entered her, Kat arched into him with a soft cry, overwhelmed by the love and passion in his eyes. Here in Mikael's arms, she had found her home, her heart, her everything.

Chapter Forty-One

The crackling fire cast a warm glow over their entwined bodies as Kat traced lazy circles across Mikael's chest. A profound peace had settled in her soul, chasing away the last vestiges of sorrow and betrayal. No longer did she feel adrift on a sea of uncertainty; she had found her anchor in Mikael.

'I don't want this night to end,' she whispered, pressing a soft kiss to his neck. 'Couldn't we stay here in the middle of the forest and live a simple life forever?'

Mikael tightened his embrace, nuzzling her hair and giving a contented sigh. 'You need not ask. My heart was yours from the first moment we met. But I don't think we'd last long in isolation like this.'

Kat grinned at him. 'You of little faith.'

Mikael kissed her long and slow, but suddenly he froze, staring at something outside. Kat followed his gaze and saw what he was looking at. There was a glow in the horizon, just visible through the tiny windows of the cabin.

Mikael was already out of bed and on his feet, pulling his trousers and jumper on.

'You need to see this!'

Kat rushed to put her clothes on, including the warm boiler suit Mikael had brought her that morning.

Outside, on the steps of the cabin, the night enveloped them, and a hush settled upon the snowy landscape. With breathless anticipation, Kat gazed upward, captivated by the ethereal spectacle unfolding before her.

A gentle breeze whispered through the frozen trees, adding a delicate melody to the air. And then, as if nature itself acknowledged her newfound optimism for the future, streaks of vibrant colour danced across the dark canvas above. Ribbons of emerald green, hues of sapphire and amethyst, and fleeting traces of rosy pink painted the heavens with an otherworldly brilliance.

The celestial brushstrokes of the Northern Lights weaved and swirled, creating a tapestry of enchantment.

Hand in hand, Kat and Mikael marvelled at this stunning spectacle. The weight of the world dissolved in the presence of such sublime wonder. In that moment, they were no longer separate souls but intertwined spirits, intimately connected to each other and the magical realm unfolding above them.

Overwhelmed, Kat blinked back tears. She had spent her life searching for a love like this, only to find it in the unlikeliest of places. Yet in that moment, as the Aurora Borealis danced across the velvet sky and the pine-scented air cooled her flushed skin, it felt as though she and Mikael were the only two souls in the universe.

That evening in the tiny wooden cabin, they talked more honestly than they had before. In the sauna, which Mikael warmed up using logs piled up inside the small porch, they revealed their dreams and desires.

Kat opened up to Mikael in a way she never had with anyone else. He listened with empathy and understanding, sharing bits of his own hopes and fears in return. There was a tender honesty to their exchange that resonated with her.

Later, while they were sipping wine by the fire, Mikael told Kat about his family, and how his father didn't approve of his career as a ski instructor. He told her how Victor had always been the favourite, even though in Mikael's view, he was selfish and a womaniser.

'I'm sorry,' Mikael said when Kat lowered her eyes at the mention of that word. 'That was stupid of me, I don't want to remind you of Jacques. That's the last thing I want to do.'

'I don't want to talk about him. Not now, not here, not ever,' Kat replied.

'That's a deal.'

They sat quietly for a moment, watching as one of the logs in the fire dropped on top of another and crackled.

Mikael drained his glass and turned to Kat, stroking her neck.

'I love your short hair,' he murmured.

Kat thought about how Jacques had been horrified by her new style. She silently admonished herself for thinking about him again.

'Thank you,' she said simply.

Mikael gazed at her in awe. 'You are the most fascinating person I've ever known.'

Heart pounding, she leaned in to give him a kiss that ignited another wave of passion. She tasted the tanginess of the wine and spice on his tongue and felt the warmth of his gentle caress on her skin.

They fell onto the bed again, keen to explore even more of each other.

The second round of lovemaking was gentler and less hurried than the first, as if they were now appreciating each other's bodies. Mikael moved inside Kat with a tenderness that made her heart melt. Each kiss, each touch, was infused with deep reverence and devotion. They held each other close, lost in the moment, as the fire crackled in the background and the snow fell silently outside.

Afterwards, they lay entwined in each other's arms, the world beyond their cocoon of warmth and love forgotten. Their breaths mingled in the air as they whispered words of adoration and promises of forever.

'I never knew I could feel this way about anyone,' Mikael said at last, his voice heavy with emotion. 'You have changed me, Kat.'

'And you have shown me what true happiness is,' Kat replied, tracing lazy patterns on his chest with her finger.

'I never thought I could be this content in my own skin until I met you.'

The next morning as they woke, the outside air was scented with pine and woodsmoke, a heady combination that made Kat's senses swim. As she and Mikael strolled along the snowy path towards their snowmobile, their hands entwined and breaths misting in the frigid temperatures, a fierce longing rose within her to get as close to him as possible.

'The Northern Lights were something last night,' Mikael murmured, his eyes on the blue-grey skies overhead. 'Have you ever seen anything like it?'

Kat smiled, gazing at Mikael. 'It was stunning. But I can think of something even more amazing.'

He turned to her with a quizzical look. 'Oh? And what might that be?'

She squeezed his hand, coyly meeting his eyes through the veil of her lashes. 'Can you not guess?'

Mikael's lips curved into a smile, lighting up his face like the sun breaking through the clouds.

'You're a real flirt,' he teased. 'Do you always try to charm men like this?'

The warmth in his tone belied the mock sternness of his words.

'No,' Kat protested, nudging Mikael in the ribs. 'Only when it comes to you. I'm afraid I have no self-control.'

She edged closer as they walked, wanting to absorb his radiant heat.

'You bring out the romantic in me,' she added.

'As you do in me,' he replied softly, all teasing gone from his voice. 'When I'm with you, Kat, the rest of the world fades away.'

His confession shattered the last of her restraint. Kat stopped in her tracks, turning to cup Mikael's beautiful face between her hands.

'Then take me home,' she whispered, standing on tiptoes to brush her lips over his.

A low moan escaped from him as he gathered her close, returning her kiss with a passion that ignited her blood. In that perfect moment, wrapped in his embrace beneath the vast blue skies of the north, Kat was happier than she could ever remember being.

Chapter Forty-Two

Later that same day, Kat and Mikael were in bed in Kat's chalet. Over the last wonderful twenty-four hours, which they'd spent exploring the beautiful snowy landscape and each other's bodies, neither had mentioned the future.

'I booked another week here and cancelled my flight home,' Kat said, running her fingers down Mikael's stomach, following the trail of hair that led lower.

'Oh.' Mikael lifted himself up on his elbows, causing her to drop her hand.

'Well, I thought I could stay another week since I don't particularly want go back to London ...'

'Right.'

He turned to face Kat with an unreadable expression. Was he not pleased that they'd have another seven days together?

In the past few hours, he'd talked as if he'd wanted to spend the rest of his life with her. Had he been saying that just to get her into bed? Could she have misread him?

Doubt began to build inside her. She got out of bed and picked up her dressing gown from the bottom of the bed. Wrapping it tightly around her naked body, she headed for the bathroom.

'Kat, come back!'

Mikael was on his feet, naked. As she turned, she saw his muscular body and his penis on full display. She couldn't help but smile.

'Come back to bed. I have something to tell you.' Mikael was hesitant, almost guilty sounding.

Kat stood there for a moment, but walked back to Mikael, opening her gown and pressing her body against his. She wrapped the fabric around them and murmured into his neck.

'You'd better be quick if you want to talk to me, because I think *he* has other ideas.'

She felt Mikael harden more against her lower tummy.

'Oh, Kat, you drive me crazy.'

Afterwards, when they were once again breathless and in a tangle of sheets, Mikael stroked Kat's hair. With a serious expression, he sought her eyes.

'To your question about the future: I do have plans. And you can be part of them – if you'd like to be.'

Kat tried to ignore the knot of worry forming in her stomach. During the few days she'd gotten to know him, she'd grown accustomed to Mikael's carefree joy. She wasn't used to hearing a serious tone from him.

'What is it?' she asked.

Mikael took a deep breath. He was quiet for a moment, but then began to speak.

'You know I told you that my mother was born near where we were in the cabin, which is why we came up here a lot during the winter holidays? My grandparents are gone now, but they lived a simple life tending to a herd of reindeer.'

'Yes,' Kat said. 'That's why you know so much about the place?'

'Yeah, I guess it's in my blood.'

He was quiet for a moment and Kat let him be. She wanted to hear more, and was glad when he continued, his face illuminated by the fire.

'My family, well, they're quite rich. They own a few mines here in Finland and in Sweden. You wouldn't know since you haven't lived in Finland, but my family name is quite well known. I guess that's why you are so wonderful to be with because you don't have any hang-ups about us.'

Kat straightened her back. Mining was notoriously bad for the environment.

'What kind of mines?'

'Oh, all sorts.'

Mikael looked at Kat and continued. 'My father wants me to join the family firm. He hates the idea of me being here, working as a ski instructor. He calls me a "ski bum".'

'Oh.'

'It occurred to me during the past day that my position here isn't exactly safe. It's fine now, but what if something similar happens again? My parents keep going on at me about the future and how I should be thinking about it. Trouble is, if I can't work here, I have no alternative but to work for my father. My older brother joined the firm straight from university, as my mum keeps reminding me.'

'Right.'

She thought hard. She'd seen leaflets all around the resort about opposition to a proposed mine that would destroy the local eco system. Kat had taken one in the first restaurant her ski group had eaten in. She'd forgotten all about, but she was certain the leaflet was still somewhere in her chalet.

Was Mikael's family behind the project? Mikael didn't seem to be exactly supportive of the way his father made his living. But Kat could not even consider being friends with anyone connected with such a terrible exploitation of the land.

They sat silently for a while.

Just as Kat was about to buck up the courage to ask about the mines his family owned, Mikael carried on talking.

'My father has given me an ultimatum. He wants me to help oversee a new mining project. It would mean that I could still live here in Lapland.'

Kat jerked upright, the sheets pooling around her waist.

'And if you don't?'

Mikael shrugged his shoulders. 'My father is a powerful man. Most people do as he says.'

She regarded him for a moment. He had his head bent and his eyes were downcast.

Her heart began to pound; a foreboding crept over her. Did his family own the land where the mine in the leaflets was supposed to be built?

She'd known as soon as she'd set eyes on him that Mikael came from money, that his family was wealthy. But she had no idea that what they did was almost the worst kind of industry she could think of. She'd chosen to ignore that part of his background, too caught up in their whirlwind romance beneath the Northern Lights.

'The proposed mine is a little north of here,' Mikael said. He ran a hand through his hair, looking miserable. 'My family own the land. It could be hugely profitable.'

'At what cost?' Kat demanded.

She thought of the reindeer that grazed on the tundra, the golden eagles that soared through the mountains, the Sami people who still lived as their ancestors had for centuries. All of that would be destroyed for profit.

She shook her head, overcome by a swell of anger and disappointment. The man she'd fallen for was willing to ignore all that?

'You can't do this,' she said. 'You know what it will do to the local environment and its people. They are your ancestors! How can you even consider it?'

'Kat, please try to understand,' Mikael pleaded. 'My

father is not an easy man. I can't keep refusing him forever.'

'Some things are more important than family or money.'

Kat pulled away from Mikael and began to gather her clothes, her hands shaking.

Her heart filled with bleak bitterness.

She stood at the foot of the bed, staring angrily at Mikael.

'I don't think I know you at all. And I think you should leave.'

He stared back, his blue eyes clouded with uncertainty. She could see the conflict raging within him, torn between his love for the land and his duty to his family. But in the end, she already knew which side would win. His silence was answer enough.

Kat zipped up her jacket with angry, jerking motions.

'I see,' she said. 'I'm going to cancel my plans to stay. I don't expect you to be here when I get back.'

She walked past the bed, where Mikael was sitting up with his head in his hands.

Chapter Forty-Three

Kat banged the door shut and stood outside, breathing in the cold night air. She glanced at her watch. It was past ten o'clock. It was freezing outside, but she couldn't stay in her room. She needed to be out of sight of Mikael and the bed where they'd just made love.

She walked into reception and the woman who Mikael had been so friendly with smiled at her.

'Everything OK? Can I help you?'

Something about her made Kat uncomfortable. She sounded friendly, but there was an underlying hostility there.

'No, thank you,' Kat replied, trying to raise a smile but failing.

She walked back out into the bitter cold.

Then it occurred to her. Perhaps the receptionist was smitten with Mikael? They'd appeared to be very chummy with each other. Had they been an item before Kat came on the scene? Was this a fling?

She had no idea what kind of person Mikael was. She couldn't trust anything he said right now.

Not knowing what to do or think she paced in front of the hotel, trying to control her emotions. How had she got in this position again – being betrayed once more? She should have done what she had vowed to and kept away from all men.

Suddenly a figure emerged from the shadows, and she saw that Mikael had followed her out. He held his palms up in surrender.

'Kat, please. Don't do this. Try to understand.'

'Understand what? That money is the most important thing to you?' she spat out, glaring at him. 'More important than the fragile ecosystem of this breathtakingly beautiful place?'

With that, she turned on her heels and made her way back along the dark, snowy path back to her chalet.

Her heart felt like it was shattering into a thousand pieces, but she held her head high. She had been willing to compromise on many things for love but not this. Not when it meant destroying everything she believed in.

Mikael called after her, but she ignored him, walking faster and faster until his voice faded. The wind picked up, rattling the branches of the pines, bringing with it the sharp scent of snow.

Inside the chalet, as she peeled off her coat and boots, her limbs felt numb – from the freezing temperatures or the raging storm inside her, she couldn't tell.

She had to get away. Away from Mikael, away from the chalet, away from the pain in heart that was threatening to engulf her.

She picked up her laptop and began to research the mining project. As she read, new fury rose within her. There appeared to be a substantial amount of resistance to the plan locally up in Lapland, as well as in the rest of the country.

Sitting by the window of her chalet, she noticed that the first stars were appearing in the dark sky, pinpricks of light against the vastness of space. They reminded her of her own insignificance in the grand scale of things. But she also knew that every action mattered. Every voice raised in defence of what was right and true could tip the balance.

And she would raise her voice. She would take action. She would do whatever it took to stop the mining project from destroying this land she had grown to love in the short time she'd spent here. Even if it meant sacrificing her heart in the process.

The thought brought a lump to her throat, and she quickened her fingers over the keys. She couldn't afford weakness now. Not when there was so much at stake. Her pain would have to wait.

Chapter Forty-Four

The next day, Kat walked into the village hall, her boots clattering on the wooden floorboards. A dozen or so people were already gathered, chatting in small groups. As she entered, they fell silent and turned to stare at her.

She scanned the room, heart pounding, and spotted a woman sitting at a table stacked high with petitions and informational flyers.

'I'm here for the meeting,' Kat said. 'About the mining project.'

The woman's face lit up. 'Wonderful! We're so glad you could make it.' Her English was a little broken. She stood and extended a hand. 'I'm Tuija. Welcome.'

She shook her hand and tried for a smile, but it came out as more of a grimace. 'Kat.'

Her nerves were getting the better of her.

'Please, have a seat,' Tuija said. 'We will start soon.'

Kat took an empty chair in the back row. Her gaze

drifted around the room, taking in the mix of ages and occupations. A group of men in worn overalls and heavy coats who looked like reindeer herders or farmers sat next to a couple of women in Faroese jumpers. A young family with two small children had claimed spots near the front.

They were all here for the same reason she was: to stand up against the mining company threatening to destroy their community. To raise their voices in defence of the land they held dear.

Her heart swelled with purpose. She wasn't alone. Together, they could accomplish great things. Even if she couldn't be up here in Lapland in person, she could raise funds in London to fight the project.

The door opened again. Kat glanced up a greeting forming on her lips for the newcomer. But she froze.

Mikael stood in the doorway, scanning the room.

Searching for her.

What was he doing here? Spying for his father?

Her heart stuttered. Their argument from the night before flashed through her mind, and Kat remembered the hurt in his eyes as Mikael realised she would never support the mining project. Would never be the woman he wanted her to be.

She slouched down in her seat, clutching at the fraying edge of her sweater sleeve. Last night in the cabin replayed on a loop, a skipping record full of tender moments and whispered promises. Promises that had been shattered beyond repair.

He stepped into the room, shoulders tense, and made

his way towards her. She clenched her jaw, willing him to turn away. To leave her be.

Mikael slid into the seat beside her, the familiar scent of his cologne threatening to undo her.

'I didn't expect to see you here.' His voice was low, rough with emotion.

Heat flooded her cheeks. 'Where else would I be?'

Mikael's gaze searched her face, as if looking for something he feared had vanished forever.

'I don't know. I thought after last night ...' He swallowed hard. 'I thought you'd be on your way back to London. I didn't think you'd want to see me again.'

Guilt twisted in her chest at the hurt in his tone. The hurt she had put there.

'I'm here as an activist, not as your *girlfriend*. And you know I have nothing to go back to England for. Besides, what does it have to do with you?'

The words came out sharper than she'd intended, and she winced. 'I'm sorry, I didn't mean –'

'I know what you meant.' He sighed, raking a hand through his hair. 'I understand this is important to you. I just wish ...'

When he didn't continue, she prompted gently, 'Wish what?'

'I wish it didn't mean losing you in the process.'

His eyes met hers, pale blue and full of sorrow.

'I think I'm falling in love with you, Kat. Even if we want different things. Even if we're fighting on opposite sides. My feelings for you haven't changed.'

Tears pricked the backs of her eyes. She glanced

away, trying to blink them back. She couldn't do this now. Not here.

'I have to go.' She stood abruptly, nearly toppling her chair.

Mikael grabbed her wrist, his grip firm but gentle. Grounding.

'Don't go. Not like this.'

She hesitated, torn between the man she loved and the cause she believed in. The future she wanted and the one she was trying to prevent.

In the end, there was only one choice.

She steeled herself and met his gaze. 'Goodbye, Mikael.'

With a sharp tug, she pulled her wrist from his grasp and walked away. She moved to the other side of the small hall, not looking back at Mikael.

A few people glanced their way, clearly wondering what was going on. Did they know who Mikael was?

After the meeting, Kat strode down the narrow lane, back towards the hotel, snow crunching under her boots. Her breath came out in white puffs as she walked; her hands were shoved deep in her pockets.

The meeting with the local environmental group had gone well. Better than she'd hoped, in fact. They were well organised and funded. They didn't really need her help, but she'd donated some money to the cause all the same.

She hadn't spoken with Mikael again. From the

corner of her eye, she saw he'd been taking notes all through the evening.

A spy in their midst. She very nearly told Tuija who he was, but she felt that would have been too much.

Still, the few words they'd exchanged before the meeting tore at her heart. She kept replaying what he said in her head, remembering the sorrow in his eyes. The love she felt for him was like a knife in her chest, sharp and twisting with every move.

But she couldn't give in. Not now. Not when her deep-held principles were at stake.

The lane opened onto a wide field covered in pristine white snow that glistened under the pale moonlight. In the distance, the shimmering blues and greens of the Northern Lights danced across the sky.

Kat stopped, transfixed by the sight. The lights twisted and spun in an otherworldly way against the velvet night. A stark reminder of the wild beauty that was worth fighting for.

This display wasn't as amazing as the one she'd seen in the cabin with Mikael, but it was still beautiful.

She took a deep breath of the frigid air and steeled her resolve.

The mining project would destroy places like this. Pollute the land and water; push the Sami from their ancestral home. She couldn't stand by and love a man who would pull the levers of the project. Even if it broke her heart.

How could Mikael, whose family had deep roots in the place, even consider joining the project?

Chapter Forty-Five

Kat managed to get a flight back to London the following day. Mikael was nowhere to be seen. Had he returned to Helsinki to report back to his father on the village hall meeting?

Last night, when she couldn't sleep, Kat had resolved to put her brief affair with Mikael down to experience. He was her rebound guy, that was all.

An ill-judged holiday romance.

To her relief, she'd managed to cancel the extra days in the chalet before breakfast, during which she'd said goodbye to Pat and Reg.

'How was your excursion to the national park?' Pat asked her, with a glint in her eye.

'It was wonderful.' Kat tried to sound enthusiastic but couldn't muster much emotion.

The older woman regarded her for a moment.

'Have you seen Mikael? We wanted to say goodbye to him.'

Kat shook her head, 'Sorry.'

She turned her head, away from Pat's searching gaze.

'Did you see the Northern Lights?' Reg changed the subject, coming to her rescue.

'We saw them last night, just in time before we have to head back to old Blighty!'

They discussed the spectacle of the night before, and their respective travel plans that day. They found out that they weren't on the same flights. Kat's connection via Helsinki was leaving soon, while the older couple were on a direct one to Manchester later that afternoon.

Sitting on the bus again, Kat was dreading her return to London. She didn't want to have anything to do with Jacques or speak to her mum ever again. Yet, back at home, she couldn't avoid the two people that used to be the closest to her, yet who had broken her heart into small pieces.

For the past few days, she'd thought she had found something else, a place that she felt at home in and somewhere she could follow her real passion.

Kat sighed as she gazed out at the emerging dawn. There was a faint streak of orange on the horizon. Each time she looked out the window the scene was different. Now, the pale winter sun rose into the clouds. How could such beauty leave her so confused?

The night she'd spent with Mikael in the wilderness felt like a dream now. She really believed that she had also found a person that she could build a future with.

But her initial instincts, when he'd tried to hit on her at Helsinki airport, had been right.

How had she been so foolish to fall for him? Fall for another fake guy?

A horrible thought came to her. Was Mikael just like Jacques? Was he too just a flirt with a string of holiday romances with women he'd taught to ski? Or women he worked with, like the flirty receptionist? And now she'd learnt that what she thought was his passion for Lapland's natural beauty was just a desire to make money at the expense of local people and their land.

How could Kat have been so stupid to make the same mistake with another man?

Her phone alerted Kat with a new message. She took a deep intake of breath and checked the screen.

It was from Richard, The Culinary Kingdom's series producer. Reading the text made her gasp.

Dear Kat, I am letting you know that Jacques Beaumont's contract has been terminated with immediate effect. We'd like to involve you in deciding on the new direction for The Culinary Kingdom. Please let me know when you're back in London so we can have a chat. Best, Richard.

Kat stared at the message, and read it again two more times before she took in what it meant.

They had sacked Jacques and wanted her to take a more important role in the show!

Before replying to her boss, Kat messaged her friend,

Toni, who always knew what was really going on in the TV world.

Just heard re Jacques. Give me the goss?

As soon as she had pressed send, her phone rang. It was Toni. She answered.

'Oh my God, you have no idea!' A breathless Toni began to recount what she knew about Jacques' demise.

Chapter Forty-Six

Kat listened with a twinge of guilt, as her friend told her how Jacques had been caught in a compromising position with a junior runner, and how the show's producers had no choice but to let him go. It wasn't clear if Jacques had been aware that the girl was still a teenager, but the damage had been done, nonetheless.

Guilt washed over her. She should have warned the intern – if it was the same girl – about Jacques. But she reminded herself that she hadn't known the extent of his betrayal then. And Kat wasn't certain that Jacques had done anything other than flirt with the girl. She also hadn't known the girl's age.

As Toni continued to tell her about Jacques, she felt relief that she wouldn't have to work with him anymore.

But now that she might be offered a more prominent role on the show, she wasn't sure if she was ready for it. It wasn't just that The Culinary Kingdom was a huge production with a lot of pressure, Kat still wasn't certain if she was fully committed to the world of food and television.

Her time in Lapland had made her realise how much protecting the environment meant to her. How much she had given up for Jacques. Like Mikael, Jacques also liked his fast cars. Kat had been forced to defend her veganism. She could not understand how she could have been with someone who cared so little for the natural world, not to mention the people he supposedly cared for.

Kat's mind raced as she contemplated her future. Whatever she decided, it would be a tough road ahead. But looking at the message from Richard again, one thing was certain: this was a huge opportunity for her.

With a newfound determination, Kat boarded the plane. She couldn't help but feel excited for what the future held. Maybe it wouldn't be easy, but she needed to step up and face it head on.

The plane took off, leaving the picturesque scene of Lapland far behind. Kat closed her eyes and inhaled deeply, bracing herself for what was to come. But as she reminisced about the time she had spent with Mikael, sadness twisted her heart. She had believed they had a special connection, that he was different from other men.

She wondered where he was and if he was thinking of her.

But it didn't matter; Mikael was in the past. She would keep an eye on the mining project and do what she could from London to oppose it. If that meant a fight against Mikael, so be it.

Kat pondered whether she would ever meet someone who truly understood her and shared her passion for the environment. But for now, she needed to focus on her career and making an impact in the world.

With a sigh, she opened her eyes and gazed out the plane window at the billowing clouds outside. Love and relationships could wait until later – when she was ready for them. For now, this opportunity at The Culinary Kingdom was one she needed to seize with both hands.

As the plane descended into London, Kat felt suddenly apprehensive. Being back meant she'd have to face Jacques and Simona eventually, but for now, she was just happy to be back in the city she called home.

Chapter Forty-Seven

The biting wind nipped at Mikael's face as he gazed at the shimmering auroras dancing across the inky black sky. His heart swelled with equal parts joy and anguish – joy at the beauty before him, anguish at the turmoil churning within.

He had fallen hard for Kat during their few days together, enchanted by her passion and kindness. But his family's mining operation had come between them. Kat was passionate about the environment, but he had no idea she would react so strongly. The mine operation gnawed at his conscience. He also believed in protecting the land, not pillaging it for resources.

With a heavy sigh, he got into the taxi taking him to the airport. He'd booked the last flight to Helsinki. After hearing what had been said at the local villagers' meeting, he needed to talk to his father face-to-face.

. . .

Mikael stepped inside his parents' large apartment in Ullanlinna. The usual claustrophobic air of the place hit him immediately, and he tried to shrug off the sensation.

His father actually smiled at him when he entered the apartment. He took Mikael's' hand in both of his and shook it. There was a smell of brandy on his breath.

'Well done, son.'

His mother hugged him warmly and whispered, 'I knew you'd come around.'

'Come, join us, my son! We have much to celebrate. I'm glad you finally came to see sense.'

These words by Mikael's father were more than he'd uttered to his youngest son in more than a year.

'Don't, Erik,' his mother said. 'Let the boy settle in before you start. Besides, it's all history now. Mikael has made the right decision, and that's the most important thing.'

She pressed her hand on Mikael's arm as he sat down next to her at the dinner table. She'd made his favourite, reindeer steak with a creamy chanterelle sauce, and garlic Dauphinoise potatoes.

His father waved his hand. 'Alright, dear, you win. I will only talk of the future from now on.'

The sleet came down in vertical sheets in Helsinki. Mikael put the collar of his jacket up to avoid getting totally soaked.

After three days at home, he had finally left the oppressive atmosphere of his parents' apartment in

Ullanlinna behind and was walking along the damp pavement towards a bar in Punavuori, a place his friends rarely frequented. The last thing he wanted was to bump into one of his successful schoolmates.

Sitting in Punainen Ahven, a bar for those who wished to drink alone, he ordered a beer and stared into the foamy top of the glass.

How could he have gotten Kat so wrong? Her reaction when he had told her about his decision to join the family firm had taken him by surprise. He had hoped that she would understand, but instead, she'd been hurt and disappointed. He had tried to explain the reasons behind his decision, but she remained unconvinced.

Mikael took a long sip of his beer, contemplating his future. He had a responsibility to his family and the company. But he also couldn't ignore his love of Lapland and its unspoilt nature.

He wondered if there was a way to reconcile the two, to find a balance between his duty to his family and his passion for the land.

As he continued to drink, Mikael's thoughts drifted back to Kat. He had felt a connection with her, a spark of something special. But now, after their conversation – or fight about his plans, he wasn't sure if that connection was still there. He considered reaching out to her, to explain his thoughts more clearly. But it may be too late; he had probably hurt her too much.

Mikael finished his beer and paid the bill. He needed to find a way to move forward, to find a path that was true to himself and to his beliefs.

He stepped out into the rain again, the damp seeping through his jacket. But as he walked through the city, clarity hit him. He may not have all the answers, but he had to follow his heart and stay true to himself. He would make Kat understand why he had to do what he was doing.

There had to be a way to reconcile their differences. He simply couldn't live without her.

Chapter Forty-Eight

Mikael dialled Kat's number and nervously waited for the call to connect.

When it did, all he heard was silence at the other end.

'Hello... Kat?'

'I'm busy, Mikael.' Kat sounded cold and distant.

'Oh, OK. Can I call you later?'

'No, Mikael. I don't want to talk to you.'

His heart sank at her words. He had to make a move, to try and salvage their relationship before it was too late.

'Please Kat, just hear me out.'

There was a pause on the other end of the line. Mikael could hear Kat breathing heavily.

'Fine,' she said finally, 'but make it quick.'

Mikael took a deep breath, trying to gather his thoughts. He had to be honest with Kat and he needed to explain his actions.

'Kat, I know that we've had our differences, but I

need you to understand. My decision to join the family firm was a shock to you, but I'm still the same person. My love for Lapland and its nature hasn't changed. But I also have a responsibility to my family and the company. I want us to find a way to make it work, to find a balance between our beliefs and our responsibilities. I don't want to lose you, Kat. I really think we could have something special together. Will you give me a chance to make it right?'

There was another long pause.

Then Kat spoke, 'Mikael, I appreciate your honesty, but I don't know if I can trust you. Your decision to support the mine was a shock to me. It goes against everything I believe in.' She paused for a moment. 'I'm on my way to work. I have to go.'

Mikael's heart sank further. He had a lot of work to do to convince Kat. But he wasn't going to give up without a fight.

'Please, Kat, I understand if it will take time –'

Kat interrupted him. 'Mikael, let's call it what it was. A pleasant holiday romance. It'll never work. We are from different worlds, both in *the way* we live and *where* we live.'

Mikael was shocked into silence by Kat's words.

The weight of what she said crushed his heart more; he struggled to find the right response. For a moment, they said nothing. Mikael tried to regain his composure.

Finally, he spoke. 'Kat, I know that we come from different worlds, but isn't that what makes us special? Our differences, our unique perspectives, they complement each other. I don't want to give up on us without a fight. Can't we at least try to make it work?'

There was another long silence, and Mikael felt hopelessness wash over him.

'Mikael, I'm sorry. Maybe it's better if we just move on and forget about each other.'

His heart shattered as Kat's words sunk in. He believed they'd had something special, something worthy of preserving. But now, it appeared to be a delusion of his own making.

He took a deep breath, trying desperately to compose himself, but the agony was too overwhelming.

'Kat, I understand your decision. But I want you to know that I will always cherish the short time we spent together. You've made me a better person, and I will always be grateful for that. I wish you all the happiness in the world.'

He hung up the phone, realising that he had lost the one person who had truly understood him. His eyes welled up with tears as he thought of all the things he would miss about her. Her laughter, her smile, the way she looked at him when they made love. All of it gone in a flash.

Mikael stepped out onto the balcony, the cold Helsinki air washing over him, as he tried to clear his thoughts. He took a deep breath and stared out into the night sky, watching as snowflakes replacing the rain started to fall gently around him. It was a beautiful sight, but it brought him no comfort. He felt alone and lost, with no idea how to move on without Kat.

But as he watched the snowfall, he realised that life was just like the weather. It was unpredictable and ever-changing. Just like the snow, life could be both beautiful and harsh. He needed to embrace the unpredictability of life, to find a way to move forward and to keep fighting for what he believed in.

Mikael took another deep breath, letting determination wash over him. He may have lost Kat, but he wasn't going to give up on his dreams. He'd find a way to reconcile his love of Lapland with his duty to his family.

And who knew, maybe one day Kat would see why he had to make the decision he had.

Chapter Forty-Nine

The phone call from Mikael had unsettled Kat. She was in Toni's apartment getting ready for work when it came through.

The last few days had left her elated. She'd had several meetings with the producers of The Culinary Kingdom. They were impressed with her ideas and had given her the green light to produce the new series. This should have been her moment of triumph, but instead her mind was consumed with thoughts of Mikael.

As she stood in front of the mirror, Kat couldn't help but think about the phone call. She had been so sure that she was over Mikael, that the connection they'd had during her holiday was just that – a holiday romance.

But hearing his voice had brought all those memories and strong emotions she'd for him rushing back.

She was still hurt over his lack of concern for the people and environment in Lapland. He must have known what the mine would do to the eco system up there. Yet, hearing the sincerity in his voice, she couldn't help but long for him.

Could they really make it work?

Kat shook her head, trying to clear her thoughts. She couldn't let herself get swept up in Mikael's words. She had a job to do, a career to focus on. She couldn't let her personal life interfere with her professional aspirations.

And she wouldn't be hurt again by another man.

Me and men are over.

The production office was busy, as usual. Stepping inside the door and shaking the rain off her umbrella, she nearly bumped into someone. She lifted her head, and her eyes widened in disbelief at who she saw.

'*Chérie,*' Jacques exclaimed and opened his arms wide.

Before she knew what was happening, he had enveloped her in an embrace.

'Get off me!' Kat pushed Jacques away and took a couple of steps back. 'What are you doing here?'

She was confused. Hadn't Richard told her that Jacques had been ceremoniously sacked because of his behaviour with a young female runner? What about the various rumours and stories since then that had appeared online and in the press?

Jacques's face lit up with a wide grin. 'I'm back, *chérie.* It seems the public opinion has won. They can't film The Culinary Kingdom without me!'

'But ...'

She thought back to the newspaper headlines she had been greeted with when she'd returned from Lapland. There had also been a twitter storm, with the hashtag *Jacquesmetoo,* where several former employees had come forward saying that he had behaved inappropriately with them.

Kat had found the stories so terrible that she had stopped reading them. She had been relieved that Jacques had asked her to keep their relationship secret, citing professionalism.

When they were still together, she had been upset about the secrecy and often wondered if Jacques had been ashamed of her. His wish not to tell anyone that they lived together and shared a bed each night had caused many arguments. Once, Kat had left him for two weeks and stayed with her mum. Then the deluge of flowers and messages from Jacques had arrived and won her back.

Now, of course, it made perfect sense. He had wanted the freedom to have affairs and small flirtations with other women without having to explain his relationship with Kat.

Kat was relived no one in the production company had known about their relationship. It meant that the reporters who had loitered around the entrance to the production office her first week back in London had no reason to target her more than any of the others working there.

No one had asked her if Jacques had coerced her into bed.

Had he done that?

And was it true that he had sexually abused several women? Had he really been a sexual predator?

And if so, how come he was here now claiming to be back on the show?

Chapter Fifty

Kat left the grinning Jacques standing in the lobby. Using her key card, she let herself into the studio. She walked straight into Richard's office.

She found her boss on the phone, but as soon as he saw Kat's expression, he ended the call and asked her to sit down.

Richard was one of the only people to have his own office. Kat was grateful for the privacy, as she fought the tears that were threatening to well up in her.

'What's up?' Richard asked.

'Jacques is here.' Kat tried to control the tremble in her voice.

He raised his eyebrows. 'Yes he is.'

Silence followed and Kat fought to control her breathing. Her heart was beating hard and her mouth was so dry, she couldn't speak.

Richard got up and came around to sit on the chair next to Kat.

'What is it, Kat? He didn't do anything to you, did he?'

'No, no,' Kat said, even though it was a lie, but it wasn't anything she hadn't agreed to. Richard didn't know the full story.

'Look, I know you two worked closely together for many years, and you must have been horrified by the stories. But it turns out that's all they were. Stories.'

Kat lifted her eyes to meet Richard's. She opened her mouth but didn't know what to say.

He continued. 'The initial police investigation has shown that nothing illegal took place. We all know Jacques is a flirt – the worst kind – but it turns out he hasn't actually broken any laws.' Richard gave Kat a searching look. 'Unless *you* have any new information?'

Kat looked down at her hands.

If she told Richard everything, she would lose his and her colleagues' respect. And it wasn't exactly against the law to have an affair with your girlfriend's mother.

As Richard had said, Jacques was known to be a womaniser, whereas Kat was known for her profession-alism and integrity. How would they feel about her if they knew she had been in a relationship with Jacques all this time? Kat, the efficient food producer, had fallen for the French gigolo. And not just fallen, but lived with him for the past two years?

She was ashamed of having put up with Jacques'

behaviour all these years because there had been plenty of signs. She'd just put them down to his French way of dealing with people. He was expressive, warm – and yes, flirty. But she had honestly thought it to be innocent.

She'd been fooling herself, that was now clear.

First her mother, now this.

But it was over between Kat and Jacques; there was no point in telling Richard.

'Look, Kat,' Richard said. 'You know that the programme has millions of viewers, but they can go in a heartbeat. Jacques is popular, particularly with the female viewers, and I'm not certain the show will be the same without him.'

Kat took a deep breath in and out and after steadying her voice, began to put her argument across. She had to convince Richard not to take Jacques back, and without telling him about her mum or Kat's relationship with the Frenchman.

'What about all the newspaper headlines and what's been written online about him? Aren't you taking a huge risk in putting him back on the screen so soon? Won't the women in particular think that there's no smoke without fire?'

It was Richard's turn to sit back and take a breath. 'Wow, I thought you were friends.'

Kat sat quietly, not knowing what to say. Sometimes silence was the best policy with Richard.

He added. 'Look, the show won't air for another six months. We are still working on the concept – with you,'

– he paused and smiled at Kat, before continuing – 'and Jacques won't be in the studio until we start filming in about a week's time. So, there's time enough for the storm to die down and for everyone to forget about the rumours. And let me remind you that's what they are – rumours.'

Chapter Fifty-One

Kat left Richard's office with a heavy heart. As she walked down the hallway, her mind was consumed with thoughts of Jacques. She tried to push them out of her head, but they kept creeping back in. She couldn't help but doubt if he'd really done what they said he had.

Kat wasn't one to believe in rumours, but the fact that he had betrayed her with her Simona, and multiple women had come forward was making her think twice. Had she herself been one of many? Her heart sank at the thought.

She couldn't work with Jacques anymore, but how could she explain that to Richard without revealing their relationship? It was a difficult situation, and Kat didn't know what to do.

As she walked through the production office, she felt everyone's eyes on her. Whispers followed her. Did they know something she didn't? She prided herself on being professional, but now with Jacques being back, she was in state of pure panic.

Kat went to her desk and slumped into her chair. She tried to focus on the work in front of her, but her mind kept pulling her back to Jacques. Images of how he used to look at her and touch her filled her mind. She had thought it was love, but now she knew she had been naive.

She looked at her screen and saw a message on her computer. It was from Jacques. He was asking her to meet him for a drink after work.

She wanted to ignore it, but then she had an idea.

At the end of the day, Kat left the office and walked to the bar across the street, where she had agreed to meet him. She saw Jacques sitting at a table in the corner, looking as charming as ever. She felt a pang of longing in her chest for what had been but reminded herself why she had come here in the first place.

They exchanged pleasantries at first, but Kat cut to the chase.

'Jacques, I can't work with you anymore. Not after your betrayal with my mother and everything else that's come out since.'

Jacques looks at her with a mixture of confusion and hurt. 'What are you talking about, *chérie?*'

'You know exactly what I'm talking about. I can't work with someone who's betrayed me in the most horrible way. Or with a sexual predator.'

Jacques leaned forward in his chair, his face turning red with anger.

'How dare you accuse me of such a thing! Those women are lying. As for your mother, well, I'd say I was the one who was being taken advantage of.'

Jacque's leery grin made Kat suddenly feel sick. She shook her head.

'Don't talk about my mother like that. How dare you!'

Jacques's expression changed; he was suddenly looking at her with pleading eyes. 'But Katherine, *mon ange*, we had something special. Don't throw it all away.'

Kat glared at Jacques, her fists clenched tightly.

'Special? You call what we had special? You were just using me, Jacques. Just like you used all those other women. I was just too blind to see it.'

Jacques reached across for her hand, but Kat pulled it away.

'Don't touch me,' she said through gritted teeth. 'You disgust me.'

Jacques looked hurt, but Kat couldn't bring herself to care.

'Kat, please, I love you,' he pleaded, desperation creeping into his voice.

She snorted. 'Love me? You don't know the first thing about love, Jacques. Love isn't sleeping around with every woman who crosses your path. Love is about respect and honesty, and you have neither.'

He gazed down at his hands, looking ashamed.

'I know I've made mistakes, but I promise you, I can change.'

She turned her head away in disbelief.

'It's too late, Jacques. I can't be with someone like you. How can you even think that after what you did to me I would take you back? You must be even more deluded than I thought.'

Jacques' eyes were soft. 'I understand. I just wish things could have been different between us.'

Kat didn't know what to say. She wanted to shout at him, but she composed herself and said what she came to this bar to tell him.

'I want you to leave the show.'

Jacques looked taken aback. 'What? You can't be serious. I'm an invaluable asset to the show. Without me, the ratings will tank.'

'The ratings will tank if you show up on the screen again. The safety and wellbeing of the women who work on this show is also important to me, and I won't have you working there, making them feel uncomfortable or threatened.'

Jacques stood up, slamming his hands on the table.

'This is ridiculous, Kat. You can't just kick me off the show because of some unfounded accusations. I have a reputation to uphold. Besides, Richard asked me back.'

Kat rose from the table too, meeting his gaze head on.

'Your reputation is already in shambles. And I won't let you use this show to salvage what's left of it. If you don't agree to leave, I'll tell Richard all about us — and how you used my mother as well.'

Jacques glared at her. 'You wouldn't!'

'Try me.'

Kat didn't break eye contact, even though she had no interest in telling Richard about the disgusting family love triangle Jacques had created. Nor did she think it would make any difference to the producer's decision.

But it was the only weapon she had in her arsenal.

Jacques stared at her for a moment longer, then turned and stormed out of the bar, leaving Kat alone. She was relieved and triumphant, but also deeply sad.

She was alone, but hadn't she vowed in Lapland that just she was enough?

To do that she needed to forget about love and men, and instead concentrate on her professional life. First on the list was to convince Richard that The Culinary Kingdom could work without the famous and oh-so-popular Jacques Beaumont.

Chapter Fifty-Two

'I*t is* you!'

Kat was so deep in her thoughts after her confrontation with Jacques that she didn't notice a smallish woman and her husband come up to her.

'Pat! How lovely to see you. And Reg, hello!'

They all hugged.

Kat said, 'What are you doing in London? I thought you're based up in the Lake District?'

'We are. We just came down for a week. Reg's daughter is having twins, and we came down to give them a hand.'

Kat wondered if they had seen or heard her acrimonious interaction with Jacques, but then they talked about what a coincidence it was to meet up in a bar in town. Neither Pat nor Reg mentioned seeing her with anyone else. Although, Kat suspected they were just being polite by not mentioning the incident. She was certain their argument had been loud enough for the entire bar to hear.

Kat told them that she worked nearby, and Reg revealed that his daughter and her husband lived in Hampstead. Now, they were on their way to see a show and some of the sights of London.

'I used to work in London back in the day, you know,' Pat said, giving Kat a wink.

'Really?'

'Yes, I used to run a wine bar. Sadly, it's closed now.'

When Kat fell quiet, Pat tilted her head and gave her a searching look.

'And have you heard from Mikael, our lovely ski instructor?'

Kat blushed, and immediately admonished herself for such a silly, childish reaction.

She cleared her throat. 'Um, we had a bit of a falling out.'

Pat looked at her knowingly. 'Oh, I see. Well, you know how fond we were of him. We always thought he was such a nice man.'

Kat nodded, her heart aching once again at the thought of Mikael. She wished things with him had gone differently. At the same time, she couldn't take the risk of being disappointed by another man. Or having her heart broken to pieces again.

Reg interrupted her thoughts. 'Anyway, Pat, we'd better be going. Our show starts at seven. It was lovely to see you, Kat.' He gave his wife a loving little squeeze. 'If it was up to this lady, we'd talk all night and miss the whole thing!'

Pat smiled at her husband and then turned to Kat. 'Take care of yourself dear. And don't forget, love often turns up when you least expect it. All you need to do is to open your heart to it.'

Kat smiled at the couple. 'It was great catching up with you both. Have a great time in London.'

As she watched them leave, she couldn't help but wonder what it would be like to have a relationship like Reg and Pat's. To be with someone who truly respected and cared for her. Surely, she too could find someone like that?

She remembered the wonderful night she spent in the cabin with Mikael. She thought they had a real connection. But had they really? Wouldn't he have stepped away from his family's project if he'd truly loved her?

She was aware that love like Pat and Reg's was difficult to find.

Not with the way her life was now.

She was too jaded, too guarded, too afraid to let anyone in.

Right now, she was content with her work and her friends, and that would have to be enough for her.

Chapter Fifty-Three

The next morning, when Kat arrived into work, she saw that Richard's office door was closed. She walked towards his PA's desk, located just outside the glass-walled office.

'Is he in?' she asked the twenty-something guy whose colourful wardrobe usually cheered Kat up. But today, she could barely raise a smile when she saw Gavin's yellow shirt and bright-pink hair, due to her worry about the producer's reaction to Jacques leaving the show.

'No, girl, he's out all day?'

Kat sighed. 'Just my luck.'

'He's reading his emails today, so I'd send him one?'

Each of Gavin's sentences ended in a question mark, something that also usually made Kat smile. He was one of London's many Aussie expats and spoke with a broad accent, even though Kat knew he'd lived in the UK since his early teens.

Gavin waved his hand at Kat and lowered his gaze back to his screen.

Kat walked to her own desk and turned on her computer. To give herself time to think what to say to Richard, she checked her mailbox. To her surprise there was an email from her boss.

Kat,

Just spoke to Jacques. He has decided to postpone his return to The Culinary Kingdom indefinitely. Says it's a personal decision. What this means for us is that the search for a replacement is on again. As you know, we haven't got much time with filming starting next week. I'm seeing two candidates today, but can you send me the list of chefs you compiled again?

Thanks,

Richard.

Kat leaned back in her chair and audibly exhaled. Relief flooded through her that Jacques had decided to do the honourable thing and tell Richard he was leaving the show. Seeing Jacques yesterday evening had finally confirmed to Kat that she'd done the right thing by cutting off all ties to him.

During the night, as she'd lain awake in her friend's apartment, she wondered why she had fallen for such a fake guy as Jacques. She'd come to realise in the early hours of the morning that she'd known for a while he was both a flirt and likely unfaithful to her many times, so why had she stayed?

He had been influential in the TV circles, which Kat had appreciated. Although they never went anywhere as a couple – this Kat also understood should have been a huge, red flag to her – he'd still been useful to her career. In TV, there was no such thing as a permanent position, so it was vital to connect with people who were hiring in one's field. And Jacques knew a lot of people.

Kat had always loved the cooking programmes. Jacques had been instrumental in getting Kat the food producer role on The Culinary Kingdom. Although he hadn't recommended her, or even been involved in the hiring of production staff, he'd given Kat the heads up about the show before anyone else had known it was in the works. She'd got her foot in the door early.

But Kat hadn't been sleeping with Jacques to get ahead in her career. No, if she'd thought for even a second that was what she had doing, she'd have been horrified.

Jacques could be very, very charming. He'd wined and dined her when they'd first met during another cookery show, one less popular than The Culinary Kingdom.

Jacques had also been a safe haven for her. Because of his age he'd seemed happier and more settled in his skin. He knew what he wanted, and Kat stupidly thought that had included her. She'd imagined them as the perfect couple. Working in the same industry, they shared a love of food and wanted to be the best at what they did.

Jacques had already been a famous, even revered, chef, and Kat had been on her way to becoming a celebrated TV producer.

They had a bright future together.

Because Kat's past wasn't much to be celebrated. Life as the eldest child had been anything but glamorous.

Or easy.

Kat's dad had abandoned them after her mum fell pregnant with Daniel, Kat's brother. For years, they'd heard nothing from him, apart from the money he regularly deposited into Simona's bank account at the end of each month.

Kat had known nothing about his 'generosity' until her father whisked her off to meet his new family in Dubai when she was twelve years old. She had hardly remembered what her father looked like, and when she met a tanned old man with blond hair, she'd felt as if she was meeting him for the first time.

'How's my Kitty Kat?' he'd said.

When her estranged father had hugged her, Kat had remained rigid. She'd been exhausted from the long flight and the time difference.

The rest of the week-long holiday had been one disaster after another. Her father's new wife and two younger children – Kat's half-siblings – had made it clear they resented her presence. The five-year old twins, both boys, kept kicking and punching her, something their parents had found 'charming'.

When it was time for Kat to return to London, she couldn't get to the airport soon enough. The heat of the desert, the opulence of her surroundings and the millionaire lifestyle her father enjoyed had made Kat feel like the poor cousin visiting her rich relatives.

When she had hugged her father goodbye, she knew it'd be for the last time.

Kat hadn't shed one tear.

Just before she finally fell asleep, she wondered if her father's actions had made her incapable of picking the right man. Was she ill equipped to spot the good and the bad in the opposite sex because her father had abandoned her?

Chapter Fifty-Four

Their meeting in the city office of Andersson Oy Ab was set for 8am. Mikael's father believed in arriving early each day by 7.30am at the latest, before the rest of his staff. Mikael had woken up in good time and was sitting next to his father in Erik's Range Rover at exactly 7.10am.

'The early bird gets the worm,' Erik said, as he started the engine.

The roar of the car made Mikael think of what Kat had said about gas guzzlers. Looking at the cream leather and teak trimmings of the interior, Mikael noticed for the first time how luxurious his father's lifestyle was. Not to mention wasteful. For as long as he could remember, his father would get a top-of-the-range, 4-wheel drive every two years.

There was no way Erik needed a powerful off-road vehicle on the streets of Helsinki. His office was only a ten-minute ride away, a distance he could easily cover on foot.

Why hadn't Mikael seen this before?

'Would you ever consider getting an electric car?' Mikael asked him, trying to sound as nonchalant as he could. He was aware of what his father thought of the 'tree-huggers', his name for anyone expressing even the slightest concern for the environment. He didn't want to cause an argument on his first day in the company.

Erik Andersson turned his head to Mikael, his eyebrows knitted together.

'No, I haven't,' he said in his usual curt manner, meaning the end of the conversation on the matter.

A few minutes later, Mikael sat in one of the leather chairs reserved for visitors in his father's large office. It was located on the top floor of an art deco building in the corner of Mannerheim Street and the Boulevard. While his father was reading something on his computer, Mikael scrolled through pictures from Lapland. Outside, the rain was coming down in sheets. How he missed being up in the north. In this office, he felt like one of the reindeer being forced into a pen. Hemmed in. All he wanted to do was to get up and flee.

But he had made a promise to his father.

Mikael glanced at the time on his phone. It was well past eight and there was no sign of his brother. Apparently, Erik had insisted Victor handle Mikael's induction into the company.

Erik had said, 'He's the best man to introduce you to everyone and tell you how things are done here. Besides, I'm too busy.'

But by 8am, Victor had still not turned up.

Mikael regarded his father, expecting him to get up and begin ranting about his eldest son's tardiness. But no, Erik Andersson appeared to have limitless patience when it came to his favourite son.

Finally, just before 9am, the door to the office opened and Victor entered.

'Sorry, Pappa, terrible traffic.'

'So, the little brother comes around,' Victor sneered at Mikael, as they stood outside their father's office. 'Ran out of money, did you?'

'Yeah, something like that,' Mikael lied.

Walking behind his brother, as Victor gave him a tour of the offices – which occupied the two top floors of the prestigious building – he wondered what the real reason behind his decision was.

A combination of duty to his family, and fear for his financial future, perhaps?

When Victor insisted they have lunch in one of the best restaurants in Helsinki, he joked, 'This is one of the perks of the job and being an Andersson. All you need to do is mark it as a business meeting, and hey presto, it's free.'

In the afternoon, his brother disappeared, leaving Mikael alone to read through proposals for the mine in

Lapland. He was shocked by what he read. The project would swallow up acres of land right next to the national park. This would mean that thousands of reindeer would lose their grazing grounds, and several wild animals would suffer, not to mention the damage it would do to the fragile eco system. There were many endangered species living in the park, such as arctic foxes and wolverines. How could his father and brother even think of building a mine in such an ecologically rich area?

That night, Mikael couldn't sleep. He had been reading online reports for and against the project late into the night, and only managed to fall asleep in the early hours.

That morning, he joined his father for breakfast and told him he'd made a mistake.

'What did you say?' Erik roared.

'I can't work in the company. I just can't.'

His father glared at him. If looks could kill, Mikael would be lifeless on the floor.

Erik left the kitchen and banged the front door hard on his way out of the apartment.

'Mikael, please, don't do this,' his mother said, tears running down her cheeks.

'I have to do what's right.'

He hugged Ulla and returned to his bedroom, shaking. His father's anger-filled silences were worse than if he had shouted insults at Mikael. His mother's tears were even harder to bear. Despite the emotional upheaval he'd felt to quit, there was a huge amount of relief in him too.

He could suddenly breathe more easily.

His thoughts turned to the only woman who had opened his eyes, made him see his family's actions with new clarity.

Kat.

Perhaps now that he was no longer working on the mine project, she would see a future with him. There had to be a way to convince her to change her mind.

Suddenly Mikael knew exactly what to do.

As the airplane approached Heathrow, Mikael glanced out at the world below in vibrant miniature. The tangle of the Thames snaked through the city's heart, its sinuous path dotted with architectural jewels. The awe-inspiring Tower Bridge emerged from the cityscape, its twin towers reaching skyward. Farther down, the distinctive circular form of the London Eye greeted his gaze. On the North Bank, the Palace of Westminster appeared like a Gothic fairy tale and its crowning glory, the colourful Big Ben, marked time for the bustling metropolis.

Mikael wondered if he had made the right decision.

At home in Helsinki, making this trip had seemed like the only course of action. He wanted to make a life together with Kat and the only way he felt he had any chance of convincing her was to speak to her in person.

But was it foolish to make the journey without letting her know?

When he'd had the idea back in Helsinki, Mikael had felt a jolt of electricity surge through his body. It was as if his entire being was telling him this was the right thing to do. He had to see Kat, he had to speak to her, and he had to convince her to give him a chance.

As he sat in the taxi heading towards his hotel, Mikael could feel his heart racing. He wasn't sure what he'd say to Kat when he saw her, or how he'd explain his sudden appearance in London. All he understood was he had to try.

The hotel lobby was bustling with people, and Mikael felt excitement building in his chest. He checked in and headed up to his room, sensing he was on the verge of something big.

But what if during the past two weeks Kat had reconnected with Jacques? He understood the pair worked closely together. Was that why Kat had been so dismissive to Mikael on the phone last week?

He felt the doubt creeping in, but he pushed it away. He had to have faith that Kat would hear him out. He couldn't let the thought of her being with Jacques again stop him from trying.

He unpacked his bags, and decided he had to put all negative thoughts aside now and focus on the task at hand.

He took a deep breath and set out for the production company offices where Kat worked. As he walked through the bustling London streets, anticipation filled his whole body. He wasn't sure what he'd say to Kat when he saw her, but he knew that he'd regret it if he didn't speak with her face-to-face one more time.

The production company offices were a vibrant hive

of activity, with people rushing around clutching papers and chatting animatedly on their phones. Mikael took a deep breath and headed towards the reception desk, where a cheerful woman greeted him with a smile.

'Hi there, how can I help you?' she asked, her fingers flying over the keyboard.

'I'm here to see Kat,' Mikael said, trying to keep his voice steady.

The receptionist looked at him and raised an eyebrow. 'Do you have an appointment?'

Mikael shook his head. 'But it's urgent. Can you please tell her that Mikael is here to see her?'

The receptionist frowned, clearly not used to unannounced visitors.

'I'll see what I can do,' she said, picking up the phone.

He paced back and forth, his heart hammering in his chest. He couldn't believe he had taken such a huge risk, but he had to do it. He had to tell Kat how he felt and hope she'd give him a chance.

After what felt like an eternity, the receptionist put the phone down and looked at Mikael.

'Kat will see you now. She's free for the next ten minutes.'

He nodded and followed the receptionist down a long hallway and into an elevator. The ride up to the top floor seemed to take forever, but at last, the doors opened, and Mikael stepped out into a brightly lit office.

Kat was sitting at a large desk, her back to Mikael. She was typing furiously on her computer, and he couldn't help notice how beautiful she looked in her bright-orange jumper and short skirt.

'Kat,' Mikael said softly, not wanting to startle her.

She swivelled around in her chair.

'What are you doing here?'

'I had to come and see you,' he said, his voice breaking.

Kat stood up and looked at him, her expression unreadable.

Chapter Fifty-Five

Kat couldn't believe her eyes. Was it really Mikael standing in front of her in the busy production office?

He looked as handsome and tall as she remembered, but there was something different about him. He seemed so much more mature than the last time she had seen him. Perhaps it was the long winter coat he was wearing? She'd only seen him in sporty ski gear.

Kat didn't know how to process all this. One minute she had been working away, trying to get to grips with Jacques and her relationship with him falling apart. And dealing with the consequences of his departure from The Culinary Kingdom.

She'd tried to forget Mikael – easier to do with all that distance between them – and now he was standing in front of her, looking like he was about to cry.

She had to admit that she hadn't been able to stop thinking about him since she left Finland. Her heart ached with every beat every time she remembered the way he'd made her feel.

The attraction was as strong as ever, but Kat couldn't forget his involvement in the Lapland mine. She wouldn't give up on her principles again. Besides, could she trust her own heart? She didn't want to get involved with Mikael only to let him down later. She cared enough about him not to do that.

Mikael saw the doubt in her eyes, and his spirits fell. Would she reject him again? Would she tell him to go away and leave her alone? He felt like he'd been hit by a truck.

He'd been stupid to come all this way without telling Kat he was coming. Of course she was going to reject him.

His heart was pounding in his chest and all he could feel was fear. But he needed to be brave. He had to convince Kat that he would resist his father and the mine project in Lapland if she gave him a chance.

Perhaps she wasn't even interested in the mine or whether the ecosystem of the north was preserved. Perhaps her feelings hadn't been as genuine as his? Had she just been a tourist on holiday, and him a pleasant distraction?

Mikael shook his head.

No, what they had was real.

'Kat, I know I should have called you,' he said, his

voice wavering, as he struggled to find the right words, 'but I had to come. I had to see you. I had to try.'

There was desperation in Mikael's eyes. She took a step closer and put a hand on his arm.

Even through his thick winter coat, Kat felt the firm muscles underneath and suddenly her heart dropped into her stomach. She lifted her eyes to Mikael and saw his lips were parted.

'Mikael...'

Someone coughed in the office and Kat noticed it had become very quiet in the room.

Everyone was staring at them.

Kat felt her cheeks flush with embarrassment as she realised that they'd been watched. She quickly removed her hand from Mikael's arm and stepped back.

'Sorry,' she murmured.

Mikael nodded quickly. 'No, it's my fault. I shouldn't have come here unannounced. Can we go somewhere to talk?'

Kat nodded. 'Let's go outside.'

They stepped into the busy London streets. The cold air hit them and they huddled closer together.

'Why did you come?' Kat asked, breaking the silence.

Mikael took a deep breath before he answered. 'I came to talk to you about us.'

Kat's heart started to pound in her chest. She wasn't sure if she was ready to have that conversation with him. Not after everything that had happened.

'What *about* us?' she asked, trying to keep her voice steady.

Mikael reached out and took her hand. Kat could feel the warmth of his touch spreading through her body, and just like that, she knew she was in trouble.

'I came here to tell you that I'm not going to join my father's company. I'm going to fight the mine project.' He said, his voice full of conviction. 'I want to be with you. But that isn't the only reason I want to fight. I understand now what a disastrous effect the project would have on Lapland and the environment there. To be honest with you, I was never comfortable with what my family does. That's why I prefer to teach skiing than be a big shot in my family's company.'

Mikael looked deeply into Kat's eyes and squeezed her hand harder.

'You made me realise that my reluctance was because I care about Lapland's wild beauty. You made me understand that instead of just choosing the easy option, I can fight and protect the delicate ecosystems up in the north. I needed someone like you to show me what's important. I need you to continue doing that.'

Kat peered into Mikael's eyes and she saw the truth in them. She understood that he was being genuine, but she was still unsure if she should risk trusting him again.

'That's wonderful Mikael, but...' she began, her voice barely above a whisper.

Mikael stepped closer to Kat, so that their heads were almost touching.

'I love you,' he said, his voice hoarse.

Chapter Fifty-Six

Kat couldn't quite take in what Mikael was saying. First, she'd been shocked by his willingness to sacrifice the Lappish nature for profit, and now he'd had a complete change of heart. Could she trust him now?

'Have you told your dad you are going to fight the mine?'

Mikael's eyes shifted from hers to the ground and Kat knew the answer. He hadn't acted on his convictions. They were just words to him.

Did he really think she would believe his complete 180-degree turn, that all he had to do was *tell* her he feared for the harm the mine would do in Lapland? Fighting the impending global disaster needed actions, not words. Too many people talked the talk, but very few walked the walk. Kat couldn't respect a man who said action was needed but never did anything about it.

Jacques had been such a man.

She sighed and pulled her hand out of Mikael's grip, turning back towards the office entrance.

'Have a nice life.'

Mikael grabbed her arm and turned her to face him again.

Kat crossed her arms and waited.

'I told my dad I wasn't going to join the family firm and he was pretty pissed off about that.'

Kat raised her eyebrows but remained silent.

Mikael hung his head, not meeting her gaze. He looked so dejected that for a moment, Kat felt sorry for him, but she just couldn't be let down again.

'Look, Mikael. I like you but I'm not ready for another relationship just now –'

'Well, well, what have we here?'

Kat spun round and was shocked to see Jacques standing next to Mikael.

'What are you doing here?' she said.

Jacques gave a laugh which sounded more like a snort.

'I could ask your lover boy the same thing. What's the Lapp doing here?'

Mikael took a step closer to Jacques, forcing him to face the taller and bulkier man.

Mikael's eyes were bulging with anger. 'I came here to talk to Kat.' His voice was low, dangerous.

Kat felt the tension building between the two men and feared that things could turn ugly quickly.

Trying to defuse the situation, she asked, 'Why are you here, Jacques?'

Jacques turned his attention to her, a smirk on his face.

'I have a meeting with Richard.'

'That's a lie. He's not in the office today.'

Jacques looked about shiftily, as he tried to think of something to cover his fib.

'You heard her. You're not wanted here,' Mikael growled.

Jacques laughed again. 'Oh, this is rich. The Lapp is jealous.'

Mikael moved even closer to Jacques, his fists clenched at his sides. Their bodies were now almost touching, and Kat could almost smell the testosterone.

Surely, they wouldn't start a fight here in the middle of a busy London street?

'Guys, please!' she said, stepping between them. 'This isn't the way or the place.'

Jacques scoffed and took a step back, eyeing Mikael up and down.

'You're not worth it,' he said, before turning on his heel and walking away.

Mikael stood too still for a moment, his chest heaving with anger.

He turned to Kat, his eyes blazing. 'I can't believe you were ever with that man.'

Kat took a step back, surprised by the judgement in his voice. She could see the fury still boiling inside of him. His breathing was shallow and laboured.

'You have no right to criticise me,' she said, trying to keep her voice level. But she heard the tremble in it.

She was embarrassed about her association with Jacques, but they'd also had good times together. Besides, she hadn't known the whole truth of who Jacques was when she'd met him.

But it was her mistake. How dare Mikael berate her choices when he'd been prepared to work for a project that could destroy an ecosystem?

At least her relationship wasn't robbing the world of its resources!

A fuming Kat barely got out the next words. 'Go back to Finland, Mikael. There is nothing here for you.'

Kat spun round and hurried inside the office. She didn't stop until she was sitting at her desk, staring blankly at her computer screen. Tears were threatening to fall, so she walked quickly into the bathroom and a sat in a cubicle. She let her tears flow freely down her cheeks. They were tears of anguish, as well as fury towards Mikael and Jacques.

Kat realised now that she had made a mistake with both. Neither were who she thought they were.

Enough was enough.

She spent the rest of the day trying to shake off the knowledge that she'd been betrayed and hurt once more. She tried to concentrate on her work, but her attention kept straying back to Mikael and Jacques, and how they seemed so determined to dominate her. She couldn't believe she'd fallen for it once more, allowing herself to be enticed by another man's charisma and pledges.

Kat inhaled deeply and blinked back more tears that threatened to fall. She wouldn't let another man control her. She would be an independent person and make her own choices.

On her way home at the end of the day, she heard footsteps behind her. She turned around to see Mikael walking towards her, his face filled with remorse.

'Kat, I'm sorry,' he said, his voice soft. 'I shouldn't have judged you like that. I was jealous and angry, and I didn't know how to handle it.'

She gazed at him, unsure of what to say. She was exhausted by her work and the emotional turmoil caused by both Mikael and Jacques. All she wanted was to sink into her bed and fall asleep.

'I appreciate your apology, Mikael,' she said, her voice guarded, 'but I need some time and space to think about things.'

Mikael nodded. 'I understand. Take all the time you need. But can we at least remain friends?'

'Of course,' Kat said.

Mikael touched her arm her arm briefly.

'Thank you, Kat.'

With that, he walked away, leaving Kat to continue on her journey home alone.

As she walked, she thought about the conversation she'd had with Mikael earlier that day. She understood now that the reason she was so angry with him was partly because she was also angry with herself. He'd said what she herself thought. She had been blind to Jacques' faults and she could understand why Mikael was surprised she'd been with a man like that. Was her lack of confidence in her own ability to assess a person's true character the reason she now couldn't bring herself to trust Mikael? Perhaps she was the one who was judging him too harshly.

Chapter Fifty-Seven

Mikael walked away from Kat and wandered along the bustling London streets. He had no idea where he was going, and after a while he realised he was lost.

He'd been to London only a few times before, and his last visit was years ago. He pulled out his mobile from his trouser pocket and saw it was low on battery. He swore under his breath and checked his messages, but there was nothing from her. Disappointment washed over him, but he wasn't surprised.

He'd made a complete ass of himself in front of Kat. But that man, the Frenchman, brought out the worst in him. Mikael wasn't the type of guy to start fights – he'd rather hide under a table than brawl in a bar. But that afternoon, he would gladly have punched the French-man's lights out.

Trying not to think about the disastrous meeting with Kat, Mikael quickly put the name of his hotel on a maps app. But he didn't even get to glance at the directions before his screen went blank.

'*Saatana,*' he swore in Finnish.

Stopping on a hectic interchange appeared to be eliciting angry glances from passersby, which made Mikael hesitant to ask anyone for directions.

And then it started to rain.

He ducked under a canopy by a theatre. But when he tried the ornately carved double doors, he found they were firmly shut. He checked inside. It was pitch-black inside.

He sighed and wondered how he had got himself into a situation like this.

Lost, alone, and freezing on a rainy street in London.

Mikael had had a completely different image of how his trip would go before he'd left Helsinki. He had convinced himself that all he needed to do was to tell Kat he loved her. After he revealed that he would not take the job his father had offered him, she would let him kiss her and tell him she loved him too.

But it had all gone horribly wrong.

Maybe his father was right: he was a useless ski bum.

With the echoes of Kat's rejection still ringing in his ears, he walked on. A wave of rainwater washed over his shoes. As if things couldn't get worse, now his shoes were soaked.

Mikael took a step back to avoid being splashed by the cars speeding by on the busy street.

Squinting across the road, he spotted a bookshop. Focusing on the street sign next to it, he read Charing

Cross Road. He remembered this street, but not whether it was close to his hotel or not.

He decided to buy a map in the bookshop and walk back to the hotel to rethink his options. One thing was clear: he needed to get into somewhere dry and warm first.

About an hour later, having found his hotel and changed into a set of dry clothes and trainers, Mikael nursed his second beer in the hotel bar. The rain was still pouring down in sheets outside. Even if he'd wanted to sample a typical English pub on what was now his last night in London he couldn't face getting wet again.

Besides, he felt anything but sociable.

When he'd finished the second pint, he ordered a third and wondered if he should send Kat a message. He needed to know what was going on in her head, because he didn't understand why she had been so angry. All he'd done was to point out what she already knew. That Jacques was a jerk. But it had come across as a criticism of her. That's not at all what he meant.

Before Jacques had appeared, he thought their conversation had gone well. She might even have let him kiss her, had that bloody Frenchman not come between them.

Mikael was livid at Jacques. He couldn't comprehend how anyone as intelligent as Kat could be taken in by the silver-tongued words of a womaniser such as Jacques.

Perhaps he should call her?

No, she said she needed time, so he would let her be.

Mikael took a deep breath, feeling a mix of sadness and frustration. He never imagined things would end like this. He had come to London with so much hope, so much excitement, and now he was leaving with a broken heart.

He decided to have one more drink before heading up to his bedroom. He ordered a whiskey this time and sipped it slowly, savouring the warmth it brought to his body.

As the night wore on and the bar emptied out, he found himself staring into his empty glass, wondering where it all had gone wrong.

He had left his career as a ski instructor because he thought there was no future in it, and caved in to his father's wishes. But his conscience wouldn't let him join the family mining enterprise, something which, no doubt, would raise fury and contempt in his father.

As he paid his tab and made his way back to his hotel room, Mikael made a decision. He was going to take control of his life and make something of himself, on his own terms. He would earn Kat's love and respect with his actions, not words. He slipped into bed, closed his eyes and took a deep, calming breath.

Tomorrow would be a new day, a new beginning. And he would make the most of it.

Chapter Fifty-Eight

The café Kat had chosen to meet her mother in was in Covent Garden, one that they hadn't been in before. It was rather large and not too noisy, and it had a Nordic influence which Kat thought would put Simona at ease.

She didn't want an argument.

The only reason she was meeting her mum at all was because of her two siblings. Lily had been phoning and texting her constantly since she came back from Lapland, and she even had another message from Daniel asking her if everything was alright. Simona had been phoning him several times saying that Kat was "cruel" and "cold".

Those messages had made Kat angry at first, but then she phoned her sister and as they talked, Kat understood that if she was going to keep the sordid affair between her ex and her mum a secret, she needed to stop Simona from involving her other children.

Meeting and talking to her was the only option.

As she walked along the busy streets from the Tube station, it started to rain. Kat cursed under her breath for not bringing an umbrella. She ducked between shop awnings, trying to avoid getting wet, as well as the sharp edges of other people's umbrellas. Covent Garden was eternally popular with tourists, even on a wet Saturday morning in March.

'Oh, darling, it's so wonderful to see you!'

Simona was already sitting at a small table by the window when Kat walked into the bustling café. She saw that her mother had bought coffees and two cinnamon rolls.

'I know you like them, so I got one for you.'

Her mum pushed a small plate with the sweet-smelling bun towards her and got up with her arms outstretched for a hug.

Kat didn't meet her mum's eyes. Instead she sat down, ignoring the gesture.

She wasn't there to make up.

Kat tried to keep her fury at bay, but the way Simona was acting as if nothing had happened was making her even angrier.

She fussed with her coat, which was soaked from the rain.

'Don't you have an umbrella?' Simona asked.

There was the usual, thinly veiled criticism in her mum's voice.

Kat lifted her eyes to her. She noticed Simona's eyes were heavily made up, and her bright-red lipstick had run outside the lines of her mouth. She looked older than the last time Kat had seen her.

For the briefest of moments, Kat felt sorry for her mum, but the pity was quickly replaced by the memory of her and Jacques tangled in the sheets.

'I didn't come here to talk about the weather,' Kat snapped.

Simona lowered her eyes. 'Of course,' she muttered.

She took a sip of her drink, black coffee, as usual.

Kat lifted the bun to her mouth, but the smell was making her feel queasy. She put it down again.

'You're on a diet, are you?' Simona glanced between the roll and Kat's stomach.

Without thinking, Kat pulled in her tummy.

This is ridiculous. She let it out again.

'Mum, I'm here because you've been telling some sob story to Lily and Daniel about me being so cruel to you. If you don't stop, I'll tell them what really happened.'

Simona leaned back in the chair and took a sharp breath in, as if Kat had hit her. She held up her hands in a defensive gesture.

'I haven't seen him since that awful day. Please believe me, it's over, Kat. Even though he promised me –'

'I don't want to hear it!' Kat shouted.

A couple at the table next to them turned to look at her. She leaned closer to her mum and continued in a lower voice.

'I don't want to hear any details. Jacques and I are over. I don't care whether you two get married and live happily ever after as long as I don't have to see or hear about it. I can't see or talk to you for a while, and you need to leave me, Lily and Daniel alone. You hurt me, mum. More than you can imagine.'

Kat was fighting tears. She looked away from her mum's face and tried to calm her breathing.

Before she could stop her, Simona placed a hand on hers.

'I'm hurt too. That son of a ...' Simona swallowed. 'He did a number on both of us.'

Kat lifted her eyes to her and pulled her hand away.

'You're incredible!' She couldn't listen to any more lies.

With tears blurring her vision, she rushed out of the café onto the street.

As she walked along wet pavements, not knowing where she was heading, she thought about how foolish she'd been not to have seen something was going on between her mother and Jacques.

But how could she have seen it, when something like that never even entered her most tortured thoughts? She'd seen Jacques was a flirt, and the fact that he'd wanted to keep their relationship secret was a sign that he hadn't respected Kat or wanted a proper relationship.

But to betray her with her own mother, that was something else.

As for her mum, even though she had always been self-centred, how could she do that to her own daughter?

Kat stopped suddenly in the middle of the road. She had reached Shaftesbury Avenue. Thankfully, it had stopped raining.

For her peace of mind, she needed more from her

mother. She had to put a stop to the torturous questions in her mind.

If she hurried, she might still catch Simona in the café.

Kat started walking quickly back along Neal Street.

Chapter Fifty-Nine

Kat returned to the café just as Simona was putting her fashionable bright-red Rains coat on, ready to leave. She was more stooped over than Kat remembered her being, but once again, she pushed away the guilt. Pity was possibly the right emotion she should feel for Simona, but not yet. Perhaps later, in a few months – or years, when her hurt had subsided.

'Mum, don't go yet.'

Simona's face was full of puzzlement as she sat back down. The wrinkles on her forehead were pronounced as she frowned at her daughter.

'I have to know why you did it.'

Her mother looked away and sighed.

She was quiet for a long time, but Kat resisted the temptation to fill in the silence by telling her what she was feeling. She must let Simona speak in her own words, however painful they may be for Kat to hear. She would never be able to move on with her life until she knew what was going through her mum's mind.

'When your father left, I didn't think I would ever be able to feel anything for anyone else again.'

Simona's eyes met Kat's.

Kat shook her head. She couldn't believe she was using that old excuse.

'I've never heard *that* one before,' she said, failing to take the sarcasm out of her tone.

'You don't know what it was like. We were happy and then suddenly, he was gone. And I was left with three babies ...'

'I wasn't a baby,' Kat said.

'No, but a child. OK, I was pregnant with one baby, a toddler, and a young child. But not only that. I'd lost my confidence in men completely. And in myself. Before your father left, he told me he couldn't stand me anymore. He had no choice but to leave his family because he couldn't live with *me* anymore. Can you imagine how that made me feel? It was my fault you, Lily, and Daniel had no father. Mine, and mine alone.'

Kat hadn't heard this version before. All she had grown up with was tales of what a rat her father had been to leave them. For a long time, Kat had blamed herself, but at some point, she had realised it couldn't have just been her. And when she'd seen her father and his new family, she'd understood he had no interest in any of them.

'You haven't told me that before.'

Tears were running down Simona's face and Kat

couldn't help herself. She took hold of her mum's hand. She squeezed it and Simona gave her daughter a tearful smile.

'Well, it wasn't something I often thought about. I tried not to. It was his loss anyway. He never got to see you grow up or see what an accomplished woman you became.'

There was a silence while Kat thought about her father and how his leaving had coloured her whole life. She saw now that she would never have gone with Jacques had her father not abandoned her. She was certain she wouldn't have accepted the kind of fatherly relationship he'd been offering either.

'But, mum, Jacques! He was my boyfriend. You did the same – worse to me that dad did to all of us.'

Simona squeezed Kat's hand and took it between hers.

'I know that now. I don't know what I was thinking. Honestly, Kat, it was like I was a madwoman under some kind of crazy spell.'

Kat fought tears and had to whisper the last words. 'You broke my heart for the second time.'

'I know darling, and I am, so, so sorry.'

'Is everything alright here?' A young woman in a dark-blue apron and golden plaits came to stand next to their table.

'Yes, thank you.' Kat tried to smile at her.

'Are you finished? Can I get you anything else?'

'No, we're fine!' Simona barked, letting go of Kat's hands. Simona's outburst made the girl widen her eyes.

Flicking one of her plaits behind her, she turned and walked away.

'The nerve of some people...' Simona said it loud enough for the girl to hear.

This made Kat smile. It was so like her mother to raise her hackles at an innocent query like that.

Simona continued. 'She should have seen we were both in tears and in the middle of something!'

'Yeah, but she didn't mean any harm,' Kat said, reasonably.

Simone shrugged and took hold of Kat's hands again.

She sighed deeply. 'Can you ever forgive me?'

'Maybe one day. Not yet,' Kat said.

She pulled away her hands, but gentler this time. 'I need to heal, mum. You can understand that, can't you?'

Her mum nodded and looked pensive for a moment.

They were both deep in their thoughts. Then Kat asked, 'What did he promise you?'

She couldn't believe she was discussing Jacques with her mum, but suddenly she needed to know the details of their relationship.

Simona looked up, surprised. Tears had smudged her makeup now; she looked older and more vulnerable.

What her mum had done was so very wrong, but Jacques had hurt Simona too, Kat could see that now. Still, she couldn't forgive the treachery of Simona's actions.

'Oh, he promised to stay,' Simona told Kat. Once again, her eyes filled with tears.

Despite this, she continued to talk, looking down at her hands instead of Kat.

'I told him what your father had done. How he had abandoned me. Jacques promised never to leave me.'

Kat didn't say anything. Images of a tense moment between her mum and her ex-boyfriend filled her mind. She fought the urge to leave again.

Simona lifted her eyes to look at Kat. 'I was surprised that he didn't know about your father. You didn't tell him?'

She simply shook her head, unable to speak.

Simona continued. 'And Jacques? I read all those reports in the papers and to be honest, I'm not surprised. Every time we were out, even before, you know, you found out... he always had eyes for other women.'

Kat shook her head. 'Mum, I don't want to hear it. Jacques and I are over. He resigned from the show and they promoted me to producer. So, I can decide who the new judge, or judges are going to be.'

Simona's face broke into a wide smile. 'That's fantastic, Katherine! I am so proud of you!'

She got up and made a move towards Kat to give her a hug, but Kat shifted backwards.

'Mum, I can't...'

There was disappointment in Simona's face as she sat back down. She nodded and said, 'OK, sorry. Of course. You need time.' She changed the subject. 'Tell me, how was Lapland?'

'It was fine, Mum... I can't do this now. Things aren't

the same between us and it will be a long time before they are. Perhaps never.'

Simona pressed her lips together in resignation and replied, 'OK, darling. I am just so happy that you agreed to see me and that we talked. At least a little bit. I will wait, I promise.'

'I also want you to promise that you will stop telling Lily and Daniel how "cold" I am.'

Simona looked sheepish when she replied, 'Of course.'

When Kat walked out of the café for the second time that morning, she was strangely relieved. Simona had promised not to complain again about Kat to her sister and brother, and she seemed to have accepted that Kat needed time to get over the betrayal.

Even though Kat was still angry with her mum and baffled at how she could have had an affair with Jacques, she was relieved that they had talked about it.

She thought that she'd wanted to find out more about how it had happened, but right now, the whole affair was still too sensitive for her.

She hadn't wanted to tell her mum about Mikael, or how fantastic Lapland had been.

Besides, Mikael and her were over.

It had just been a holiday romance, nothing to tell anyone about, least of all her mum. What they had was in the past and she would get over it, just as she would get over her father's abandonment and try to forgive her mum.

When that would happen she had no idea, but she felt a little better about it all.

With Jacques history, she needed to focus on the future.

Kat thought about calling her friend Toni and suggesting they go out. She needed to be amongst happy people tonight.

Her friend had just finished filming and was back in the flat that they currently shared. That was another thing Kat needed to sort out – her accommodation. Toni had told her that she could stay with her indefinitely, but it wasn't practical. Toni had a boyfriend and with only one bedroom in the small apartment, three was a crowd.

Perhaps she'd talk to Toni about it all tonight.

Chapter Sixty

'You cannot tell me what to do. I'm a grown man and can make my own decisions.'

Mikael stood in front of his father in the family apartment in Helsinki. The snow was falling outside, something which made Mikael yearn for the fells of Lapland. Instead of sliding down the virgin slopes, he was in a dark-wood panelled library which also served as Erik Andersson's home office.

'Then act like a man!'

Mikael squared his shoulders.

His father, with grey hair and a slightly stooped gait, still cut an impressive figure.

Mikael paused, trying to calm his nerves. No one ever stood up to Erik Andersson. Even Mikael's many cousins and his father's own siblings feared the company CEO.

Somehow, over the years, – Mikael didn't really know how –Erik had gained total control over the company. He was the major shareholder, as well as the head of the concern.

'That means I, and I alone make the decisions,' he'd proudly told Mikael the week after he had graduated from university.

He had proceeded to give him a certificate showing that Mikael was now the proud owner of one percent of the company's shares.

Although Mikael didn't want anything to do with the family firm, the graduation present hadn't come as a surprise to him. His brother, Victor, had received the same gift, presented to him two years prior.

Victor had started working in the company the next day, a fact that he or Erik Andersson never missed an opportunity to remind Mikael about.

When Mikael had told him that he was going to work as a ski instructor in Lapland instead of joining his brother and father, Erik had disapproved, but had begrudgingly allowed his youngest son to have 'a year of freedom', as he put it.

Mikael had been too much of a coward to tell Erik that he had doubts about joining the mining firm.

But now, newly returned from London and with the memory still fresh of the disappointed look on Kat's face when he'd told her that he hadn't yet talked to his father, he felt stronger.

Despite his strength, his throat felt dry when he said, 'I think it's wrong to start mining in Lapland. The ecosystem there is sensitive, and a mine can do huge harm to the environment. And to the people. In fact, I don't approve of any of your company's activities, whether here in Finland, or in Sweden. Not to mention the shares you have in mines in South America. Who knows how the staff there is treated, let alone what the environmental impact has been?'

Erik stood opposite his son with his mouth slightly open. He looked as if he was stunned into silence.

But not for long.

'And you are now an expert on the ecological effects of mining? And here I thought I paid for you to study engineering.'

Erik's voice boomed around the dark-panel room, so loud, Mikael imagined the windows overlooking the small Ullanpuistikko park were vibrating.

He replied, 'You don't need to be an expert to understand how harmful the operations of Andersson Oy Ab are.'

'You know absolutely nothing about it! We use the latest technology and offset our carbon use. Plus, we give hundreds – thousands of people jobs. Doesn't that count for anything?'

Mikael regarded his father. He knew he'd hit a sore point. In the last few years, there had been several negative newspaper reports, and even a few demonstrations outside the company offices in the centre of town.

'Not when the world is burning,' Mikael said softly.

Suddenly, the mighty Erik Andersson looked tired and old. He sat himself down at his desk. His face was ashen and his eyes watery when he looked at his son.

'If you do this –'

'Your threats won't change my mind, father. I'm selling my share and if you want to buy it, that's fine. But I don't want any part of it, so I will sell to whoever wants it.'

One of his cousins, Jacob – Erik's sister's son – was very keen on taking a more active role in the business. He'd been buying up any shares he could get his hands on, and Mikael also knew that Erik couldn't stand him. He wasn't certain why, apart from the fact that his father didn't want anyone else but his sons to head the firm.

He wanted to be in full control.

Erik Andersson straightened up in his leather seat and the colour returned to his cheeks.

'Fine. I will buy it back. This is rich of you, though. I won't forget what you are doing in a hurry.'

Erik's eyes bored into Mikael's, but he felt stronger to deal with it. He imagined Kat's face as he told her about his actions today – if he ever got the chance to tell her.

Finally, he put into words what he really came here to say.

'I will be helping to fight the plans for the Lapland mine.'

Erik stood up too fast. 'What?'

Chapter Sixty-One

Mikael had only been in Helsinki for a week before he was sitting on another plane, this time bound for the north. Before he'd left his childhood home, his father had told him never to return. He'd hugged his mother and told her to come and visit him in Ylläs, but he doubted whether she'd be brave enough to.

Erik Andersson had barely said two words to Mikael since their argument the night before.

'If you carry on this course, you will be dead to me,' had been Erik's last words.

'I always knew money was more important to you than family,' Mikael had retorted.

He gazed out of the small aircraft window at the snow-capped pines below, his thoughts travelling back to the fight, and when his father's face had gone bright red. He had been speechless and for a moment, Mikael feared he'd been having a heart attack.

Instead, Erik had stormed out of the room, banging the door shut behind him so hard it had shaken the large painting of his great-grandfather on the wall.

Later, when Mikael had been packing in his room, he'd heard his mother talking to his father in a low tone. Then there were tears, followed by Erik's raised voice.

Mikael felt sorry for his mother. Always the peacemaker in the family, she'd had to step in between Erik and his sons many times.

His father's parental style had been learnt from his days in the military, while Ulla Andersson preferred a more lenient and modern approach to child rearing.

Mikael felt a pang of guilt when he thought about his mother, crying as they'd said goodbye. Not only would he miss her, but knowing his father, Erik would be in a bad mood for days, perhaps even weeks, because of him.

Ulla would no doubt have to tread carefully to avoid Erik's bad-tempered outbursts. It relieved Mikael to know that, although his father was an old-fashioned man without any patience whatsoever and always had to be right, he wasn't a violent man.

But Erik Andersson also wasn't a man who would easily change his mind. Mikael would not be welcome at home anymore. His father had told him Mikael was no longer his son.

After the plane had landed and Mikael was travelling on the bus towards the Ylläs ski centre, he pulled out his phone. He had decided he would try to at least remain friends with Kat, if nothing else. Blowing air out of his lungs, he sent her an image of the setting sun against the white snow.

Guess where I am!

To his great delight, the reply had come almost immediately.

Lapland?

Mikael replied, telling her he was moving back permanently.

I'm pleased for you.

Thank you.

Mikael wanted to say more, how much he missed her, and how their separation was ridiculous. It was clear she had feelings for him. He wanted to tell her of his exact plans for the future, but it would have to wait until it was all in place. He needed to be certain everything was going to work out as he'd planned.

When Mikael stepped off the bus and onto the snow-covered pavement of Ylläs, excitement bubbled in his chest. The air was crisp, and the sky was a dark shade of bluish-black, a winter evening that made everything look brand new. He couldn't wait to start his new life here, away from the pressure of his father, to fight the mining project.

He made his way to the small cabin he had rented, taking in the scenery along the way. There were five similar houses nestled in the trees, the snow piled high around them.

The silence was deafening. It was a far cry from the

hustle and bustle of Helsinki and the tense atmosphere in the family apartment in Ullanlinna.

As he stepped inside the cabin, calm washed over him. It was cosy and warm, and it already felt like home. He spent the next few hours unpacking and settling in and, as the darkness settled over the trees, he started making plans for his future.

Mikael was going to face a lot of opposition from his father and his family, but he was determined to fight for what he believed in.

He pulled out his laptop and began to read more about the environmental impact the proposed mine would have on the region. As he delved into the information, his anger grew. How could anyone be so callous and greedy as to destroy this pristine wilderness for their own profit? He felt shame that he was part of the family that was doing it.

He now fully understood Kat's hesitation. He felt ashamed that it took her rejection of him for Mikael to fully comprehend the catastrophic consequences of the project.

There were many local groups, including the one he'd followed Kat into, so Mikael wasn't alone in this fight. He needed the support of the locals, the environmental groups, and anyone who cared about the future of Lapland. He could already feel the passion and determination growing within him.

Something suddenly occurred to him. What if the locals didn't accept him into their ranks?

The people in Lapland could be suspicious of Southerners, let alone anyone with the surname Andersson.

Of course, they loved the tourists and he had never had any problems while living up here as a skiing instructor, but what would they make of the son of the boss of the mining company turning up to fight against the project?

Mikael would have to earn their trust and prove himself to them. He would go back to the local community meetings and get involved in their activities. He also planned to volunteer for environmental projects and show the locals that he was truly committed to protecting their land.

The thought of meeting and interacting with the locals excited Mikael. He had always been a people person, and he looked forward to making new friends and allies. He'd have to work hard to overcome their initial suspicions, but he was determined to win them over.

Chapter Sixty-Two

In the darkness of his new home, Mikael's thoughts kept straying to Kat. He wondered if she'd be proud of him for taking a stand against his family. He also wondered how she was doing and if she was thinking of him. He decided to call her.

Kat answered on the first ring.

'Hey,' she said, sounding cautious.

Was she regretting taking his call?

'Hey back,' Mikael replied.

He'd missed her so much, and it felt good to hear her voice again.

'How is it up there in Lapland?' she asked.

Mikael could not decide if she was just timid talking to him after a tumultuous time in London, or if she was being indifferent. Perhaps she had already moved on?

'It's amazing,' he told her. 'It's cold but clear, with a scattering of stars. No Northern Lights tonight, though.'

Kat didn't reply. He could hear her breathing down the line.

Had Mikael said too much? Was it a mistake to remind her of the wonderful night they had spent in the cabin? Did she regret everything?

'I feel like I'm finally where I'm meant to be,' he added.

'Good for you,' she replied. 'I'm glad you're happy.'

Mikael felt a swell of emotion in his chest. He wanted to tell her everything, to share his plans and dreams with her. But he hesitated, unsure of her reaction.

'Listen, Kat,' he said finally. 'I am going to fight the mine. I don't understand how I didn't see what you saw before. I was blind to the horrific consequences of it. I want you to know that the reason I'm here is to do the right thing. Finally.'

There was another pause on the other end of the line, and Mikael held his breath, waiting for her response.

'Wow,' she finally said. 'That's really brave of you, Mikael. I'm proud of you for standing up for what you believe in.'

A rush of relief and happiness flooded through him. Kat's support meant everything to him, and he was grateful that she believed in him.

'Thanks,' he said softly. 'I wouldn't have gotten here without you.'

'It was all you. It took a huge amount of courage to go against your family,' Kat replied.

Mikael couldn't interpret Kat's mood from her jovial tone. He wanted to tell her again how he felt about her, but he wasn't sure if she was ready to hear him.

'Hey, listen,' he said, changing the subject. 'Why don't you come up for a weekend? My cabin has a guest bedroom, so...'

'I don't know...'

Mikael heard the hesitation in her voice.

'We're still friends, aren't we? You could join me in the meetings and hone your excellent skiing skills.'

Mikael,' she said slowly. 'I'm not sure if that's a good idea.'

He felt his heart sink. He had been hoping that she would jump at the chance to come back to Lapland.

'OK,' he said, trying not to sound too disappointed.

'It's just...' Kat trailed off, and she sighed. 'I don't think it's a good idea for us to see each other right now.'

Mikael felt a knot form in his stomach. He had been afraid that she would say something like this. It wasn't that he didn't understand her reservations, but it still hurt.

'Right, I understand,' he said finally, trying to keep his voice steady.

'Listen, Mikael, I'm really busy with filming The Culinary Kingdom. And... I think I need more time to process everything. Jacques, what happened between us, and the thing with my mum. You know, it's a lot.'

'Of course,' Mikael said quickly.

There was hope, he thought. She wasn't saying no. She had said, in a few more words, perhaps.

'I bet it's raining in London,' he added. 'When I was

there it rained all the time, just as all the tourist guides say.'

That made Kat laugh and the tone of the conversation lightened.

'Funny you should say that, because I've just walked through a downpour!'

'You should take up water skiing,' Mikael joked.

They talked a little more about skiing and how the snow was still deep in Ylläs, even in early April. When Kat said goodbye, there was genuine warmth in her voice, something Mikael hadn't heard at the beginning of the conversation.

As he hung up the phone, he had hope that there might still be a chance for him and Kat. He needed to give her space and time to work through her issues, but he was willing to wait for her.

He would prove to her that he was serious about resisting the mine and that he was exactly the man for her.

Chapter Sixty-Three

When the filming of The Culinary Kingdom began, Kat barely had time to go home to her new flat in Dalston. Her commute was a lot more complicated now that she no longer shared with Toni, whose apartment was closer to the studios in Camden.

Without the famous French chef, Jacques, as the face of the programme, there were concerns expressed in several forcefully written emails from up high in the production company. According to them, Kat would be wholly responsible for the equal success of the new format, which included three lesser known chefs as judges and a food critic.

Richard, her boss, was visibly nervous around the set and that made Kat even more concerned about the future of the programme – and her career in TV.

As she worked, directing the food team, and helping

with the prepping, she tried to push aside her worries. While inspecting the cod fillets being prepped for a fish chowder that would be cooked by a Norwegian contestant later, Kat thought back to the conversation with Mikael the night before.

She had been delighted to hear from him, and was surprised to learn he was fighting his father on the proposed mine. That showed real courage, and compassion.

Last night, she'd dreamt about Lapland and Mikael, and when she'd woken up in the morning, she had doubts about her decision not to take their relationship further.

Had she been wrong to think that a future together with Mikael was impossible?

They lived in different countries and came from completely different backgrounds. He had grown up in Helsinki, in a wealthy family, whereas she had been brought up by a single mother, not in poverty but certainly not in luxury.

Kat often had to step up to look after her smaller siblings when Simona was on a deadline with her translation work. There was no father to ask for help, nor any other family members who lived close by.

It had been difficult for Kat to trust a man after her father had abandoned them. But Jacques had somehow broken through Kat's defences. He had offered stability. But how wrong Kat had been!

How could she possibly trust herself to make the right decision about Mikael now when she had been so wrong before?

As the day wore on, Kat's emotions towards Mikael grew stronger. She tried to focus on work, but her mind kept wandering back to him. She imagined him up in Lapland, preparing to fight for what he believed in, and she felt a pang of admiration mixed with sadness. It was hard for her to envisage a future with him in Lapland. She had lived in London all her life, and she thought herself quite independent, although the years spent with Jacques had put a dent in that. Would she be able to adapt to life up in the wilderness of the north? She didn't even speak Finnish, although almost everyone seemed to speak English up there. It was a tourist resort, after all. But what would she do for work?

These practical concerns completely disappeared when she thought about Mikael's smile and their magical night in the cabin under the Northern Lights. The attraction she'd felt had been animalistic, but she'd also admired his character – and still did.

Unlike Jacques, who had none.

Mikael was a brilliant, patient, and inspiring teacher – and he spoke English like a native. He was friendly with everyone, and thinking about it now, she hadn't seen him flirt with any other women. Her suspicions about the receptionist had been an overreaction to Jacques' behaviour, she was certain of that.

Mikael was so very different from her ex. He was trustworthy, and he cared for her deeply.

. . .

At the end of the day, it was pitch-black outside, but at least it wasn't raining. Kat finished up her work and headed back to her flat. She was exhausted, but her mind wouldn't switch off. She couldn't shake the impression that something was missing in her life. She poured herself a glass of wine and sat down on the couch, trying to clear her mind.

Suddenly, she knew exactly whose voice she needed to hear.

'Hey, Mikael,' she said, trying to keep her tone casual.

'Hey, Kat,' he replied.

Kat could hear the smile in his voice.

'I hope I'm not interrupting anything.'

'No, not at all. What's up?' Mikael replied, his voice warm.

'Nothing really. I'm tired from work and wanted to hear a friendly voice. We're still trying to get everything sorted after Jacques left.'

Kat bit her lip. Why had she mentioned his name to Mikael?

'It's funny, because I was just thinking about you.'

Kat felt her heart flutter at Mikael's words.

'How about you?' she asked.

'I'm OK,' Mikael replied, and continued, 'I've been doing some research. I think I've found a way to slow the mining company down.'

Kat relaxed as she listened to Mikael describe his plan. She could hear the passion in his voice, and it made her heart ache. He was doing this for the right reasons, and she was so proud of him.

'Sounds like you're really making progress,' she said, trying to keep her tone neutral. 'I hope everything works out for you.'

'Thanks.' His voice was soft, but Kat could still hear the disappointment. 'I really appreciate your support.'

There was pause, and Kat felt the tension rise between them. She wanted to tell Mikael how she felt, but she wasn't sure if she was ready to take that step.

'Mikael,' she said finally. 'I've been thinking about you.'

There was a moment of silence, and Kat wondered if she had made a mistake.

'Kat,' Mikael said, his voice low and hesitant. 'I don't want to pressure you into anything.'

She took a deep breath, trying to steady herself. 'I know. I just need to figure things out. But I want you to know that I care about you.'

'I care about you too,' he said. 'More than you could ever know.'

Mikael's voice was soft, and Kat felt her chest fill with a promise for a future.

They fell into a comfortable silence, the tension between them slowly lifting. Kat sipped her wine, warm and content. She still had a lot of doubts and fears, but for the first time in a long time, she felt hopeful about their relationship – whatever that turned out to be.

Friendship or something else ...

'Listen, Mikael,' she said finally. 'I have to go, but can we talk again soon?'

'Absolutely. I'll call you tomorrow.'

'Goodnight, Mikael,' Kat said softly.

'Goodnight, Kat.' And with that, the call ended.

Kat set her phone down on the coffee table and took a deep breath. She felt at peace; she'd made the right choice in being honest with Mikael.

Chapter Sixty-Four

The next morning, Richard caught up with Kat as soon as she walked into the studio.

'Bad news, I'm afraid. We've had the initial results of the focus group, and they aren't good.'

'Oh?'

They walked along the corridor running alongside the various studio sets.

'Only fifteen percent said they liked the new judges. Most of them, eighty-five percent, said they wanted Jacques back.'

'But –' Kat hurried to keep up with her boss, her mind whirling with questions. Richard didn't slow down, nor did he seem to want to hear what Kat had to say.

'This is a disaster.' He stopped abruptly, turning around to face her.

His expression was set, and he had his arms crossed.

'I think we can safely say that your little experiment has failed.'

'What?'

'The powers that be' – Richard looked up at the ceiling, as if the head of the production company was God – 'want to scrap the new format and go back to the old one.'

Kat was speechless. She stared at Richard, unable to articulate what she was thinking.

'You agree?'

Finally, Kat found her voice. 'No! We can't bring Jacques back.'

'We have no choice. We can't afford to have a flop. That will mean they'll shut the series down all together and neither of us want that now, do we? All these people would lose their jobs, along with me and you. Well, perhaps not me, since all this was your idea, but, you know, it wouldn't be good for my career either.'

Richard was talking to her as she were a child or a stroppy teenager.

Kat's rage began to bubble inside of her, and she could feel her heart beating hard against her chest.

This couldn't be happening...

'Look, all you need to do is give Jacques a call, Kat. I'm sure he'll be delighted to return.'

Of course, she couldn't tell Richard that she never wanted to see him or hear his voice again.

'But what about all those other allegations of sexual harassment? Surely, we can't overlook those in this day and age? Especially as this programme's viewers are predominantly women?'

Kat gave him the same arguments she had before she'd managed to convince Jacques to resign. Would she have to meet up with Jacques a second time and threaten him again?

And just when she was finally moving on.

Richard gave her a puzzled look. 'You haven't heard? Police have abandoned the initial investigation due to lack of evidence.'

Kat stared at Richard.

Her boss added, 'Right, that's settled then. You firm up plans with Jacques and once that is done, pass on the news to the crew and the contestants. We need to call...' Richard rubbed his chin. 'What's his name? You know the American guy who was kicked out last week and have him start again.'

He patted Kat on the shoulder and walked away.

She stood in the corridor for what felt like an eternity. How could Richard not see that Jacques' reputation was in tatters, that he was a liability?

Plus, the new format was something she and Richard had worked on together, and Kat had sought his approval at each step. She hadn't made one important decision on her own – Richard had approved everything. And now he was washing his hands of it all.

The first focus group on a new format for programme was always bad. That was a fact. It took time for viewers to get used to new faces, especially after such a high-profile TV personality as Jacques.

The door to the studio opened and one of the floor directors popped her head out.

'We're ready, Kat.'

In that moment, it occurred to her that not only had

Richard put the blame for the non-working new format on her shoulders, but he had also passed the buck on telling the crew about the focus group results. As well as expecting her to sweet-talk Jacques into coming back.

'I need ten minutes.'

The woman gave her a puzzled look, but nodded her head and disappeared back inside the studio.

Kat turned around and started running after Richard.

He's not going to get away with this!

Chapter Sixty-Five

That evening, when her mobile pinged with a message from Mikael, Kat wasn't sure what to do.

Can I call you?

She was so disappointed and angry at the turn of events of that day and was dead on her feet with exhaustion.

During the last twelve hours in the studio, she'd had to reorganise everything and deal with the angry TV chefs who were being sacked. She'd had to tell the contestants who thought they'd already got through to the second stage of the competition that they had to restart the whole thing. Finally, she had to negotiate with the productions staff to try to make them understand why it was necessary to scrap everything they had done in the past week and start filming again.

And she had to beg Jacques to return to the programme.

That she had done by email. There had been an immediate reply.

Jacques Beaumont was returning to the show.

The last thing Kat had done before she'd left the studio around 7pm was to write her resignation letter.

She had no idea what she would do now. She had a new flat which was costing her a fortune each month, and obviously she needed an income. Luckily, she had some savings, but she couldn't live off them forever.

She needed a new job, but would anyone employ her after her unsuccessful revamp of The Culinary Kingdom? In TV, you were only as good as your last programme.

How could she possibly recount all of that during a phone conversation with Mikael?

Kat decided to open a bottle of wine before replying to Mikael, but she hadn't even had time to take a sip out of her glass when her phone pinged again.

I have great news. Please can I call you?
Sure.

Her phone rang almost immediately. She picked up.

'Hello, Mikael.'

'Are you OK?' There was concern in his voice.

Kat smiled, despite how she was feeling. How did he know she was down?

'Not really, but I want to hear your good news first. I need cheering up.'

'What's happened?'

'Mikael, please, I'll tell you after.'

He took a deep breath before he spoke. 'You know

how much I love skiing and teaching others, right? And that I want to fight the mine but I need to earn some money too?'

'Yes.'

'Well, my father – reluctantly, I have to say – bought my share in the family firm so I have some funds, but I don't want to sink it all into a new venture. And today, I got an offer from someone we both know to set up a new ski school up here!'

'Who?'

'Pat and Reg! You remember them? Apparently, they bumped into you in London and after, they contacted my old employer, who passed their details onto me. They thought I was such a good teacher that I should set up on my own. They've done some research and thought it would be a good investment. They're flying up here next week to finalise it all. Isn't that great? I can set up the school for next season and fight the mine at the same time.'

As Kat listened to Mikael, she could hear how excited he was. He had a passion for skiing and Lapland and his enthusiasm was making her feel better too. It was contagious.

'That's incredible. I'm thrilled for you.'

But Mikael wasn't finished.

'This could be good news for you, too.'

'What do you mean?'

'Are you happy with your job?'

Mikael's question could not be timelier. 'Well, since you mention it, I actually resigned today.'

'That's wonderful!'

'No, Mikael it isn't. I don't have another position to go to.'

'You do. That's what I wanted to phone you about. I'd like you to – no I'd *love* you to join me in the business. I need someone to kick ideas around with and to look after the practical things. You would be perfect.'

Kat was taken aback by Mikael's news and his offer.

She'd never expected him to set up his own ski school, or that Pat and Reg would be investors. Not to mention that he'd ask Kat to be a part of his new venture. It was a tempting opportunity, but she wasn't sure she was ready to take that leap of faith.

'Mikael, I don't know what to say,' Kat replied, filled with uncertainty. 'I've never worked in a ski school before. And although I love Lapland, I was only there for a week. I don't even speak Finnish! Living there would be a huge change for me. Besides, I don't think I'm right for the job.'

'Don't sell yourself short, Kat,' Mikael retorted. 'You're a quick learner, and you're great with people. And you're practical. Your skills as a producer would be incredibly useful, I'm sure. I know that you'd be an asset to the business.'

Kat took a moment to consider Mikael's offer. She had been feeling lost and uncertain about her future, and the thought of working alongside Mikael in Lapland was enticing. It was perhaps the complete change she was looking for.

The last few weeks working for The Culinary

Kingdom had been a slog and she now realised that she hadn't enjoyed one minute of it since her return from Lapland.

But she was also worried about the risks involved in moving abroad to a completely different place to London, let alone starting a new business.

Mikael filled the silence.

'And I saw how you were up in Ylläs. You learnt to ski incredibly quickly, and you made friends fast with the local environmental group. You took everything in your stride, the husky ride, a night out in the deserted cabin, and an avalanche! Honestly, I'm not just saying that.'

Kat smiled at the memory of the Northern Lights, and how, during the day, the sun had reflected off the bright snow on the dark pine trees. It had been a magical trip, but was that only because she had been there on holiday? Like the relationship with Mikael, hadn't that just been a holiday romance after all?

'Mikael, I've had a terrible day. I'll tell you about it later. And I appreciate the offer, but I need some time to think about it,' Kat said finally. 'Starting a new business in a new country is a huge risk, and I'm not sure if I'm ready to take that on just yet.'

'I understand,' Mikael replied, sounding disappointed. 'But don't forget this isn't a new country or a new industry for me. I hope you seriously consider it. I truly believe that we can make something great together.'

'I will.' Kat promised. 'I'll think about it, and we can discuss it more when we talk tomorrow.'

'Sounds good,' Mikael said, his voice brightening. 'I

can't wait to hear what you think. And hey, even if you don't want to join the ski school, we could still work together to fight the mining company. We make a great team, Kat.'

She smiled, with warmth spreading through her chest. Mikael was right. They did make a great team. A small spark of hope ignited inside her about their future together.

'Thanks,' she said, her voice soft.

Chapter Sixty-Six

As soon as Kat had finished talking to Mikael, there was a knock on her door.

She wasn't expecting anyone. Plus it was unusual because if anyone was visiting, they had to press the buzzer on the front door on the street.

Kat thought it must be one of her neighbours in the block. She went to open the door without thinking more about it.

She couldn't believe her eyes when she saw who was standing in the hallway.

'Surprise!'

Jacques had a wide smile on his face. He was holding a bottle of champagne and a huge bouquet of deep-red roses. Her favourite.

'What are you doing here?'

'*Chérie*, I just wanted to thank you for giving me another chance. I know it was you who convinced Richard to take me back.'

Kat felt her heart sink as she looked at Jacques. Since talking to Mikael, she'd been increasingly excited about the possibly of a different future, and now Jacques had come to ruin it all.

She took a deep breath and tried to keep her voice steady. 'What are you talking about? I didn't speak to Richard about your job.'

Jacques' smile faltered for a moment, but then he quickly recovered.

'Oh, I must have misunderstood. But it doesn't matter. I'm just happy to see you.'

He stepped forward, trying to kiss her cheek, but Kat pulled back.

'Please go.'

Jacques looked stunned at Kat's reaction. He'd obviously expected her to be happy to see him, not to reject him like this. She could see the hurt in his eyes, but she didn't want to let her guard down. Not after everything he'd put her through.

'Kat, please,' Jacques pleaded. 'Let me come in for a quick drink.'

'No,' Kat replied firmly. 'You lied to me, Jacques. You made me believe that you were someone you're not. I can't trust you anymore.'

Jacques looked defeated, and for a moment, Kat felt a pang of guilt. But then she remembered his betrayal and all the times he had manipulated her into believing his lies, and she felt her resolve hardening again.

'Please, just go,' she said firmly. 'I can't do this anymore. You know it's over between us.'

Jacques looked like he was about to say something else, but Kat shut the door in his face. She leaned against the door, her heart racing.

She stood there for a long time with her back to the door, still in shock at what had just happened. She couldn't believe that Jacques had the audacity to come to her new flat after everything he'd done.

She slid down slowly until she was sitting on the floor, exhausted and overwhelmed by all her emotions. She had made the right decision by rejecting him, but it still hurt.

She thought of Mikael, and the hope he had given her for the future. She felt a surge of determination, knowing that she'd made the right decision in cutting Jacques out of her life.

Kat got up and headed to the kitchen to pour herself a glass of water. As she drank it, she wondered if now was the time to believe in herself and to take a chance on something new.

Chapter Sixty-Seven

Mikael scanned the dark horizon, sipping on a glass of whiskey. He had heard that there may be Northern Lights that evening, so after he put the phone down with Kat, he turned off all the lights in his cabin and settled himself on a chair next to the floor-to-ceiling windows. Even if there was no show tonight, it didn't matter. It was a chance to have time with his own thoughts.

Kat had sounded positive about his suggestion to join the ski school venture, although he could hear the hesitation in her voice. But he would work on her. How wonderful it would be to have Kat by his side. During the past few days, spent in his new rented cabin, he had missed her every single moment. Especially when his father had dropped by with the news that he had transferred the funds for the sale of Mikael's share into his bank account.

As he watched the sky, littered with tiny sparkling

stars, his thoughts returned to the awkward meeting with his father.

'So what are you going to do with your money?' he'd asked.

He'd stood with his feet slightly apart and his hands on his hips just inside Mikael's front door. He hadn't even taken his heavy overcoat off.

Mikel had almost asked him to come in and sit down, but they were beyond such niceties now.

'What I do with it is none of your business,' he said.

He saw the twitch on his father's face, which quickly disappeared.

He took one step towards Mikael.

Erik Andersson's imposing bulk and his growly voice used to cause dread to rise inside of Mikael. But that was before he'd met Kat. He now saw that his father was just using him and his brother to make money off the backs of the people and the land in the beautiful north. Mikael was no longer scared of him.

He straightened up and crossed his arms over his chest. He said nothing while his father's pupils grew darker; he tried to stare his son down.

'That may be so, but I tell you this young man,' – Erik Andersson's voice was low and threatening –'you will regret this.'

Mikael shrugged his shoulders. 'I doubt it.'

His father pointed a leather-gloved finger at his face and growled, 'When you've lost all your money and are in trouble, don't come running to me because I won't help you. And neither will your mother. She's very disappointed in you, so you can forget about holding onto her apron strings any longer. She'll never see you ever again.'

Mikael shook the memory from his mind and shuddered, despite the heat from the roaring fire. He took another sip of his drink.

He could only imagine what his father would say when he heard of the ski school project.

If only Kat were here with him.

Mikael enjoyed the tanginess of the whiskey, which warmed his throat as it went down. He couldn't shake off the memory of the way his father had threatened him and brought up his mother.

He couldn't believe he'd never see her again. He would convince her to visit his new home in secret, after the dust had settled a little. He hoped Ulla would come.

If it was impossible, Mikael would miss his mum, but he couldn't let his father's words affect him, not when he had a chance to create something new and exciting with Kat.

He looked out the window again and saw a faint-green glow in the sky. The Northern Lights. He smiled, remembering the first time he'd seen them with his mother. She had taken him out late at night, wrapped him in a thick blanket, and pointed up at the sky.

'My grandfather used to say that there was a fire fox running across the sky, creating the sparks and colours with his tail,' she had said, her voice soft and reverent.

As a small boy, Mikael had been entranced by the

lights, and the way they danced and swirled in the sky, like a mystical force beyond his understanding. He watched the sky with awe and wonder he'd never experienced before.

Now, as he gazed at the lights again, he saw hope reflected in them. He and Kat could create something special together, something that would bring joy and prosperity to the people in their community. He took another sip of his drink, determined to carry out his duty for his ancestor's land.

He would show his mother and father that he could be a success and make this venture work. And he longed for Kat to support him through it all.

He emptied his glass and headed to bed. Relief washed over him as he left his father's words behind in the living room. He understood that there was a great amount of hard work ahead of him, but he felt certain that his strength and determination would bring him success.

As he drifted off to sleep, he thought of Kat in his arms now, as she had been in the cabin in the wilderness.

Chapter Sixty-Eight

When Kat woke the next morning after a disturbed sleep and vivid dreams about Lapland, she realised that she had made a decision.

Glancing at her phone, she saw there were several messages from her work colleagues. She hadn't had time to tell anyone about her decision to resign. Even before she could make a coffee, her phone buzzed with a call. She saw from the display that it was Richard, her boss.

Or ex-boss.

Kat sighed. Should she just ignore him after how he had treated her? Getting her to take responsibility for the new format when Jacques had been dropped from the show. And when he was reinstated, getting her to do all his dirty work for him, then feigning he'd had no part in any of it.

She didn't owe him anything.

Yet, she felt a slight responsibility for the success of the show.

She pressed the green button to take the call, putting Richard on speaker while she filled her coffee machine with water from the tap.

'Kat, you can't do this to me!'

'What are you talking about?' She tried to keep her voice steady and calm.

'You can't just leave the show in the middle of the season. We need you. You're the reason why Jacques is doing so well.'

She rolled her eyes. 'I highly doubt that.'

'Kat, I'm serious. You're an integral part of the show. You can't just abandon us.'

'Well, I'm sorry Richard, but I've made my decision. I'm resigning. I've found a new opportunity that I'm really excited about.'

Richard paused for a moment, his voice tense.

'What opportunity?'

Kat hesitated. She hadn't told anyone about Mikael's offer, and she wasn't sure if she was ready to reveal it to Richard.

'It's a new project. Something that I've been wanting to do for a while. And I thought it was time for me to move on from the show.'

Richard let out a frustrated sigh. 'You can't just leave us high and dry like this. We need you.'

Her patience was wearing thin. She took a deep breath before responding.

'I understand that this is an inconvenience for you,

Richard, but you threw me under the bus when you decided to bring Jacques back. You left me alone to deal with him, the crew, and the contestants, all on my own. I've had enough! I'm going to do what is best for me for a change.'

There was a moment of silence before her boss spoke again, his voice calmer this time. 'Fine. I guess there's nothing I can do to change your mind. But I hope you know what you're doing.'

'I do. Goodbye, Richard.'

Kat hung up the phone and let out a sigh of relief. It was done. She had officially resigned from the show. Now she could focus on her new project with Mikael.

The thought of Mikael brought a smile to her face. She couldn't wait to see him again, to discuss their plans for the ski school and the campaign against the mine. She also wanted to explore the beautiful north together with him. As she finished her coffee and got dressed, she could feel butterflies in her stomach. This was a new beginning for her, a chance to do something meaningful and exciting with someone she cared about deeply.

She dialled his number.

'I'm coming to Lapland!'

Kat could hear Mikael's excitement at the end of the line.

'That's wonderful news! When?'

Kat gave him the flight details and ended the call quickly. She could have talked to him all night long, but she needed to pack and she had very little time.

Kat couldn't wait to tell Mikael her other decision,

but she didn't want to do it over the phone. She needed to be next to him, to see the reaction on his face, to feel his arms around her when he realised that they were going to spend their future together.

After everything she had been through, it felt so right returning to Lapland. She would need to come back to London after a week to move out of her flat, but now, all she could think about was being close to Mikael.

Kat packed her bags quickly, eager to be reunited with him. As she moved about her apartment, gathering her belongings, she felt liberated, like a weight had been lifted off her shoulders. She was leaving behind a life that hadn't fulfilled her, a job that she didn't love, and a boss who didn't treat her well. But with Mikael, she had found something different, something that could be the key to her happiness.

As she closed her suitcase, she felt the familiar buzz from her phone. She saw that it was a message from Mikael.

Her heart fluttered as she read the message: **Pick you up at the airport?**

Kat smiled and responded quickly.

I'd love that. Can't wait to be back in Lapland.

Chapter Sixty-Nine

The flight was long, with a stopover in Helsinki, but Kat hardly noticed, too lost in thoughts of Mikael and their future together.

She dreamt of snowy landscapes and warm fires, of skiing with Mikael by her side. She dreamt of laughter and shared moments, of love and passion.

When she landed in Lapland, Kat could barely contain her excitement. She rushed through the airport, her heart racing as she looked for Mikael. And there he was, waiting for her with a grin on his face.

As soon as she saw him, Kat felt safe. She didn't need anything else, as long as they were together. She ran into his arms, warmed by his strong arms wrapped around her.

'Can I kiss you?' Mikael asked.

They hadn't talked about the future. Kat had only

agreed to come and visit him, but Mikael was full of hope. He didn't want to take her for granted, though.

He'd been nervous all day, arriving at the airport far earlier than necessary. He'd drunk so much coffee that he felt jittery.

Or perhaps it was the prospect of seeing Kat again that had been making him nervous?

Kat nodded and he bent down to place his mouth over hers. Desire crept through his body as he deepened the kiss.

Finally, they broke free of each other.

'My beautiful Kat,' Mikael whispered into her ear. 'I've missed you so much.'

'I missed you too,' Kat replied.

He could see tears in her eyes, as if she was about to cry.

'Are you OK?'

'I'm just so happy to be here with you.'

She gave a little laugh and wiped the corners of her eyes with the tips of her fingers.

Mikael hoped that her show of emotion was a good sign, but he had promised himself not to push her into a decision. If she was ready to build a future together with him, she would need to arrive at that decision on her own, just as he had done with his plan to move up here, fight his family's mining project, and start his own ski school.

Mikael took her hand and led her outside, where a light snow was falling. The air was crisp and clean. When they walked towards Mikael's rented car, Kat felt a sense of wonder and joy. She had made the right decision in coming here, with Mikael by her side.

As he drove them through the snow-covered landscape, Kat took in the beauty of the forest and the frozen lakes. She was at peace and contented, something she hadn't felt in a long time. It was as if everything had fallen into place, like she had finally found her place in the world.

Mikael looked over at her and smiled, his eyes sparkling in the dim light of the car interior.

'You're quiet,' he said.

Kat turned to him, a smile on her face. 'I'm just taking it all in. It's so beautiful here.'

Mikael nodded, his hand on her thigh. 'It is.'

Mikael had made a special effort to make the cabin cosy and inviting. He'd bought some candles, and a bunch of tulips from the shop in the centre of the ski resort. He'd made the fire ready, so all he needed to do was light a match to it.

'This is nice,' Kat said.

'Thank you.'

Suddenly, he was unsure of what she wanted him to do. Did she want him to kiss her again?

He stood there awkwardly with his arms by his sides. Then she walked over to him and, pressing onto her tiptoes, kissed his lips. He bent down and took her into his arms. Their kiss was long and passionate, but Mikael didn't want Kat to do anything she wasn't absolutely sure of.

He pulled away and walked into the little alcove kitchen.

'Would you like a drink, coffee, or wine?'

'No, I'm fine.'

Kat remained in the middle of the room. Standing there, in the fading light, she looked gorgeous. She was wearing a thin jumper over a short tartan skirt, and black tights. He could make out the outline of her breasts through the top. Her slim waist was pinched in by the skirt.

All Mikael wanted was to lead her to his bedroom and undress her. He longed to feel his naked body against hers and make her moan with pleasure the way she had when they'd made love in the cabin, weeks before.

He walked back to her and took her into his arms once more. Their kiss lasted even longer this time and Mikael had to fight his resolve.

He forced himself away again. He took hold of Kat's shoulders, looking deeply into her eyes.

'Is this what you want?'

Kat smiled widely.

'Yes, Mikael. Will you take me to bed already?'

Chapter Seventy

Afterwards, lying on top of the covers, their clothes strewn all over the bed and the floor, Kat kissed Mikael on the mouth. Pulling on her knickers and bra, she asked if he had any food in the cabin.

'Oh, I don't. I completely forgot about dinner...'

Mikael was supporting himself on his elbows. His wide, naked chest made Kat want to kiss every part of it, but she needed nourishment. She'd been so nervous during the flight that she hadn't eaten anything but a packet of nuts.

'I'm famished. For food, this time,' she said, grinning at Mikael.

Mikael glanced at his watch and said, 'Oh, no. If we're quick, we can still get into the hotel bar. I'm sure they can get us something to eat.'

. . .

While they were walking along the snowy path that led from Mikael's cabin to the familiar hotel, Kat asked if the manager was worried about his new ski school.

'Surely that's competition to her?' she suggested.

Mikael put his arm around her shoulders and grinned down at her.

'Well, you won't believe it, but I've convinced Petra to give the contract for next season to me!'

Kat stopped in her tracks. 'Wow, that's amazing. You've already got your first contract. And that's before you have even started advertising for private clients.'

'Yeah, I'm pretty pleased. She said the tourists were always so happy with me that it was a no-brainer.'

Talk of the manager brought back memories of the horrific avalanche to Kat.

'Has she forgiven you yet?'

'I should think so. The investigation was quickly over. I'm in the clear. Which is good, because I need to organise insurance for the school.'

They arrived at the entrance of the hotel. It held so many memories for Kat. She felt emotions wash over her as she walked through the glass doors.

The same young female receptionist as before welcomed them. She was visibly surprised to see Kat again but smiled a welcome all the same.

The restaurant was still open, so they got seated and ordered food.

'I'm pretty hungry too,' Mikael said. 'I haven't been able to eat anything all day. I've just had cups and cups of coffee.'

Kat leaned over and gave him a soft kiss on the mouth. They were sitting next to each other, needing to be close. Mikael put his arm around her shoulders, and she snuggled into his side.

Kat was happier and more contented than she could ever remember being.

'By the way, I've only got a week.'

After their wonderful lovemaking, Mikael had hoped that Kat's decision would be a different one. But hearing now that she would be returning to London just after a week, his hopes were thrashed.

'Right,' he said.

He could feel his own muscles tensing, but he couldn't help it.

Their food arrived and both being starving, they tucked into the delicious looking platefuls.

His research into the harmful impact of the mining on the environment had led him into articles about veganism. What had counted as normal behaviour to him before he'd met Kat now seemed selfish. Lately, he'd tried to avoid meat and dairy.

Tonight, he'd ordered the same dish as Kat, a vegetable stew with a nut crumble topping. It was more delicious than it sounded. He tried to keep his emotions in check while he ate.

He would just have to make the best of the few days he had with her. Perhaps next time, she would stay longer and the time after longer again, so that eventually he would be able to convince Kat to stay forever.

Kat could feel the tension in Mikael's body. She was just about to tell him her decision when the food arrived. She was so hungry, she had to eat something first.

When the waiter came to collect their empty dishes, she took a sip of her beer and turning to Mikael, said, 'You don't need to eat vegan food just because of me, you know.'

It hadn't gone unnoticed that he'd ordered the same as her.

Mikael's expression was strained, but it softened when he began speaking.

'I want to. It's not just to impress you – although there is some of that, too.' He grinned at her. 'I've been reading about the warming of the planet and all the environmental issues that come from that, and I am convinced by your argument. The least we can do is to stop eating meat. I will occasionally have a steak, though, but I'll try to be good.'

Kat was so delighted with his reply that she put her hand on his cheek, feeling the rough, five o'clock shadow underneath her fingers, and kissed him again.

'I love you,' she said.

'Really?' Mikael said, obviously surprised.

'I'm only going back to London to organise practical things like breaking the rental on my new flat. Then I'll be back here with you, if you'll have me.'

'What?'

'To work with you on the mine and the ski school.' Kat said, suddenly mischievous. 'Unless the offer is not on the table anymore?'

'Of course, it is!' Mikael flung his arms around her and squeezed her so hard, it almost hurt.

She laughed. 'I can't breathe!'

He let go of her, but still holding her in his arms, he said, 'This is not a joke. You are really going to move here and join me in all this?'

'Uh huh,' Kat said.

Mikael's eyes were shining so bright, and he looked so happy that it made Kat's heart burst.

'We have to celebrate this properly.' He called the waiter and told her to bring them a bottle of champagne.

They clinked their glasses and, looking deeply into each other's eyes, they each took a sip.

Of course he would order champagne, Kat thought, remembering the first time they'd met at the Helsinki airport. But now, she was happy to let him treat her. She rather liked the taste of the stuff, anyway.

'You have no idea how happy you make me, Kat,' Mikael said.

'I do, because you make me deliriously happy, too,' Kat replied.

Epilogue

Kat and Mikael stood next to each other on top of a slope, their skis pointing to the side, admiring the view of Ylläs Fell. The temperature was above freezing and because of it, Kat noticed the landscape had changed.

The pine trees bordering the slope and deep in the valley had previously been covered in snow; now they were dark green. In the distance, the small Lake Ylläs was free of ice, its teal-blue water glinting in the sun. The snow had already melted in places on the mountain too, but the piste below them was busy with skiers, some wearing just T-shirts with their salopettes.

It was the first of May, and the traditional Nordic spring celebrations, which had started last night, were still going on. On their way up the mountain on the chairlift, Kat had even spotted a guy holding a bottle of champagne in one hand while speeding down the slope.

'Some of them have been up all night,' Mikael had told her.

Gazing now at the snow beneath her skis, the strong sun beaming down on the mountain was thawing it before her eyes.

'It's a bit like skiing on sorbet,' Mikael said, his forehead creased with concern. 'You must watch out for the bare spots, too. They're dangerous if your skis get caught on them. Are you sure you're OK doing this?'

'Stop worrying. I've been skiing nearly every day for the past two months. It feels as if I've been sleeping with my skis on. I'll be fine.'

She leaned in and kissed him on the mouth. When he didn't respond, she pulled back, and saw worry on his face. The snow was a little more slippery than usual; perhaps he was just concerned they'd lose their balance if they got too close to each other.

'Let's go then,' Mikael said tersely.

He has nothing to worry about. I'll show him.

Kat pushed herself off.

The first two runs were exhilarating. With the snow a lot wetter than it had been just two days earlier, it was more difficult to control her parallel turns. Mikael had been right about that. But with a little more concentration, she managed to match his pace.

The sky was bright blue, and the sun streamed down on them as they dodged the other skiers, many of whom were going at speed but rather erratically.

After three easier runs, they took the bubble car to the topmost peak of the mountain, where the longest and toughest slopes would take them to the centre of the resort.

Standing by the hilltop restaurant, Mikael leaned on his poles and said, 'How about a little break?'

'Already?'

Kat was surprised he wanted to stop so soon. Today would probably be their last opportunity of the season to ski down the Ylläs Fell. Plus, they had yet to take the more difficult runs that Mikael preferred.

When he wasn't teaching, they would spend the whole day on the mountain, hardly taking any time out. Mikael would pack a thermos of coffee and snacks in his backpack to keep them going.

But he said, 'It's May Day, so I thought we should celebrate.'

Last night, while the rest of the resort had partied, they had stayed in their cosy cabin and shared a bottle of champagne to toast the new season in. Mikael had told Kat that the town would be so full of tourists, it would be no fun. Kat hadn't minded; she loved their new home and couldn't get enough of being alone with Mikael.

'Okay,' she replied.

They left their skis on a rack by the restaurant. The round building made from heavy logs was heaving with revellers, drinking and laughing. The tables outside over-looking the slope and valley beyond were all taken, and many drinkers were standing about enjoying the sun.

'It's busy,' Kat said, glancing at Mikael, who was striding towards the entrance of the restaurant.

'We'll be fine,' he said, not looking at her. He took her hand and led her inside the wooden structure.

'Ah, Mikael and Kat!'

The owner, a large man in his fifties with thinning hair and a large, grey moustache greeted them warmly. Kat had met him previously at a protest rally against the proposed mine.

'I have your table ready.'

He winked at Mikael and led them to a quiet corner of the room, next to a crackling fire.

'I didn't think you could book...' Kat whispered to Mikael as they sat down.

'Oh, it's a special occasion.'

He glanced at her briefly and then began fussing with their jackets. He hung them on a nearby hook made from reindeer antlers. Apparently, the animals shed them naturally during the winter, so it was only right that they would be transformed into everyday tools and equipment. In the resort, most of the shops sold everything from bottle openers to pens made from antler bone.

Kat smiled at Mikael, who had taken a seat opposite her. She wanted to tell him how comfortable she felt with the Lappish culture. But he wasn't looking at her. Instead his attention was on the bar, packed with people trying to get a drink or order food.

She noted his tension and how his left knee kept bouncing – something he did if he was nervous.

Kat reached her hand out and placed it on top of his.

'You OK?'

'Yeah, fine,' he said, glancing at her.

But his eyes were on the owner, who was fighting his way through the throng of customers. He had a wine cooler filled with ice in one hand, a bottle of champagne in the crook of his arm, and a pair of high-stemmed flutes in his other.

'This the right one?' He showed the bottle to Mikael; Mikael nodded.

Kat frowned at the personal service they were getting. The restaurant was known for its simple, home cooked food and most skiers washed it down with a beer. She didn't even know they served wine, let alone champagne. Mikael had really gone to great trouble to organise this for them. Was May Day really such a special celebration up here in Lapland?

The owner popped the cork with a flourish and poured them each a glass.

'Enjoy. I'll try to keep this pack of merrymakers away from your corner.'

He flicked his eyes to the crowded bar. Then he winked at Mikael again and gave Kat a wide smile.

She smiled back and tasted the drink. It was different to the champagne she'd had before.

'It's delicious, so velvety,' she exclaimed, smiling at Mikael.

'I'm glad you like it. It's vintage.'

'Wow! Is this what you do every May Day with your girlfriends or am I special?'

Mikael's face fell.

'I've never done this with anyone else,' he said gruffly.

'Hey, sorry, I was joking!'

Kat threaded her fingers in his and squeezed them gently.

But Mikael didn't smile. Instead, he pulled his hand back and got up. His worried eyes were now on her as he made his way around the small table. He took something out of his back pocket and lowered himself onto one knee.

Kat stared at him, not quite sure what he was doing. A shout came from someone and the noise in the place instantly dropped to a quiet hush.

Mikael opened the small velvet box he was holding, revealing a sparkling ring.

He cleared his throat.

'Katherine, Kat, the moment I saw you at Helsinki airport, I knew you were special. Over the past few months – and I know we've only known each other for a short time – I've come to realise that you are the most important person in my life. I love your smile, your firm beliefs, and your warm heart. I want to spend the rest of my life with you. I hope you feel the same. So, Katherine Wootton, will you do me the greatest honour ever and marry me?'

Kat's heart raced as she stared at Mikael in shock. She heard commotion and the occasional shout from some people in the room, but her eyes were on Mikael and the sparkling ring he was holding. Her eyes welled up with tears. She had never felt so special before in her life.

As she gazed into his eyes, she knew she wanted to spend the rest of her life with him. Every moment she had spent with him had been perfect, and she couldn't imagine her life without him. Her lips curled into a smile as she caught her breath.

She responded in a whisper, 'Yes, yes. I will marry you.'

Mikael's face lit up with a smile; he slid the ring onto her finger. The room erupted into applause and cheers as they embraced each other, lost in the moment. For Kat, it was as if everything had fallen into place, and she was exactly where she was meant to be.

'I was so worried you'd say no,' Mikael whispered in her ear. He pressed his lips to hers.

When the noise died down, the owner of the bar approached them with a grin on his face, clapping Mikael on the back.

'Congratulations, you two! I didn't think you'd ever get around to popping the question.'

Kat laughed and hugged Mikael again, happy and content. She had never believed in fairy tales before, but in that moment, she was living one.

The Anderssons Book 2
TO LOVE AGAIN

Second Chance Love Under the Northern Lights

If you've enjoyed Kat and Mikael's love story, it's time to meet the brother he never talks about...

In *To Love Again*, Elsa Berg returns from her orderly life in Stockholm to a winter wedding in Finnish Lapland – and straight into the path of Victor Andersson, the first love who broke her heart ten years ago. In a close-knit community where family secrets run deep and old loyalties are hard to shake, Elsa and Victor must decide whether some loves are better left in the past, or whether it's worth risking everything for a second chance.

Turn the page now to read Chapter One of *To Love Again*, the next emotional Lapland romance in The Anderssons series.

TO LOVE AGAIN

Chapter One

The hotel shuttle bus hummed through the afternoon gloom, its headlights cutting through the swirling snow as Elsa Berg pressed her face to the frosted window. Each kilometre north from Kittilä Airport felt like travelling backwards through time, away from her constructed Stockholm life and towards something she'd spent ten years trying to forget.

Elsa noticed the other passengers chatting in various languages, their voices creating a gentle hum that should have been soothing. Instead, Elsa gripped her phone tighter, scrolling through Tobias's irritated messages without reading them.

'Spectacular, isn't it?' said the elderly woman beside her, nodding towards the blur of snow-laden pines through the window. 'This is my first time in Lapland. Are you here for the skiing?'

'Not exactly,' Elsa replied, grateful for the distraction. 'Just visiting friends.'

'How lovely. I'm hoping to see the Northern Lights while I'm here. Although the weather doesn't look promising,' The woman eyed the grey sky.

Elsa murmured agreement, though her mind was elsewhere. Somewhere ahead, in the warm lights of the hotel that were just beginning to appear through the trees, Victor Andersson was waiting. Not waiting for her, of course. He didn't even know she was coming. However, she knew that tomorrow she would have to confront him, the first time since Helsinki. Since the events that shattered her world.

The Hotel Äkäslompolo materialised through the swirling snow like something from a fairy tale, a welcome beacon against the brief Arctic afternoon. As the bus pulled up to the entrance, Elsa's hands trembled, though whether from the temperature or nerves, she couldn't say.

'Elsa!' A familiar voice called out as she stepped into the hotel lobby, and she turned to see Mikael Andersson approaching with arms outstretched. He looked relaxed, happy, the lines around his eyes speaking of laughter rather than stress.

'Mikael.' She accepted his embrace, breathing in the scent of his cologne. 'You look wonderful. Marriage suits you.'

'Happiness suits me,' he corrected with a grin. 'I can't believe you're here. After all these years of Christmas cards and promises to visit –'

'I know, I know. Life got complicated.' She gestured, encompassing her Stockholm existence, her legal career, everything that had kept her away from Finland – and from the memories this place held.

'And your boyfriend? Tobias?' Mikael's eyes moved past her shoulder, searching the small group of guests still collecting their luggage.

'He's coming. Work crisis.' The lie came easily. She found explaining the truth, that she'd needed those few hours alone to prepare herself for what was coming, too complicated.

Mikael's expression grew more serious. 'Elsa, I should mention – '

'Victor will be here.' She cut him off, surprised by how steady her voice sounded. 'I assumed he would be. He's your brother, after all.'

'He's my best man.' Mikael observed her for a moment. 'I wasn't sure if you knew. I'm sorry if that's a problem – '

'It's not a problem.' Another lie, but what was the alternative? She'd already made the journey, already disrupted her life to be here for one of her oldest friends. 'It was a long time ago, Mikael. We're both adults now.'

Relief flooded his features. 'Good. That's – good. Because I was worried – ' He paused, then seemed to decide. 'Oh, and Kat and I are having a small pre-wedding dinner this evening. Nothing formal, just close friends and family. We'd love for you and Tobias to join us, if he makes it in time.'

Elsa felt her stomach drop. A pre-wedding dinner meant hours of proximity to Victor, forced conversation, and the pretense of normality. 'That sounds lovely,' she managed to say.

'I hope Tobias will make it,' Mikael continued, though there was something in his tone that suggested he wasn't sure about her boyfriend. 'These work emergencies – they have a way of dragging on, don't they?'

'He'll be here,' Elsa said with more confidence than she felt. 'He promised he wouldn't miss the wedding.'

'Of course. Well, I should let you get settled.' He was already walking towards the reception desk but then paused. 'Elsa? I'm glad you're here. Whatever happened between you and Victor – I'm glad it didn't stop you from coming.'

As the lift doors closed behind her, Elsa caught her reflection in the polished metal – pale, apprehensive, but determined. In just a few hours, she might see Victor Andersson again. Tonight, she might discover whether the feelings she'd buried were dead, or whether some ghosts were too powerful to stay buried.

The thought terrified her.

It also, she admitted, thrilled her.

To continue reading, get your copy of
To Love Again now!

To Believe in Christmas Love

Want to know what really happened before Lapland?

Now that you've finished *To Melt a Frozen Heart*, there's one more story to discover. *To Believe in Christmas Love* is a spoiler-filled prequel novella to *To Melt a Frozen Heart*, set in London over one fateful Christmas. It reveals the forbidden affair and devastating betrayal that change everything for Kat before she ever sets foot in Lapland.

This novella is best read **after** *To Melt a Frozen Heart*, as it contains major plot reveals.

Subscribe to my Readers' Group and you'll receive *To Believe in Christmas Love: A To Melt a Frozen Heart Prequel Novella* **free**, plus news, behind-the-scenes extras and exclusive offers. Go online here to find out more:

To download your free prequel novella (with an exclusive Author Note), *To Believe in Christmas Love,* go here:
https://dl.bookfunnel.com/io9tzvr8mg

Acknowledgements

I've wanted to write a love story set in Lapland, and particularly the Finnish ski resort Ylläs, for a long time. A very good friend of mine introduced me to the place, for which I am eternally grateful because it's one of my favourite holiday destinations. My sister also worked there for a while, and I've visited often, so I could easily imagine Kat and Mikael falling in love on a skiing holiday against the backdrop of the magical Ylläs Fell.

There are naturally a few occasions where I have taken so-called artistic liberties. Not all places are situated where they are in reality, nor look the way they do in real life. But I'm assured the general flavour of Ylläs remains in the story.

To write a new novel requires inspiration, time and space to write. I get inspired by most things I see and hear around me. Ordinary conversations on the bus, the books I read, or people I meet, all give me ideas for characters and plots.

The character of Simona, Kat's mum, was influenced by a play I saw at the National Theatre in London. In a new version of *Phaedra*, Janet McTeer played a passionate older woman in love with a young man. Her performance gave me a deep understanding of Simona, and why she did what she did.

The time and space to write is gifted to me by the eternally patient Englishman, David Frise. Not only does he support my writing efforts, but he's also an excellent cook and acts as the first reader of each manuscript. I can safely say that without his continued support, I would not be publishing my 16th fiction title.

I'm also hugely grateful for the meticulous efforts of my editor, Kate Gallagher. She worked tirelessly on the many mistakes and inconsistencies in the first drafts. Needless to say, any still left in the book are mine and mine alone.

My intrepid Launch Crew must also get a mention. I cannot thank you enough for taking the time to read and comment on *To Melt A Frozen Heart* before publication. Each time I ask you to 'turn up' for me you do it without complaint. Your comments are always astute and intelligent. I'd like to thank Jaana R, Suvi Kivinen, Linda Brown, Vicky Waters, Amanda van de Velden, Seija Hyrsky, Patty Baumeister, Jessica Bracken, and Malia Renee Lewis, in particular.

Last, but by no means least, I couldn't do any of this writing lark without you, my Readers. As long as you continue to read my books, I'll continue to write them!

London, November 2023

Also by Helena Halme

<u>The Nordic Heart Series:</u>

The Young Heart (Prequel)

The English Heart (Book 1)

The Faithful Heart (Book 2)

The Good Heart (Book 3)

The True Heart (Book 4)

The Christmas Heart (Book 5)

<u>Love on the Island Series:</u>

The Island Affair (Book 1)

An Island Christmas (Book 2)

The Island Daughter (Book 3)

An Island Summer (Book 4)

The Island Child (Book 5)

An Island Heatwave (Book 6)

<u>The Anderssons Series</u>

To Melt A Frozen Heart (Book 1)

To Love Again (Book 2)

To Risk It All (Book 3)

To Choose Love (Book 4)

To Believe in Christmas Love (Prequel novella)

About the Author

Helena Halme grew up in Finland and moved to the UK via Stockholm and Helsinki at a very tender and impressionable age. She's a former BBC journalist and has also worked as a magazine editor, a bookseller and ran a Finnish/British cultural association in London.

Since gaining an MA in Creative Writing at Bath Spa University, Helena has published 18 fiction titles, including three in her latest series, *The Anderssons*, set in Finnish Lapland.

Helena lives in North London with her ex-Navy husband. She loves Nordic Noir and sings along to Abba when no one is around.

Find Helena Halme online
www.helenahalmebooks.com
hello@helenahalme.com